ONE NIGHT TO KILL

ONE NIGHT TO KILL

VALENTINA WINTERS™ BOOK TWO

MICHAEL ANDERLE

DISRUPTIVE IMAGINATION

Copyright © 2021 by Michael Anderle
Cover Art by Jake @ J Caleb Design
http://jcalebdesign.com / jcalebdesign@gmail.com
Cover copyright © LMBPN Publishing
A Michael Anderle Production

LMBPN Publishing
PMB 196, 2540 South Maryland Pkwy
Las Vegas, NV 89109

Version 1.01, June 2021
ebook ISBN: 978-1-64971-776-4
Print ISBN: 978-1-64971-777-1

Thanks to the Beta Team
Allen Collins, Kelly O'Donnell, Rachel Beckford

Thanks to the JIT Readers

Debi Sateren
Deb Mader
Veronica Stephan-Miller
Wendy L Bonell
Dave Hicks
Diane L. Smith
Peter Manis
Daryl McDaniel
Zacc Pelter
Jeff Goode

If I've missed anyone, please let me know!

Editor
The Skyhunter Editing Team

DEDICATION

*To Family, Friends and
Those Who Love
to Read.
May We All Enjoy Grace
to Live the Life We Are
Called.*

— Michael

PROLOGUE

The Wendy Howard Hotel was a pinnacle of elegance.

Surrounded by fifty acres of perfectly manicured botanical gardens, hand-crafted rivers and lakes, and some of the finest and most exotic roaming wildlife contained by the grounds around the four long walls of the hotel, the setup was something to be admired for miles around.

The hotel stood in the center of the greenery and water-scapes, rising into the sky and losing its top in the fog. The design was abstract, with sections of balcony skimming around in long arcs, flat rooftops where hotel-goers could bathe in the sun or stare out at the city of Atlantica a short way off in the distance, and monuments of stone that stood out like shards of peanut brittle. The building had been a combined effort for the Howard family, forty years ago when the Forbes top-listers migrated to the island.

Since the family's landing in Atlantica, their wealth had only grown. Nobody knew how much money they had, nor how much the property was worth in total because the family refused to comply with the Forbes listers and give an amount. Many rumors said the family was so rich that a named number didn't yet exist to determine their accounts. Some believed that it was all a front, and the businesses were dribbling money away, the family unable to face the public shaming of being further in debt than anyone would believe.

All that anyone did know was that an evening's stay in the Wendy Howard Hotel was available only to the land barons and the ridiculously wealthy. The Howard family gave new meaning to the word luxury, and although the hotel was publicly available for anyone to stay overnight, few ever did.

The procession of cars drove down the long drive toward the building. Carefully clipped grass bordered the pavement. Agoutis ran across the lawn, scrabbling away from the rumble of vehicles. A spotted genet leaped into a nearby tree, scaling up its thick boughs and disappearing into the foliage. Dik-dik bounded out of sight, losing themselves in the hedges and verges. A rainbow-colored quetzal swooped overhead, squawking as the headlights bounced off its glorious plumage.

The cars were nothing to sneeze at, either. A caravan of BMWs, Ferraris, Teslas, Bentleys, and Bugattis purred, all of them driving reverently slower than their powerful engines would have liked. The parking lot filled as men and women in tuxedos and ballgowns emerged in a full array of glitz and glamor. They were greeted at the large mahogany doors by half a dozen butlers waiting with glasses of champagne, whiskey, rum, gin, and every other type of drink to order.

The hotel spared no expense as they headed inside the reception room, which was as large as a soccer pitch and fitted with a dozen chandeliers that stretched to the size of cars. A forty-piece orchestra occupied an island in the center of the room and played classical music under the conductor's direction.

Guests milled around, politely talking to one another and catching up on the past few months of business. Shining red lipstick caught the attention of men, a few of the older ladies and gentlemen were half-drunk from liquor, and a smattering of the youngest of the gentry roamed around, outnumbered but not outclassed in their finest tailored suits.

The reception hall filled during the hour, the guests squeezing closer as the temperature rose from their combined body heat. The ensemble reached the crescendo of their number, then drifted into a silence that pulled the others with it as a man and a woman appeared on the sweeping staircase that ascended into the hotel's upper levels.

Wendy Howard strode down the staircase with the stature of a goddess. She pulled all eyes in her direction, her dazzling silver dress catching the light and throwing an array of rainbow stars into the room. Beside her, a man who looked as old as he did wealthy supported her with the crook of his arm, using the rails to brace himself. Although they were both aged, they held all the vigor of a younger couple, their kind smiles radiating strength as they stopped on the stairs and called the announcement for the rest to follow them to the Platinum Room.

Excitement rattled through the crowd. They followed their hosts, respectful of their slower pacing, and began their ascent to the thirteenth floor. The Wendy Howard Hotel boasted that while every other hotel in history shied away from declaring the thirteenth floor, due to superstitious nonsense, they had embraced the invisible level and now used the room as a twice-yearly gathering place for Atlantica's elite.

Concierges lined the way, regarding the guests with warm smiles. Wendy and Stanley Howard made their way to the second floor, where two sets of golden doors awaited them. A receiving concierge thumbed the button, and the doors opened to reveal a large lift carriage, able to fit up to thirty people with ease. The lifts were specially constructed and rated to handle the capacity.

No one joined the Howards in their elevator. As the doors

closed on the owners, the concierge called the second one and guests began to file inside.

On the thirteenth floor, the lifts opened into an enormous ballroom, easily four times the size of the reception area. Music played from a second orchestra in one corner. In another area were tables for craps and poker. In another were hot tubs and Jacuzzis, complete with folding screens and separators, as well as stacks of bathing suits in all sizes, freshly wrapped and waiting for the guests.

A bar lined one wall with every type of drink you could name —and a few that the world hadn't met yet.

The guests slowly filled the space, sticking with their friends and laughing as the drinks lubricated any anxiety and eased people into their comfort zones. Large glass doors opened onto a balcony that lined almost the entire side of the hotel, giving an incomparable view of Atlantica's glittering cityscape.

Archie Fontana adjusted his tie with one hand. His other held a sour mash of bourbon and lime in a glass. He laughed at Brendan Schitt's jokes, wondering when the insufferable bastard would leave him alone. For years, Schitt had believed that money automatically gave him charisma, shouting for hours about his underground cocaine business and the fact that no one would ever catch him since he served most of his clients in international waters. He'd offered Archie a stake in the company many times in the past, and Archie had declined equally as many times. Archie knew the dangers associated with investing in hard drugs, and that wasn't where his line of work sat. Despite most of the corrupt and immoral in the room who used the citizens of Atlantica as the fuel for their businesses, Archie had his eye on a much bigger prize.

Archie wiped a fake tear from his eye, his two years spent in theatrical studies paying dividends, and clapped a hand on Schitt's shoulders. "Another great one, really, simply sublime. I'm awfully sorry though, but I think I need to get a little fresh air."

"Can't handle the booze?" Schitt barked, much to the disgust of those around him. "Go ahead, lightweight. I'll catch up with you later. I've just spotted Christine Jorgensen, and well, you didn't hear this from me, but that bitch owes me big. Been trying to track her down for months. Hey! Christine!"

Schitt spun away, and Archie used that moment to dash outside. The air was warm and humid as he placed his hands on the railing and looked out over the city. Lights twinkled back at him, brighter than the stars ever did above—not that you could see them beyond the fog. A small grin appeared on his face as he marveled at the city—*his* city—and let his mind drift to greater things.

A waitress approached, smooth blonde hair sleeked back into a ponytail, dressed in a clean white shirt and black slacks. "Hors d'oeuvre, sir?"

Archie studied the woman up and down before looking at the plate. "I'd rather have you."

The waitress blushed and lowered her eyes. There was no sincerity to it. Even he could see that. Howard had trained her staff well, able to take a compliment without showing offense or discomfort.

Archie picked up a morsel of food—Turkish figs with anise and walnuts. It went down easily.

As he licked his fingers, he stopped the waitress from leaving. "Answer me a question, would you?"

"Anything," she replied.

"How much are they paying you?"

The waitress paused for a moment, then answered, "I'm not at liberty to divulge that information, sir."

Archie nodded thoughtfully.

The waitress looked at the other guests, eager to continue serving. "Will that be all?"

Archie nodded. As she walked away, his eyes strayed to her

ass. It practically called his attention in her well-fitted slacks. *Not at liberty,* he thought. *That means at least six zeroes...*

"Bothering the children again, are we?" a female voice crooned, causing Archie to glance over his shoulder at a woman leaning against the balcony's railing. "Some people never change."

"I always see that as a good thing," Archie replied.

Deng Zenim smirked, her pale white face barely creasing as though her skin was the porcelain it resembled. Her dark hair was tied back into a neat plait, her gown a blazing combination of ruby and gold. Her lips were as red as her clothing as she peered over the horizon toward the same city that Archie had just marveled at. "Do explain."

Archie leaned on the balcony. "Consistency is key when it comes to business. Delivering consistently, maintaining the same values consistently, giving people what they know they should expect. Surely you understand those principles?"

Deng nodded. "Consistency has its place."

"You disagree?" Archie asked.

Deng narrowed her eyes. "If we abide by consistency, the world would never move on. Technology has only progressed as far as it has due to countless revolutions and revelations. My business is built on disrupting the norms and destabilizing what we believed to be the ideal world and structures. If we were to remain consistent, I would not be sitting on the throne of a successful company, leading the charge in the technology sector."

Archie chuckled. "You *consistently* break the norms."

Deng let out a soft laugh. "Touché."

They were silent for a long moment as the band played behind them and the murmur of chatter trickled out of the room.

"You took something of mine," Deng commented. There was no anger or accusation in her tone, only a faint tinkle of respect.

Archie shrugged. "I don't know what you're talking about."

"Don't give me that bullshit," Deng replied gently. "You know the rules of the conclave. Here there is honor among thieves.

Here we can open up and share in a safe environment, far from the dangers of the outside world." Her eyes darted toward the center of the ballroom where Wendy and Stanley were deep in conversation with an older gentleman in a motorized wheelchair. In the center of the chair was a glowing blue core, providing the power needed to function.

Archie trailed her gaze to the man in the chair. Not too far away, a woman in her late thirties who Archie recognized from the cover of several Atlantica magazines looked stunning in a buttery yellow dress. The headlines of each publication raved about Vanessa's progress in space exploration. If the magazines were correct, Vanessa Hatfield's Infiniverse program was soon to be the first-ever successful attempt at landing a manned mission on the surface of Mars.

Archie pulled his gaze away, realizing that Deng was staring at him intensely, awaiting her answer.

"So what if I did take?" Archie asked. "What can you do about it at this point? I'm sure you have a thousand other projects you're working on that make this look like a kindergarten science fair project."

Deng smiled. Again, there was no real emotion in it. "I do. I simply need to understand where to keep my beady eyes and point my security." She sipped from her glass and stared back at the city. "You're not the first to break into my compound, and you won't be the last, either. People are jealous of what they don't understand. They fear what they cannot comprehend. We are working magic at Tynamo, and the world isn't ready for what we have in store."

Archie spotted movement above. On a shallow edge of the building, a black-clad figure pointed a gun toward the men and women on the balcony. He was barely visible, but Archie knew the protocol. They were guards of the Howards. One wrong move during this conclave and they'd instantly execute their target. The Howards held a tight grip on the party, ensuring that despite the rivalries and conflicts among the rich, all could gather at least twice a year, possibly overcoming their differences and sharing ideas. Most of the time it fueled new feuds as the guests crossed each others' boundaries and people discovered their true enemies.

Archie drew a long breath. "Your AI code is sophisticated. I'm impressed by the security protocols you've set inside. It's just the type of puzzle I need to stretch my brain."

"How many levels have you broken?" Deng asked, intrigued.

"Three."

Deng nodded knowingly. "As I expected."

"How much further is there to go?"

Deng sipped her drink. "Now that would be telling, wouldn't it?"

Archie chuckled. He accepted another hors d'oeuvre, examining the female waiter's ass once more.

Deng chewed her lip, eyes narrowing on Archie. "You have a loyal pet in her, you know."

Archie almost choked as he swallowed. He cleared his throat, drawing the eyes of a few groups around him. He gave a weak thumbs up to signal that he was okay. "I don't know what you're talking about."

"The Countess," Deng insisted. "The Red Countess, to be precise. She's a loyal lapdog, Archie. I'm impressed you've managed to keep her on that string of yours for so long."

Archie cocked his head. "What can I say? Employment with me comes with its benefits."

Deng looked around to check that no one was eavesdropping, then stepped closer. She smelled of magnolia and vanilla. She was a head shorter than him at least, and he had to look down to meet her eyes. "What power do you hold over the girl?"

Archie grinned. "I told you. Employee benefits package. It's comprehensive."

"No." She shook her head, not taking any of his lies. "I know that something is up, and I know when someone is playing with fire. You have something over her, and I'm going to figure out what it is. No one can keep such loyalty from an independent contractor such as she. The Red Countess is the best there is. I've seen it first-hand. She wouldn't flip over and have her belly scratched because it feels nice. She'd bite off the hands of whoever tried to chain her, and I don't see any blood on those fingertips."

Archie looked stoically down at her. "Whatever you think you can get from me is impossible. My lips are sealed tight. You can try and take her, but I don't see that being feasible in any way, shape, or form." He grinned. "Now, if you'd please like to take a step back from me before you get blood on my coat, that would be fantastic."

Three bright red lights danced over Deng's gown. Archie saw the snipers aiming from the roof, ready to fire if anyone stepped out of line.

Deng took a step back, eyes not leaving Archie's. "Very well. Understand that once I get my sights set on a target, I don't back down. You watch your back, Mr. Fontana, because you will never know who's watching you from behind."

Archie watched her leave, unable to keep his eyes from trailing down to her derrière. For a cash-loaded bachelor in the world's wealthiest city, he sure had trouble closing the deal with the ladies. Deng disappeared into the crowd, and Archie was once again drawn to the older man lazily driving around in his motorized chair. The rig was unusual, built to the highest specifications of comfort. The blue Atlanticore in the center throbbed with power. It filled Archie's mind with images of the raw core cells he'd seen in the various functions of machinery and infrastructure across Atlantica. The power source so desperately sought by the rest of the world had people prepared to risk their lives to acquire a gram of its infinite power.

He drained his drink before saluting the snipers on the roof with the glass. He turned to the balcony and looked out into the city. To the left of the cityscape, the hills rose into great mountains that lost themselves in the fog and wilderness. He fixed his eye on the darkness, thoughts drifting to the golden sextant and the information that his search party had revealed.

Something lay deeper...a lost something...a place that modern hands had yet to explore.

CHAPTER ONE

Innocuous acoustic guitar music played over the speakers of the late-night diner. The lights were a little aggressive, stinging Isabella's sore eyes. She had been asleep for what felt like four days, but she was still exhausted.

Bradley sat across from her, a concerned look on his face. A mug of coffee steamed before him, a poor imitation of a heart shaped into the foam. "So...are you going to tell me what's going on?"

Isabella remained quiet, unsure where to begin. How was she supposed to explain the truth to Bradley? Did she even want to?

The last few days had been a colossal headache for her. Isabella was used to sharing her body with her alter-ego, but that didn't make things any easier to deal with. They had struck a good balance in the past. Valentina would do her thing mostly at night. Isabella would do hers in the day. Rarely did the two ever meet, yet here she was, fresh off a couple of days of pure torment as she panicked in the back of Valentina's mind and tried to remain subdued.

She tried telling herself they were only nightmares, but she knew that wasn't true. Waking in the middle of the night to an unfamiliar room, being surrounded by strange machines, glimpsing fights with black-clad attackers…

It was all a far cry from the kind of life that Isabella embraced. A quiet existence in the library for her, please, while Valentina spent her time and dollars trying to fix Isabella's brother.

A brother that she rarely got to see.

"Bella?" Bradley lured her from her thoughts. "You have to talk to me."

Isabella sipped her drink if only to buy herself more time. When she opened her mouth, she went with honesty. "I don't know what to tell you, Bradley. I really don't."

"Well, start from the beginning," Bradley encouraged. "That's my favorite place to start."

Isabella chewed her lip.

"Well, start with why you've been missing work?" Bradley offered. "Things must have been serious if Naomi was phoning me to find out where you were. She didn't sound happy. I'd be careful going back."

Isabella nodded knowingly. "I will be."

"So where were you?"

Isabella considered this, then leaned across the table. She took Bradley's hand in hers. "Have you ever in your life felt like you weren't in control of your body? That you were someone's… puppet or plaything, and they controlled you from the inside?"

She expected Bradley to balk at this, but instead, he considered. "Sometimes. I often feel like the actions I take, and the things I think don't align. Why?"

Isabella looked into her cup. "Sometimes I…" She couldn't bring herself to say it.

"Sometimes you what?" Bradley insisted. "Come on, Bella, it's me."

Isabella sighed. "Sometimes I sleepwalk, and I don't know where I go."

Bradley's pause showed his trepidation. "Go on…"

"It's been a problem for as long as I can remember," Isabella continued, making it up as she went along. "In the beginning, it was when I was young. 'An overactive imagination,' they said. Believing I was born in a country other than America. Making up a different childhood. They promised it would go away when adolescence kicked in, and the hormones restructured my biology. It did—for a while. My mother used to find me in empty parking lots, sitting under a streetlight and talking as if she were there."

"Sounds creepy." Bradley swept a hand through his hair. There were bags beneath his eyes, and he hadn't shaved in some time, although the hipster look was working for him.

Isabella nodded, working on her fabrication. What else could she do but lie her way from the truth? Even now, the exhausted Valentina sat in the back of her mind, and Isabella could hear her mumbling, trying to feed her lies to protect them both.

"Anyway," Isabella continued, "they stopped when I was ten and hadn't really been a problem since then. Now that I'm dealing with a new management position, and everything is changing, I—"

Bradley shook his head and stroked her hand. "You don't need to continue, Bella." He leaned over the table and raised her chin with his finger. "Change can do many things to a person. Look at me. Out of a job for a week and living like a vagabond on the streets. I'm half of what I was." His eyes narrowed as if coming to some conclusion. "You know what? We can both get out of this." He puffed out his chest and sat up straight. "We can work through the hard times. I mean, sure, our hard times may be different, but we can do it together. You make sure I'm out there, hitting up interviews and seeking a job that'll get me out of this funk, and I'll…"

"You'll what?" Isabella was afraid of what he would say. The last thing she needed was someone who relied on her. Although, at the same time, it felt nice that someone was taking a genuine interest in looking out for her. How long had it been since Isabella was allowed a true friend? Someone who understood her inside and out and who helped her through the tough times?

No one has tough times like you, the voice insisted. *No one will understand the truth of your life. A lie is how you were born, a lie is what we will be when we die. Empty is better than hurting those around you.*

Unwanted, a vision of Kit emerged in her mind. It was a time when he was well and mobile, waving Isabella off after a few drinks down at a local pub near his hometown. That had been the last time Isabella had seen him awake.

"I'll keep an eye out for you," Bradley replied. "Make sure you're not sleepwalking. Set up cameras at your door, sit outside all night. Hell, I'll even sleep at the end of the bed if you need me to."

"No!" Isabella snapped a little too quickly. The serving staff looked their way for a few seconds before pretending to distract themselves with the one other customer in the place. "No," Isabella repeated, softer this time. "Look, I appreciate the offer, and I'm happy to help *you,* but... Don't take this the wrong way, but I don't need a stalker looking over me."

Bradley's mouth dropped theatrically. "A *stalker?*"

Isabella made to protest.

"Relax," Bradley soothed. "I get it. I do. But, just know that I can't not look out for you, Bella. If you're roaming the streets in the middle of the night, stuck in a lucid dream, you're going to run into trouble. Atlantica isn't safe in the daytime, let alone at night."

Don't I know it, Isabella thought, remembering the cold, strange room and the panicked man with the stale, whiskey breath.

Isabella offered a smile. "I know. Look, I'll soothe things over with Naomi tomorrow and get it all sorted, okay? You can stop me if you see me roaming the corridors at night, but otherwise, I'll be fine. Let's focus on you. Let's get *you* a job, yeah?"

Bradley chewed his lip while scrutinizing Isabella. At last, he offered, "Fine." He extended a hand to shake.

"Really?" Isabella asked.

Bradley nodded to his hand. "I insist."

Isabella took the hand and shook it, not missing Bradley's curious look at her calloused palm and the bruises on her knuckles.

What little sleep Isabella did get was wildly disturbed, interlaced with visions of guards clad in black, and waking up in strange rooms. Figures stalked her in kabuki masks, and as the sun peered through the windows and brought the world to life, she kicked off the sheets and sat up sharply.

Sweat peppered her forehead. The knock on her door had been forceful, followed by a gruff voice muttering words she didn't understand. Somewhere deep inside her, Valentina moved, shifting in her disturbed thoughts and dreams.

Bradley beamed as she pulled the front door open. "Morning sunshine!" His smile slipped as he glanced down at the short length of her nightdress. Isabella had been so bleary-eyed that she didn't realize how revealing it was.

She slammed the door shut, then fetched her gown. Wrapping the tie around her waist, she returned to the door. She opened it as Bradley made to knock on the door again. "Sorry, I didn't mean to catch you…like that."

Isabella waved a hand, her head throbbing with a dull ache. "Don't mention it. What do you want?"

"Just checking you were heading to work." Bradley's cheeks

flushed. He answered Isabella before she could ask the question. "Naomi told me that you were due in at 8:00 a.m. today. It's…" He checked his watch. "Seven."

Isabella ran a hand down her face, then stifled a yawn. "We didn't get in until four."

"Then that's three hours of glorious snooze time." Bradley's peppiness upset her. "Come on. Rise and shine. Go, go, go."

Isabella turned back to her room, grumbling, "Remind me again why I let you stay across the hall?"

"Because you're a diamond," Bradley called, following with a soft, "And you like me."

Isabella shot a look over her shoulder. Bradley raised his hands defensively and closed the door.

Her coffee eased her headache some, but it didn't help her for long. Naomi swept up to Mission Control when Isabella reached the station, practically grabbing her by the hand to lead her to her office.

The office door slammed shut behind them. Naomi fell into her chair and stared daggers at Isabella. "Well?"

Isabella raised her eyebrows.

"Don't make me ask twice," Naomi warned.

Isabella cleared her throat. There was a large glass of water beside Naomi, beading with condensation. Isabella's throat went dry, and her only thoughts were of drinking it.

Naomi slammed a hand on the table.

"I'm fine, thanks for asking," Isabella replied at last.

Naomi's eyes blazed. She rose, back hunched and hands on her desk, leaning on her arms. "That's all you have to say to me? You go *missing* for *two* days, and all you have to say is that 'you're fine?'"

Isabella yawned. "I'm sorry. Is that better? I'm sorry, and it won't happen again."

Won't it?

Naomi drew a long breath and skirted the desk. She sat on the edge and folded her arms as she stared down at Isabella. Isabella knew this was a power move and one that she wouldn't submit to. "Do you know what I did to the last supervisor who went AWOL on me, Isabella? The last time someone upped and left and didn't so much as come back with a sincere apology? Do you know what happened?"

Isabella raised an eyebrow. "There hasn't been a supervisor for as long as I've been here."

"Right!" She slammed her hand down again. "Because people who let me down get thrown out into the garbage. You should ask your friend Bradley all about that. Good riddance to bad news."

"So, you're saying I'm fired?" Isabella asked, heart beating faster.

Naomi smirked, a devilish look. She let her arms relax. "No. Fortunately for you, you are not fired. Despite the last couple of days of absence, you are a stellar employee and one whom I wish to see go far in this place."

Go far? There's like one level between you and me. "Oh?"

Naomi's voice softened, the edges laced with honey. "One can forgive just *one* simple mistake. As I understand it your...medical emergency...was the primary feature of your absence, correct?"

Isabella sighed. Had Bradley spoken to Naomi? Despite all she did to him. "Right..."

"Is this something that we have to get used to?" Naomi asked.

Isabella shook her head, not fully believing herself. "No. Have you known this to happen in the last few years I've been here?"

"No," Naomi answered. "I admit, I haven't." She studied Isabella once more, then moved to a stack of yellow, blue, green, and pink sheets of paper piled precariously on the table. "These are all files that need to be archived in the old archive room. Can you ensure that these are taken care of by the end of the day?"

"Of course," Isabella replied begrudgingly. She moved to the stack of papers.

Naomi stopped her. "Uh, uh, uh." She smirked. "Get your minions to do it for you. Power comes with its advantages." She leaned closer toward Isabella. "Don't worry, Bella. Stay with me, and I'll show you the true way to lead in this dump."

CHAPTER TWO

One week later

What the hell is it with people and diamonds?

The picture was printed in Valentina's mind, a diamond as big as her fist, its gleaming edges catching the light and throwing out an array of rainbow colors. It looked almost cartoonish, too perfect to be anything other than hand-carved. She wondered what it would look like in real life instead of on her phone screen, captured in a photograph behind a thick, glass case.

Valentina stood in the shadows on the rooftop, her back to the wall. Around the corner, two guards roamed the upper levels, the distance between the walls and the drop no more than ten feet. The building was five stories high with guards walking around all levels in small numbers. She knew there were more guards inside, and they would soon come if she screwed up. The challenge was to get as close as possible without raising suspicion. For that, she felt prepared.

Traffic flowed by below. Cars hummed and muted the soft steps of the guard's feet on the gravel surface. Somewhere in the distance, music thumped as Atlantica's nightlife hit fever pitch.

Valentina listened closely. A few more steps and he would round the corner.

Three. Two. One.

The guard appeared, clad in black uniform to hide from view. If only the uniform masked his face. His pale skin caught the soft moonlight blurred by the Atlantica fog and stood out in the darkness. He strode along, oblivious to Valentina, who even now clung to the small window shelf above and looked down on him.

She waited until he was beneath her to strike, descending like a Nosferatu on her prey. The guard managed a muffled grunt before Valentina's hand stifled his mouth. He wriggled in her grasp, but not for long as she maneuvered the concealed mask with its attached dose of sevoflurane to cover his nose as well. She triggered the inhalant and it performed its duty, sending the sleep agent into his system. The guard grew limp in her hold. She lowered him to the roof where he would lie unconscious for the next thirty minutes.

One more to go on this level, which held the access hatch. Scaling the building hadn't been all that hard since she knew its layout like the back of her hand. She dragged the guard out of the way, then peered around the corner, looking for the second one.

He was nowhere in sight.

Not an issue, Valentina thought. She tapped her cell phone, and the screen came to life. The black and white image displayed minimal light as Valentina guided her camera drone around the building and searched for the remaining guard. It wasn't until she'd nearly performed a complete loop that he came into sight.

He was coming around the other corner.

Valentina drew a small pistol from her side holster and waited patiently. She held her arm straight ahead, eyes fixed on the corner now that the soft *crunch* of gravel reached her ears.

The man appeared, turned, and walked toward her. He stopped, eyes narrowing as they peered into the darkness.

For a moment, all was still.

The guard's lips parted, and Valentina shot. The tranquilizer spat from the gun, finding its place in the guard's neck. His hands reached up, but he was already going limp. She held her arm straight, waiting until the man had fallen to the roof. When he stopped moving, she holstered the pistol and hunted for the hatch.

As Valentina unscrewed the cover of the ventilation duct, she wondered when buildings would stop installing them like this. Functionally, the shafts were a great way to regulate air and temperature, but they left a vulnerable access point in nearly every building in Atlantica. Hadn't people seen *Star Wars*? Didn't they know that they were installing their two-meter-wide shaft in their Death Stars? Didn't they know that anyone with Valentina's skills could break in?

To be fair, not many people possessed Valentina's skillset.

She wriggled inside, leaving the hatch cover beside the entrance. As she entered the darkness, she pictured a trail of blood ahead of her, a man struggling to pull himself through the vents. At least this time Dick Chambers wasn't joining her. At least this time he wouldn't mess up her outfit and slow her down.

At least this time she knew her way inside.

She took her time, moving arm over arm as she worked toward the correct drop-in room. The steel chamber magnified every tiny sound, so she worked to ensure that only silence prevailed. As she made the correct lefts and rights, dropping and climbing as the system allowed, her mind drifted to Dick Chambers, wondering how he was. In the week since leaving him in the hospital to recover, she had looked through his apartment window and saw him hobbling around with a white patch secured to his hip, yet she hadn't visited him personally. She didn't know how or what to say. Dick Chambers had put himself in harm's way, almost endangering her mission with Deng Zenim. How was she supposed to approach that conversation with him? How was she supposed to explain that her work was dangerous, and it didn't matter how skilled you were in your profession. Even being associated with Valentina was a death sentence.

Valentina stopped at a grate that looked down into a darkened room. She twisted a small lock and allowed the cover to swing open on its hinges. She dug into her pocket and found a small remote control with a single button on its front. She pointed it into the room and pressed the button. Easing herself out, she gripped the vent above until she could lower herself no more and dropped. She bent her knees, using her hands to balance on the floor and shrink her size.

The room was quiet. The room was cold.

Around her, exhibits glinted in the glow of the city lights. Large windows with thick, tied-back velvet curtains took up most of the wall space. Gold pieces of strange artifacts littered the glass cases. There were coins and goblets, compasses, ornaments, and more. Display signs informed museum viewers about the history of the items.

A red LED flashed in the far corner of the room—a CCTV camera.

Valentina rose and strode confidently to the corner where the camera was situated. There was a panel on the wall. Using an instrument with a flat head, she popped open the panel's casing, then let her fingers dance across the digital keypad. A screen only four inches wide showed grainy black-and-white footage of the room. She examined the last minute of the video, checking to see that it hadn't detected her presence.

There was no sign of her.

With a cocky grin, she made her way across the room toward a set of large oak doors.

She pressed her ear to the wood, listening for any sign of people wandering outside, stalking the hallways. The room she wanted was four doors away, protected by a combination lock that had been stupidly easy to determine. A quick break into the director's associate's apartment to grab his address. A well-placed tapping program on his computer, downloaded without his knowledge over the internet. A day or two later and the code was hers.

If only people were more tech-savvy. At least then this job might be a challenge.

She eased the door open after disrupting the sensor trigger that informed the guard's control desk that there was activity in the relic room. The hallway was dark. A long woven rug ran the entire stretch of the floor and covered the slate tiles. Great pieces of art hung on the walls, at least twice Valentina's height. She crept along the hallway, walking softly across the rug and listening for any signs of disturbance.

Muted footsteps came from somewhere around the corner. Valentina tucked herself closer to the wall, finding a nook where an exhibit might have once stood. A figure dressed all in black appeared, silhouetted in the milky light coming through the window. The figure touched a finger to its ear. Valentina made out the strange static hiss from radio instructions muttered directly into someone's ear although she couldn't distinguish the words.

Valentina stood perfectly still, barely daring to breathe. Her hand hovered by the tranquilizer pistol.

The figure stopped outside the diamond room, the door rimmed in gold with an ornate carving in the shape of a diamond on the oak surface. The figure tapped a code into the panel, the door *clicked* open, and the figure entered the room.

Shit, Valentina thought. She needed that room to be empty. She had tried to find a thousand ways inside the room, but her current route had been the safest and most efficient. With some of the highest-priced valuables in the diamond room, the museum had been careful to allow no easy access points. There was one door in and one door out. That was it.

Valentina thought for a moment about her next move. She

had two options to choose from. On the one hand, she could continue with her mission and wait for the guard to leave the room before attempting the heist again. On the other hand, she could leave now, undetected, and try again another day.

Valentina didn't like the second option. She was so close, now. The diamond was a whisper away.

She stood, gaze fixed on the door for a beat of time, wondering when the figure would emerge. The person exited the room a short while later, carefully easing the door closed behind. Judging by the figure's gait and the way they moved, Valentina assumed them to be female. What she didn't understand was why a guard was so careful when closing the door.

She followed the figure with her gaze as she departed the way she had come. Valentina's skin prickled, sensing something awry. The moment the woman was gone, Valentina snuck to the door and punched in the code she had acquired from the director's computer. She eased the entry open, thumbed her remote disrupter, and slid inside.

The room was silent, the weight of its value thick in the atmosphere. There was no natural light in here, nowhere for glass to smash and people to break in. Sconces hung on the wall to compensate for the lack of natural light, though now all were off. Valentina spotted the LEDs on the security cameras, noting that all their lights were flashing, indicating the frozen feeds.

Good.

Valentina shone a light, unable to pick up anything before her. That didn't matter, though. She knew that lasers scattered in all the directions she'd have to face. She'd done her research. She'd seen the scenes from old spy movies in which the agents had to manipulate themselves into strange and exotic positions to navigate the labyrinth of beams.

It was all so cliché. Technology had come a long way in that time.

Valentina moved to the nearest wall where another panel sat.

She inserted the key she had stolen from one of the guards into the lock and opened the casing. The digital screen needed a thumbprint. She took out her acetate sheet with the imprint from one of the guards and was pleased to see the reader accepted it.

Piece of cake, Valentina thought while striding across the room. There wasn't a part of her that worried about getting caught, no lasers to trip, no more nearby guards.

She headed to the central dais, approaching the glass casing where the diamond sat inside on a plush velvet pillow. Red rope cordoned off the display, but Valentina stepped over it gracefully, pausing at the showcase…

Where the diamond was missing. An object carved in its likeness but made of wood replaced it.

Valentina gave a knowing nod, her mind going back to the figure she had seen emerging awkwardly from the room.

That was when the alarm tripped.

CHAPTER THREE

The sound was unbearable, screeching around the room as a green light flashed and pulsed.

Valentina returned to the door, hearing the shouts and footsteps of the guards sprinting toward the room. She looked around, finding a place to grab the wall nearby, where the wood paneling was carved and shaped in ornate features. She pulled herself up to a shelf that lay above the main door into the exhibit room. She crouched and waited in the dark.

The door burst open. Four guards raced inside, flashlights waving back and forth as they approached the glass casing.

"How?" one of them exclaimed, flashlight aimed at the wooden structure.

Another inserted a key in the side of the casing, then pushed a button. Hydraulics hissed as the display rose from its mechanism and revealed the inside of the exhibit.

The second guard picked up the wooden object in both hands, turning it over to examine. "There's no marker. There's nothing."

"Could have been fingerprints," the first announced. "Not anymore, though. You've seen to that."

Valentina tensed as they stood straight and panned their flashlights around the room. "Are they still in here?"

The flashlights lit up the exhibits, light scattering as it hit the contours and angles of the glass casings. A couple of times Valentina shielded her eyes from the bright sparks, but the guards paid no attention, only looking behind the exhibits and at floor level.

"Nothing. Fuck," the first guard declared. "Seriously? We're going to have to call the AJS."

A third guard ran his fingers through his hair. "We have to tell Rogers first. He's going to be pissed. How can this happen on your watch?"

"You think Rogers doesn't know?" the woman snapped. "He has his home system rigged to our security. Fuck. Fuck, fuck, fuck."

"Reckon anyone else picked anything up?" the first guard asked.

The others debated this as they wandered over to the door. The woman patched through on her radio, getting a response a moment later. "Someone ran past the weapons displays. They gave chase but were too slow. Said they jumped from the window on level three."

"Jumped from the window?" one of the guards replied. "How did they manage that? From level three? That would've been east-side out onto Primment Road."

The woman frowned. "That's what they said, okay? I'm not going to argue with them."

They made their way toward the door. Valentina tracked them below.

The guard continued, "That's an impossible jump. Forty feet at least. They'd smash their heads and die."

Another spoke up. "Imagine if a car sped by, too."

The woman ran a hand over her face. "I don't care about whether it's possible. I'm saying what I heard. Thompson,

Kurshtu, you stay in here and check the place for clues. Don't fuck up anything until the AJS get here, though."

Thompson rolled his eyes.

"Problem?" the woman challenged.

"No," he replied.

She closed the door behind her and left the room in silence. With the absence of the other torch, Valentina let out a brief sigh of relief.

"Fucking AJS," Thompson grunted.

Kurshtu wandered over to the dais, shining his flashlight around the base and looking at the floor as if expecting to find footprints. "What's your issue with the AJS?"

"Government pigs," Thompson replied. "Spent three years in one of their gritty precincts. Worst three years of my life. Bureaucratic bullshit, y'know? Spend a thousand years to pass a piece of paperwork and get shit done. They'll come here, sniff around a while, cordon the place off, but they won't find anything. They never do. I never did while I was with them."

Kurshtu ran his finger across the carpet, then inspected the tip. "Maybe it was you being shit at your job." He grunted as Thompson clipped his head with one hand.

"I was great at my job," Thompson snapped. "Whole reason I went into private security, to get away from those pigs. If Rogers gave us the tools to inspect and chase, we might have a chance at catching people. We're neutered here. Obeying fucking government policies and guidelines and giving people rights when they perform acts of injustice."

Kurshtu shrugged, clearly unbothered by it all. "This is a public organization. AJS jurisdiction. You don't like it, work as someone's home security detail. No rules there. Kill a guy on sight. Could be more fun for you."

Thompson waved his flashlight at the ceiling, sending the light sparkling off a crystal chandelier. Valentina held her breath once more.

"Nah, I don't think so," Thompson replied absently.

Kurshtu laughed.

"What?" Thompson asked.

"You're scared," Kurshtu declared. "Can't stand the heat of being on the real firing line."

Thompson growled. "Bullshit."

Kurshtu held up his hands. "I get it. Really, I do. Don't fancy being murdered on site, do you? Those billionaires in their penthouses and mansions have all manner of Atlantica scum looking to break in and make a quick buck, all of them out of sight of the AJS. Some fleabag breaks into a private residence to steal ten bags of coke or a stash of cash from under the owner's bed, and what can the AJS do? Nothing. It's on private property, so it's out of their hands."

"I could handle it," Thompson replied.

"Okay." Kurshtu's grin grew. "If you say so. I mean, I'm happy to admit that security in the city is better than bleeding on the floor in a stranger's house with no ability to call the authorities and get justice. But if you want to pretend that you're above it all—"

Kurshtu shut up as a fist pounded into his cheek. He fell to the floor, cracking his head on the dais. Thompson stood over him, chest heaving, flashlight aimed at Kurshtu's face. "Shut your fucking mouth."

"All right, all right," Kurshtu protested. "It was only a joke. Jesus."

Thompson nodded. "Better be—"

Kurshtu lashed out, kicking at the back of Thompson's legs. Thompson fell to his knee, eyes blazing with rage. He lunged at Kurshtu, who raised a knee to defend himself. Thompson's face crashed into it. He grunted. They fell into each other's arms, punching and kicking as they rolled around on the floor.

Valentina seized her moment, slipping down from her perch. The beams of the flashlights shone all around, but the two guards weren't paying attention. She opened the door, then slipped out.

The closed door muted the sounds of their scrap. Valentina crept to the far wall and found a space to tuck away behind a miniature Grecian pillar with a vase standing proudly on top. She could hear several guards all around her, commotion coming from somewhere nearby.

She looked at the door where she'd entered. Two guards stood outside it. She cursed, reached for her pistol, lined up a shot, and took it.

The dart flew through the air, finding its bed in one guard's neck. She fired the next one too quickly, which compromised her aim. The dart stopped in the lapel of the man's jacket.

The first man gasped, hand finding the dart. The second man instantly reached for his pistol. "Halt! Who's there?"

Valentina broke cover, shooting the tranquilizer gun once more. The guard's eyes widened as he pulled the trigger, but Valentina had leaped to the side, using the wall to bounce back and run toward the man now collapsing on the floor.

She shoved the door open, the echo of the man's shot sounding through the hall and drawing a series of cries from the other guards. Valentina raced to the center of the room and used one of the central exhibits as a launching platform. She deftly jumped for the open vent in the ceiling and pulled herself up.

The shouts gathered outside. Someone entered the room. Valentina made out their flashlight beam as she crawled farther into the ventilation shaft. She knew the way, but she needed to be quick, and quick meant making noise.

She shuffled along. Then her foot kicked the metal shell with a resounding echo. Shouts rang out, followed by several gunshots. Valentina sped up, throwing caution to the wind as she made progress and got out of harm's reach.

Cool air kissed her face as she emerged on the roof, empty-handed and rattled. She grimaced, hating that someone had bested her on a mission. It rarely happened, and there was a reason for that. Valentina was the best in the business.

She looked out across the city, hunting the horizon for signs of another thief. She remembered the guards mentioning the east side of the building, so she ran around the corner.

The museum's east side offered a view across a broad street with four lanes of traffic. Nightclubs and bars made up most of the bottom sections of the large skyscrapers although a few buildings slotted in between, fitted with irregular designs that looked like they belonged in another city or country.

Valentina scanned the horizon, sure that she would have missed her chance to find the other thief. The moon was full but blurred behind the veil of fog above, spilling down a faint milky light in the darkness.

Something moved—a tiny shape on a building across the next street.

Valentina didn't question it. She ran.

She skidded at the edge of the building, using the gravel to provide the momentum for her legs to slip over the ledge. Her fingers gripped the edge as her body lowered against the wall. She dropped five feet, landed, and twisted over the next roof, working her way down to level two, then level one.

A guard caught her moving. She shouted something, and a projectile whizzed by Valentina's ear. Valentina kept moving, arms pumping as she sprinted across the road. A car honked its horn as Valentina dive-rolled over the top. She landed safely, wove between two driverless cabs, then darted into the shadows of the alley across the street.

Valentina knew the city like the back of her hand. She found the fire escape leading to the rooftop where she'd seen the movement and scaled her way up. The first level was a leap off a dumpster, but after that it was easy. She sprinted past the windows of residents, most of them dark or curtained. A few had their lights on, enjoying late-night TV as questionable smoke leaked from their air vents.

Valentina emerged onto the flat rooftop, eyes scanning for what she had seen. She ran to the farthest edge and looked across to where something was moving, four buildings across.

A woman. An agile woman, leaping across the gaps and escaping from sight.

Valentina gave chase.

When she reached the edge of the first rooftop, she sprang off one foot, arms pinwheeling in the air as she flew toward the next roof. This building was slightly lower, which helped her gain some distance although she still had to roll to soften her landing.

On approaching the next building, Valentina looked up at the wall in front of her as she drew out her grapple gun and aimed it at the roof's lip. She leaped. The hook gripped the edge, and the line went taut. She softened her impact with the wall by using her feet and bending her knees. She pulled against the cable and made her way up.

The woman was only two buildings away, now. It seemed she was slowing as if satisfied that the museum guards were no longer giving chase and she was out of the danger zone.

Valentina heard Kenny Loggins belt out a riff in her mind.

She lowered her head and dug her feet into the pebbled surface. She vaulted over the metal construction of a rooftop vent, then stopped as she reached yet another edge.

The woman had disappeared.

Valentina glanced down at the next rooftop, easily a ten-foot drop onto its surface across a fifteen-foot gap. Near the edge was an old mattress, its surface stained, the corners ripped. Valentina wondered if the thief had placed it in advance, knowing what her escape route would be and that she'd need to soften the impact of landing.

Valentina made the jump.

Wind whipped her hair as the city unfolded below. Cars sped

by. The rooftop grew closer. For a brief moment, she felt weight-less, immortal, like some kind of superhero from the movies her parents made her watch as a child.

Not that she needed much encouragement.

Then she was on the mattress, executing the roll and pushing off and onto her feet.

She slowed and walked the remaining distance to the edge of the roof, eyes peeled for the woman who was still nowhere in sight. Around her, ventilation systems spewed clouds of conden-sation into the night. Despite the vibrant activity below, there was a calm to the rooftops. That was why Valentina liked them. The city was a bustling hive of action through most of the night, depending on where you went in its heart, but the rooftops granted a brief reprieve from the chaos—a breath in the eye of a hurricane.

The vapor clouds were warm, flitting around Valentina and masking her view. They snaked around her, giant metallic-smelling cobras that she cleared as she made her approach to the final rooftop.

Not that she needed to bother. Someone moved behind her.

Valentina gripped her tranquilizer gun and spun, arms straight out in front of her, pistol aimed at the throat of the other woman.

CHAPTER FOUR

"You still have it," Gabriella "Gabby" Torres exclaimed, a grin on her face as she stood with her hands on her hips. Despite the gun aimed at her throat, there was no concern in her eyes. "You don't miss a beat, do you?"

"Apparently I do." Valentina lowered her weapon. "I didn't foresee the fact that someone else would be here to do the same job at the same time."

Gabby chuckled. She was only an inch shorter than Valentina, but they were similar in many ways. Their athletic builds matched, they were both natural brunettes, and their fatigues were close in style but not in color. The differences were somewhat less subtle. While Valentina's wig was a vibrant red, Gabriella chose not to disguise herself so. Valentina's skin was light, whereas Gabriella's was caramel in color, hinting at her Latina roots. Valentina hadn't seen Gabby for years, not since she'd spent time in Madrid, but over the last few weeks, she'd picked up many signs of Gabby's work, having crossed her path once already.

"It's about time there was a bigger fish," Gabby crooned. "The legend of the Red Countess is fading, Val. You've been in hiding from the public eye for far too long, and people need a new figure of notoriety. I figured I'd step up for you. Maybe drive my prices up a little." She drew the diamond from a small backpack, then tossed it casually in the air.

Valentina shook her head. "Seems like a stupid move to me. There's a reason I laid low for so many years. Notoriety increases your chances of capture. Sure, the pay packets are good from those who still trust you and want to work with a celebrity, but sooner or later they come at you from all sides. Those walls close in. After that is just torture."

"Sounds like the attitude of a quitter," Gabby replied. "If you didn't like the limelight, you should have said. I'd have been happy to swoop in."

"As we established last time," Valentina commented, "I had no idea you were in the city. What is it with you and following in my shadow? It's like you enjoy being in second place."

Gabby's smile slipped.

Valentina continued, "There will always be those who eat the leftovers off the shark's body. Birds that peck the fleas from the hippos. Greater animals eat their prey while others simply take what's left. If that's what you want to be, then fine. I'll get used to you being an irritating thorn in my side."

Gabby's eyes lowered, and her grip tightened on the diamond. "We used to be friends, Val."

"Then you couldn't stand the heat," Valentina replied. "There's a reason I left everything behind, okay? There's a reason I jumped ship without a word, traipsing halfway across the fucking world to this island."

"Is that reason Dick Chambers?" Gabby had a knowing look in her eye.

Valentina faltered.

"Hit a nerve, have I?" Gabby continued.

Valentina let out a breath. "You don't know the truth. That's okay. No one does. Sure, Dick's a fun plaything to occupy my time, but if you think he's my sole reason of service, then you're mistaken."

Gabby looked hurt by Valentina's words, looking up at her in the way a little sister might look up at her older sister after she refused to let her go to the mall with her and her friends. "I tried to save his life, y'know."

Valentina's eyes narrowed. "Excuse me?"

"The night he was taken by Zenim's minions," Gabby explained. "I warned him. Broke into his apartment and urged him to flee. He was too slow, of course. Or, maybe they were too fast. Either way, I did you a solid."

Valentina ran a hand down her face. "I didn't ask for your help."

"You don't need to. I'll give it without you asking. That's one of my faults, I guess. I've always got a soft spot for you, Val."

Valentina shrugged off her comments. "Give me the diamond."

"No." Gabby returned the diamond to her bag, eyes glued to Valentina.

"Hand it willingly, or I take it by force," Valentina warned.

Gabby shook her head. "My employer has his sights set on this baby. I can't even begin to tell you how many zeroes he's offering in return."

"You said you'd help me," Valentina stated. "Hand me the diamond."

"No." Gabby fixed her gaze on Valentina, sizing her up.

"You wouldn't have stopped if you didn't know that I would win this fight," Valentina remarked. "You would have kept running."

Gabby's grin returned. "It's nice catching up with an old friend. Besides, I wanted to test myself. Since I got to the diamond before you did, I'd say there's a fair chance that I'm one step ahead of you."

"Is that so?" Valentina replied.

"Mmhmm." Gabby chuckled. "I'll see you around, Val."

She turned to leave. Valentina broke into a sprint. Something exploded beside her, a small detonation that created a hole in a nearby vent and spewed a cloud of warm steam directly at her.

Valentina coughed and waved a hand in front of her face as Gabriella faded from view. She continued her run, finding Gabby leaping across the next rooftop and making her escape.

Valentina lined up her tranquilizer gun and shot. The remaining dart missed the target as Gabby took a sudden right step, as if she knew what was coming. Valentina ran and took a leap of faith. She landed on the rooftop as Gabby made it to the far end.

Sirens rang nearby, the AJS finally turning up the museum. *Thompson was right. Those fuckers are slow.* Valentina pursued, sprinting across the roof to where Gabby had disappeared.

She reached a fire escape and hopped down. Gabby was several floors below her, speeding toward ground level. Valentina was at a disadvantage, but an idea came to her. She shot the grapple gun at the lip of the roof and waited for the line to go taut. Once it caught, she swung away from the fire escape, nothing below her but air until it met concrete.

She thumbed the trigger to release more of the cable. She sped down, falling fast until she was ten feet from the ground. There, she pushed the button again, and the line caught. Valentina jerked and swung, then tapped the button again, falling until she hit the ground.

Gabby made it to the ground and turned to see Valentina. Her eyes widened as she sped toward a dark object protruding from the dumpster. She straddled the object, then started it and revved the throttle. The motorbike's headlights flashed to brilliant life. Valentina moved an arm to block the light from her eyes as Gabby accelerated out of the alley.

Not one to allow defeat, Valentina ran out of the alley and into the street. Gabby was gaining ground. Valentina reached for her holster and drew a pistol that was half the size of the one she held before. She tapped a button, and a green light indicated the power had switched on. She closed one eye, took a second to breathe and line up the shot, and pulled the trigger.

The device sped through the air, catching up with the bike. A moment later, the tiny bullet buried itself in the rubber of the rear tire.

Gabby sped away, oblivious.

Valentina drew a long breath and watched the bike speed out of sight. Somewhere in the streets behind, the AJS sirens silenced and the night returned to its usual chatter. She crossed the road and made her way toward a fast food restaurant. There was a small alley tucked behind with a staff parking lot.

Striding toward a moped, she drew out her cell phone and tapped through a series of folders and files. She clicked an application, and her screen displayed a map of the surrounding city. The map gently scrolled by as the screen tracked the flashing green pin in the center. She straddled the moped and clipped the phone to a convenient mount before tearing out a panel beneath the handles and fiddling with the wires. Electricity sparked.

"Hey! What are you doing?" a voice called as a back door opened and spilled light into the dark parking lot.

Valentina grinned as the engine kicked into life. The man swung a laden trash bag at her as she walked the moped back and lined up with the mouth of the alley.

"Hey! Stop!"

Valentina blew a kiss before hopping on and kicking the moped into action. Although the vehicle was small, the engine barely powerful enough to haul a second person, it screamed its call into the city.

She emerged onto the roads and twisted the throttle to its maximum. The moped lurched, threatening to unbalance Valentina and dump her in the street. She lowered her body and braced her feet as she chased the tiny green dot.

The wind roared by. A smile grew on her face as the adrenaline kicked in and drove her forward. The moped wasn't the fastest vehicle she'd ridden, but its steady progress allowed her to take the corners with precision and a fair speed. With Gabby oblivious to her chase, Valentina could clock up those extra seconds and gain ground.

The dot continued through the city, making its way toward an acre-wide strip of gardens set in the city center. A tag above her location read "Vivant Gardens."

Valentina took a hard right, knowing a shortcut that the map wouldn't pick up. She continued along the road, then turned a sudden left into the belly of a pedestrian cut-through between the buildings. Stairs descended, and Valentina bumped down them, flashing the headlight to move the odd few people who walked in her way.

At the bottom, she skidded around the corner, the rubber fighting to grip the pavement as she rebalanced. She accelerated as the gardens came into view.

Pedestrians shook their fists as she passed. Her heart raced, fearful of losing the diamond. As she drew level with the corner, Valentina slowed, taking a left before neatly parking the moped on the sidewalk beside the fence.

She checked her phone. The dot was nearby. She peered through the metal fencing bordering the gardens, moving her head around to see through the bushes, and finally spotted her.

The park was empty, save for Gabby. Valentina knew better than anyone that this part was locked up after hours, primarily to protect its beauty from drunks and vagrants who roamed the city after dark. Graffiti and vandalism had marked Atlantica's greatest public areas too many times in Atlantica's formative years.

Gabby sat on a bench by the fountain. Valentina looked around, waiting to see who would come to meet her.

She was aware of the man creeping behind her before he

arrived, but curiosity drove her to remain still as the knife pressed into her side.

"Spying, eh? My employer knew that you would be a tough bit of work. Difficult to shake off, like herpes, he said."

Valentina scoffed. "You'd know all about that, wouldn't you?"

The hands grabbed her from behind and led her around the fence toward the gate. Few people batted an eyelid as they passed. As far as they were concerned, it was merely another couple having problems on their midnight walk.

The man fitted a key into the lock, then opened the gate. He crudely shoved Valentina ahead of him, then ordered Gabby to keep an eye on her as he closed the gate behind him.

Gabby's lips parted a fraction as she struggled to contain her surprise. After a few seconds, she smiled, her gun pointing at Valentina's chest. "You're really pushing your luck, aren't you?"

Valentina shrugged. "It's what I do."

The man's shoes *clicked* on the stone path as he approached. He was taller than the average, wearing a long brown trench coat with his hands lost in the pockets. A hat shadowed his eyes, the arms of his glasses the only evidence of what sat on his face.

"You said you had it handled," he directed at Gabby. "Is this how you handle your business?"

Gabby shook her head, sneering. "Not usually. Although most of the time, my demands don't clash with the Red Countess."

"They said you were the best," the man replied. "I suppose I had my doubts, and they've been proven right."

Gabby rolled her eyes. "She tracked me, but we have her here at gunpoint. What's she going to do? Steal my gun from ten feet away and shoot us both?"

Valentina smirked.

"Don't even think about it," Gabby commanded, her smile slipping.

The man stepped around to face Valentina, fingers laced behind his back. His chin stuck in the air as he looked down at her and she could now see the dark glint in his eye as the soft moonlight exposed his face. "The Red Countess..." he mused. "Such an honor to see you in the flesh. The tales they tell...they're rather...extraordinary."

"Legends are twisted truths," Valentina replied. "I wouldn't believe everything you read or hear."

The man's lips parted in a pained smile. "Ah, but you're too modest. Your infamy extends far beyond Atlantica, far beyond this continent we find ourselves on. The Red Countess is revered across the seas, used as inspiration in many Japanese comic books and TV shows. The Red Countess is the tortured soul who stalks our streets, exchanging her integrity for change, able to perform death-defying feats and turn invisible at the click of her fingers."

He moved closer and stared at her. "That's you, right?"

Valentina's lips thinned. "If you think anyone is capable of that, you might need to go and see someone."

The man punched Valentina in the face, arm moving like a cobra striking its prey. Valentina spat to the side. Gabby moved toward her, offering a protective hand until she realized the man was looking at her.

"I knew it," the man hissed. "You two are in cahoots." He drew his gun and aimed it at Gabby. In that beat of distraction, Valentina drew her pistol and aimed it at the man. The three of them stayed still, caught in a strange triangle.

The man kept his gaze on Gabby but spoke to Valentina. "I saw you once, you know? Five years ago, running through the street. My wife didn't believe me, said I was seeing things, making things up because I was overworked, overstretched. I pointed you out, but before I could track you again, you dissolved into thin air. Gone. One minute you were there, the next...poof." He drew a deep breath, finger flexing on the trigger. "I never forgot that moment. I vowed that if I ever saw you again, I would prove that your talents were only fictional. That you are human like the rest of us, and all the stories, the legends, the myths...I would prove them all false."

He swung his gun from Gabby to Valentina, both hands on the grip. "So, prove it, then."

Valentina narrowed her eyes. "What do you want me to do?"

Gabby interjected. "Hans, we should finish the transaction. We don't have time for this."

"We can do it in a minute," he replied, eyes fixed on Valentina. "What're a few minutes going to mean when the Red Countess is either dead or disappeared? You'll get your money, don't you worry, Torres. It's coming your way."

"Not if you're dead," Gabby replied, shuffling uneasily and glancing between Valentina and Hans.

Hans let out a loud laugh.

"I'd listen to her if I were you," Valentina reinforced.

Hans shook his head, still chuckling. "Or what?"

Valentina stared levelly at him as his tension increased. Her little finger flexed on the gun's grip. "Or...this."

Valentina smacked the barrel into Hans' hand, redirecting his shot away from Gabby and somewhere into the bushes instead. A car horn blared, and someone shouted. Valentina grabbed his hand and pulled him toward her, lowering his center of gravity so that his head was near her chest. She drove an elbow into the back of his neck and sent him sprawling on the ground.

Gabby stayed where she stood, gun tracking Valentina. Valentina strode confidently toward her. "You're not going to shoot me."

"No?"

"You would have done it," Valentina stated. "If you wanted me dead, it would have been simpler on the roof."

"I gave you a chance," Gabby explained.

Valentina shook her head. "That was your mistake." She stomped on the man's hand as he reached for her ankle. She walked to Gabby, only pausing when the barrel aimed at the center of her forehead. Somewhere nearby, someone was shouting to call the AJS and report a shooting.

Valentina fixed her eyes on Gabby. "Pull the trigger."

Gabby's eyes shimmered. "You're really making me do this?"

Valentina pushed her head against the gun, testing Gabby's resolve. Gabby took a step back. "Pull the trigger."

"Val, you're making this happen," Gabby stated as if reassuring herself that it wasn't her fault.

Valentina roared at her, "Pull the goddamn trigger, now!"

Gabby's finger tensed, but before she could shoot, Valentina uppercut her hand and sent the gun into the air. A swift kick in Gabby's stomach sent her flying back against the fountain. Her back hit the stone, her hair touching the water. Valentina dove for her chest, arms reaching for her backpack straps.

Gabby propped herself up on the fountain and kicked with both feet. The move pushed Valentina back. She recovered, then came at her again, managing to grab an ankle and twist it.

Gabby kicked again. Valentina lost her grip. Gabby sidled away, then lunged for the gun that lay on the ground near Hans. The man was on his hands and knees, pushing himself to his feet.

Valentina spun, grabbing Gabby before she could get much traction. She swung her around, throwing her at the fountain. Gabby fell over the edge and into the first stone bowl. Valentina grabbed the pistol, snatching it a moment before Hans could reach it.

"You stupid bitch," Hans shouted. "You don't know what you've done."

Valentina looked past him to where several civilians had gathered and were peeping through the iron bars. She gritted her teeth, then turned her attention back to Gabby.

Gabby climbed out of the other side of the fountain, dripping wet, dark hair clinging to her face. Valentina raced after her, gaining ground, but Gabby had spotted her and was making her escape. Valentina aimed the pistol and fired at her feet. Gabby cried out and stumbled. Valentina pounced on top of her. She dug through Gabby's backpack and snatched up the parcel.

The diamond was heavy in her hands. Valentina slipped it in her pocket, then leaned closer to Gabby's ear. "Nothing personal, you understand."

She ran for the fence before Gabby could cry out again. Scaling the top, she hopped down into the street beyond and ran for cover, ducking into a dark alleyway and losing herself to the city.

Triumphant, and a little sore.

CHAPTER FIVE

Valentina scaled the walls of Archie Fontana's residence in near silence. No cameras tracked her. She barely left a mark on the way in.

The building was quiet, with most of the staff either asleep or home for the night. Valentina took her time roaming along the cold, clinical halls, allowing herself a moment to think in the quiet solitude. A wash of moonlight filtered through the glass windows and cast long quadrilateral shapes on the floor, glittering and filling the corridor with a mystic haze.

The diamond was heavy in her pocket. She couldn't trust a driverless cab to get her here, so she had been forced to joyride once again. Ironically, she took no joy in the ride, but she had to get things done. No obstacle stood in the way of Valentina Winters.

Her headache was mild and was a soft reminder of the days she had a week ago, her alter-ego appearing in the middle of the night and taking her over. Valentina would never say it out loud, but those moments of losing control had been some of the most frightening of her life. She had previous inklings that perhaps it could happen, but knowing that it was there and was indeed more than possible—it had happened—unnerved her.

She drew the diamond from her pocket and eased open the gathered material, gaining a glimpse inside. To Valentina, the diamond was only a rock. It was pretty, sure, but pretty wasn't always functional. What did people do with diamonds? They *owned* them, crafted them into jewelry, or used them as strange societal status symbols.

Valentina didn't get it one bit.

Yet, here she was, delivering another stolen jewel to another bidder. The corridor fell behind her as she made her way toward Archie's office, ready to hand over the goods, receive the pay check, and allow Isabella—and herself—a good night's sleep.

Archie didn't answer the first knock. Nor did he answer the next three. Valentina picked the lock, easily bypassing the digital panel on the side with a small device of her creation. She nudged the door open and peered inside.

The room was empty although the desk lamp was still on. The air was smoky from the dregs of a cigarette left still burning in the ashtray. A faint whiff of something malty hung in the air.

Valentina closed the door behind her and roamed around Archie's office. She strolled, taking in the place, marveling at his collection of leather-bound books. There was a snootiness to his space as if Archie had modeled his primary quarters after offices seen in the likes of Arthur Conan Doyle novels. Rich woods made his furniture, and dusty bottles of vintage liquors showed in glass cabinets.

The computer screen was still active. Valentina looked around the room, then snuck a glance at the monitor.

Strings of code cycled across the display. Elements of the code were green, while others were red. Between the lines of varying colors were white algebraic equations that would look like nonsense to a layperson, but which now drew Valentina's attention.

She studied the riddle for some time—for a puzzle, it was. A sophisticated use of mathematic formulae led to a simple override code that Valentina tried now, using a finger to tap the letters on the keyboard.

F.U.C.K.T.A.N.A.

The minute she hit the final "A" the screen flashed in a series of violent lights. Valentina shielded her eyes, unable to look at the monitor for too long. When the flashing stopped, she watched as the green color bled into the proceeding sections of code, running through at least a hundred lines until it blocked at the next riddle.

Archie cleared his throat from the corner of the room.

Valentina looked up and smirked. "It's easy when you know the answer."

For a moment, Archie looked confused until he skirted the desk and looked at the screen. "You solved it? But... How? I've been working on that one all evening."

Valentina rolled her eyes. "Look past your hubris."

"What was the code?" Archie asked.

Valentina told him. Archie's face fell, anger creasing his eyebrows. "That bitch."

Valentina dropped into his chair and kicked her feet up on the desk. "She may be a bitch, but she's got you sussed. It's almost like she specifically knew who was going to be stealing her code."

Archie looked at her for a moment as if wanting to say something. He bit back his words, instead choosing, "I trust you successfully attained the package?"

Valentina cupped the diamond in her hand. She proudly tossed it in the air a few times and smirked.

Archie's gaze fixed on the jewel. "It's even more beautiful than I'd imagined."

Valentina rolled her eyes. Archie reached out to take the diamond, and she slapped his hand away. She spun in the chair and gracefully rose to her feet, putting distance between them.

Archie scowled.

"Honestly," Valentina mused. "What is it with people and diamonds? I've never understood the appeal."

Archie composed himself, standing straighter as he adjusted the buttons on his waistcoat. "*You* don't understand the value of diamonds? *You*? One of the greatest jewel thieves of this age? Someone who spends her time roaming around the city and lifting the unliftable? *You...*"

Valentina shrugged.

Archie scoffed, moving closer to Valentina. Valentina stepped back, and Archie stopped again as if knowing that he could scare Valentina away with his prized possession. "Women have swooned over diamonds for decades. The tiniest of sparkles fitted to the bands of their rings were enough to make women drop to their knees and vow to be with a man for the rest of their lives. Wars have broken out over the gems. People have spent more money than I care to count on their exchange, and *you're* telling me you don't understand it?"

Valentina held the diamond to her eye, the light from the lamp refracting through its edges. "Can't say I do. It's a rock. You can't do anything with it. Except maybe kill a guy."

Archie, who had been advancing again, stopped. Valentina smirked. It was the one power-play she had over Archie. He might have Isabella's brother fitted to a machine, binding her to his service until her brother recovered, but Valentina saw the respect in his eyes in Valentina's presence.

Archie held up his hands. "But women..."

"Women?" Valentina laughed. "*That's* the angle you're coming from? Because I'm a woman, I should be hypnotized by this thing? Entranced? Wet in the lips because of this...rock? This marvel of geological creation?" She wagged a finger and tutted. "It's compressed carbon, Archie. The same as coal, but with a different molecular shape. You think that kind of shit impresses me?"

"What does impress you?" Archie stepped back toward the chair. He sat and laced his fingers together. "What impresses the great Valentina Winters?"

Valentina paused, uncertain how to answer.

"I've got you, haven't I?" Archie commented smugly. "You don't know *what* you like."

Valentina's eyes lowered. "I'm impressed by the courage of the small people. I'm impressed by great deeds delivered by honorable men and women. I'm impressed by technological advances that can save a man's life when all signs suggest that he should be long buried in the grave. I'm impressed by people's abilities to exceed expectations and find a ray of light in the darkest caverns of their lives."

A silence followed.

"Poetic," Archie replied at last. "I only wish the rest of the world could share your vision." He rose from his chair and extended a hand. "Now, hand me what is mine, and you can have what is yours."

Valentina examined the diamond one more time, then tossed it to Archie. His eyes widened as he clawed for it, terrified that it might drop on the floor and lose some of its flawless shape.

Valentina helped herself to a bottle of wine from the rack. She sipped straight from the neck of the bottle. "Let me ask you a question. What is it that *you* want with a diamond? I thought a man of science and progress would be more interested in things that could help humankind, not just playthings for the shelves which will collect dust."

Archie studied the diamond, rotating it in his hands beneath the light. There was a hungry look in his eye as a smirk plucked his lips. "You are right, Miss Winters. This diamond, while utterly hypnotic, wouldn't do well for a man of my desires and tastes. That's why I have acquired the diamond for a colleague of mine. Someone who holds leverage in an arena in which I have none."

Valentina's brow creased. "The diamond isn't for you?"

"Oh, no, my dear." Archie pulled a soft piece of material from a drawer and delicately wrapped the gem. "Of course not. What could I do with something like this? Like you say, it's a rock. It doesn't provide energy and cannot be manipulated into components of medicine. It's densely packed carbon. That's something we can both agree on."

Valentina stared at Archie, an uncomfortable feeling roiling in her gut. "So you used me to fetch you an item? I'm the proxy for your trade deals with your friends and enemies?"

Archie raised an eyebrow. "Valentina…" He spoke as if addressing a child, convincing her that her response was silly. "You understand our situation, don't you? I help you, and you help me. That's the way it's been for years. That's something we have in common. I'm pulling my full resources into bringing Kit back from the brink of death, impossibly holding him together when he should otherwise be dead, with medicines and science that *no one* else has access to. In return, you're helping me. I thought we understood this?"

Valentina's fists flexed. "I didn't agree to be a work-for-hire pet you could lease out to your chums." She gritted her teeth. "You should know better than that."

Archie faltered and glanced at the diamond. He inhaled a long breath. "Miss Winters, I'm afraid you don't have too much choice. Does it matter whether the task is for me or others? Truly, the only thing that should matter is the extensive time and effort I'm putting into performing the impossible. Everything else is collateral."

Valentina drew a steadying breath, her nerves tingling. "It's been years."

Archie nodded solemnly. "That it has. That…it…has… Although, we're performing something that has never been done before in the history of the Earth. And we're making progress. Progress can be small, but every step forward is one in the right direction. All you have to do is trust me."

Silence lingered between them. Valentina strode over to Archie, stopped by the chair, and loomed over him. She bent closer, her face inches from his, eyes dark. "I am not for rent. Understand?"

"Valentina…" Archie chuckled weakly, fear in his eyes.

She drew her pistol, pressing the barrel into his side. "I don't mind the odd hit job for you. I don't mind working on things that are going to help Kit in the long run, but if I find out that you're advertising me as some kind of pet for hire to your goons, I will not hesitate to turn you into soup and spray these walls with your guts. Got that?"

Archie adjusted in his chair, the diamond forgotten. His hand moved to the pistol. He grabbed the barrel and pushed it away from him, the tension between the pair shaking the gun as his gaze locked onto hers. When there were a few inches of room, he let go. Valentina kept the weapon where it was.

"Need I remind you that I don't have to help you," he grumbled, upper lip peeled back, thunder on his face. "I am going to tremendous lengths, pushing the boundaries of what we know to keep him alive. I don't have to do any of this, Valentina. One switch of the button and all of this will be over. You can live your free life in the city, and I can pretend we never met."

Valentina's eyes narrowed. "Switch that machine off, and it'll be the worst decision you've made in your life. You think I wouldn't come for you? You think you wouldn't find yourself staring up from hell, your face on the morning papers?"

Archie nodded, humor coloring his cheeks. "Then it appears we're at an impasse."

Valentina held the gun for a few more moments. Eventually, she holstered it and stood straight. "Don't fuck with me, Archie. I'm not your rent girl. We have a good thing going on here. Don't get greedy and fuck it all up." Her eyes flashed to the screen where another line of code was waiting. "Dustbox?"

She said it before she realized she had. For a moment, Archie's face screwed up in confusion until he glanced at the screen. "You know the answer?"

Valentina shrugged. "What can I say? Computers and I go hand in hand. Plus, Deng isn't as smart as she thinks she is. I could read that one from a mile away."

Archie kept his face straight, but Valentina took smug pride in the fact that he was baffled about how she came to that conclusion, based on the equation, numbers, and letters on the screen. "Dustbox?" He typed in the letters.

A red error code flashed.

Valentina rolled her eyes. "The answer isn't to type 'Dustbox.' It says that the next answer lies *at* the Dustbox."

Archie frowned. "What's the dustbox?"

Valentina leaned over the man, seizing control of the keyboard and mouse. She opened a browser window and pulled up a series of images. "The Dustbox is one of the most notorious drug dens in Atlantica. It's a private residence at the bottom of East and Third where dealers and users from all over Atlantica come together to do blow."

Archie raised a questioning eyebrow.

Valentina looked at him incredulously. "Blow? Cocaine? Powder? Dust?"

Archie nodded as realization sank in.

Valentina scanned through images of darkened rooms, concrete walls littered with graffiti, and murky windows filtering light onto sleeping bodies. Wife-beater tops, tattoos, floors strewn with piss-covered cardboard, needles, and white powder filled the pictures.

"A real-life drug den," Archie commented. "Great news…"

Valentina returned to the code screen. "It says that the answer to the riddle lies in the Dustbox, in the place where the powder filters."

"What does that mean?" Archie asked.

"No idea." Valentina's eyes narrowed. "Good luck working

that one out, big boy." She leaned back and stretched. "Valentina needs to go home and get some shut-eye." She moved to the bookcase with the hidden entrance and folded her arms. "I'm waiting."

Archie stared at the images of the drug den for a little longer before finally relenting and moving to Valentina. He triggered the door, and they both entered the clinical hallway.

Archie was deep in thought with his eyes narrowed. Valentina kept silent, knowing what he would ask but hoping he didn't. She only wanted to see Kit before she headed home to rest. She didn't need to go down another rabbit hole that Deng had carved out.

"Name your price," Archie instructed at last.

Valentina sighed. "I'm not a pirate searching for lost treasure."

Archie stopped outside the door to Kit's room. A cleaning robot buzzed by gently, disinfecting the places where they'd walked. Archie looked at her. "Do you know the single reason that the AI you acquired from Deng is so sought-after? Do you have any idea what power lies in the depths of that code?"

Valentina shook her head. "Honestly, no. I figured it was a bravado power play from one rich bitch to another."

Archie laughed—the first genuine one of the night. "In a sense. Understand, though, that Deng is on the cutting edge of technology. She's a smart one, and she can build things the likes of which the world has never seen. Yes, the AI can break into some of the greatest unlockable systems in the world, but it can be manipulated. There is a glimmering of hope that the code might have the capacity to explore the genealogy of a human and unlock the secret behind the body's neural networks."

He unlocked the door. They walked across the short bridge leading to Kit as the lights triggered and illuminated the unconscious man. "The body is run by electricity. Small impulses tell each nerve and neuron what to do. A break in a synapse is like cutting the wires to a power source. But, imagine if we understood more of the body, could fix the broken, could reignite the parts of the brain that have otherwise died."

He circled Kit's body, staring down into the peaceful, pale face. "Kit's brain has been the primary reason we have been struggling to make progress. Certain functions have returned, and readings show us that he is healing, but progress is infinitesimally slow." He paused, eyes lighting up with morbid curiosity. "Imagine what we could do if we could break into the world's greatest computer. If we could hack into the same computer that Dr. Frankenstein played with in fiction all those years ago? The possibilities would be limitless. We could bring back the brain dead, wake the *actual* dead—although, let's be careful, there. We could eradicate all the restrictions we have as humans if an AI can stimulate, control, and fix the broken." A strange twisted grin appeared on his face. "Valentina...we could bring Kit back in seconds. All we need is that code."

Valentina's heart thumped in her chest. She had heard of biologists and medicinal experts worldwide experimenting with the brain and working to understand its intricacies, but this seemed impossible.

Yet, not entirely implausible.

The body *did* run on electricity. Human thoughts and emotions were mere signals sent along tiny pulses of energy through the body. Was that all that Kit was missing? Something to trigger the responses and kick him into gear? It couldn't be true...could it?

Valentina had held the code in her hands and acquired it for Archie. If he knew the AI had this kind of power, why had he waited until now to tell her?

Because he doesn't want to lose you.

Valentina blinked the thought away, banking it for later, at a time when she wasn't in the presence of Archie and Isabella's brother.

Valentina laid a hand on the glass, her breath fogging up her view of Kit. "So your theory is that you could use Deng's software to resurrect the brain dead?"

Archie nodded. "That, and so much more."

"Here's a question." Valentina's mind strayed to her conversation with Deng in the middle of the Tynamo compound and the brief address of Valentina's relationship with Archie. "Why all the riddles and clues from Deng? What does she get from all of this? I went through hell and high water to claim that AI, and it looks as though she preempted it all. She knew I was coming, and she knew I was delivering it to you." Her eyes narrowed. "There's something you're not telling me, and I want to know what it is."

Archie's lips thinned. "Unfortunately, some of this is *not* your business."

"It's my business if it concerns using me as some kind of pawn in your games," Valentina growled. "Do I need to be any more explicit about the hell I could make your life?"

Archie didn't reply. He smiled and nodded at Kit as if using Isabella's brother as a prop and proof that he had the upper hand.

Valentina had to admit that he did, but that didn't make it any easier for her.

Archie laced his fingers behind his back. "Suffice to say that mine and Deng's relationship is...complicated."

"She accidentally 'super-swiped' on Tinder?" Valentina asked. "She won't commit on her Facebook status? What do you mean your relationship is complicated?"

Archie thought for a moment. "That's all I have to say on the matter. Suffice to say that she's a smart woman, and preempting our move wasn't out of the realm of possibility. All we have to do now is work through her clues and unlock the source code in its entirety. Once we have the AI up and running, we may have some hope to heal." His eyes drifted to the man lying unconscious before them.

Valentina's expression steeled. "Then we better get to work."

CHAPTER SIX

Isabella watched her colleagues pack up their things as they prepared to set out from work.

The world had turned dark, the windows leading to the streets outside lit up with the glare of streetlights. The library had emptied some time ago, and now only a few stragglers remained as time drew to its close.

Isabella waved goodnight to her staff and thanked them for their hard work that day. Although there was a smile on her face, her heart was heavy. Naomi had given her a to-do list that was as long as her arm that morning, and Isabella had only made it halfway through it.

Ten minutes after the library was due to close, Isabella heard Naomi's telltale clip of heels as she sauntered over to the main entrance and locked it up tight. The main lights shut off, and only the emergency lights illuminated the library's interior.

"Good riddance to bad news," Naomi muttered, fiddling with a ring of keys as she approached Mission Control. She paused as if noticing Isabella for the first time. "You're still here."

"I am," Isabella begrudgingly replied.

"Why?"

Isabella sighed, trying her best not to snap at her boss. "Because there's plenty of critical tasks that need completing before morning, and they aren't all done."

Naomi's face darkened. "You're doing it all yourself?"

"I am," Isabella repeated.

Naomi shook her head then busied herself with checking that the others had turned off all the machines. "You'll learn one day."

Isabella laid a book down a little harder than intended. "Learn what?"

"To let the minions do the work." Naomi lifted her chin with a smug grin. "The minions can do all the busywork. Their lives depend on our pay check. Tell them what to do, and they'll serve as instructed."

"But they get paid less," Isabella replied. "Their responsibilities don't extend as far as ours."

Naomi laughed, the harsh cackle sounding around the empty library. "Bella... One day your moral walls will crumble, and you'll be standing where I am. Successful and proud. It doesn't matter who you need to tread on to get here. You just have to make it happen. If you don't swim, you sink. And you, my dear, are sinking right now."

Isabella made to answer, but Naomi cut in.

"Look at you, drowning in paperwork and to-dos." She clicked her tongue. "That list was a test. To see if you could delegate. Make the bees in the hive serve the queen. You don't win by being nice. You win by getting shit done." She watched Isabella for a moment, then shook her head. "Well, *I'm* heading home at least."

Isabella raised an eyebrow. "How do I have all of this stuff to do while you can finish when you like?"

Naomi didn't turn back, but she did laugh. "Because I know how to play the game, Bella. Best get studying up on the rules if you want to make it in this business."

Naomi disappeared through the side door, a crash following as it closed. Isabella remained in the ringing silence.

She grumbled and growled, eyes tired, as she ran a finger down the list. In front of her, a trolley of books needed reshelving, there was a pile of return slips to address, and several late fees that she needed to chase. She had no idea how long all of this would take her, but she struggled to put this work on the others. Isabella had been nothing if not independent for years, and she'd always much rather do something herself if it saved someone else aggravation.

She stared forlornly at the clock. It could be hours before she made it home that night.

Deciding there was no point in wasting more time, she got to work. She grabbed the trolley of returns and wheeled them into the long rows of books, standing like strange sentinels in the dark. Each squeak of the wheels was a giant declaration in the quiet, and after a while, Isabella noticed she was humming.

The city whispered outside, most of the sound blocked by the thick walls of the ancient library. Occasionally she fancied she heard a noise somewhere in the cavernous building. However, she soon discovered it was her footsteps echoing, and once, a pigeon circling in the rafters. It had somehow made its way inside the building earlier that day.

The clock ticked the day away. Isabella grew more tired, her eyes blurring as her body moved to autopilot and took over in the driver's seat.

The trolley was near empty when she finally heard a noise that pricked her attention. A voice in the back of her mind, laced with impatience. *Are you going to be much longer?*

Isabella pinched her eyes. For the last week, she had worked hard to pretend as though the events at that strange building hadn't happened. She didn't know what it would mean if it was all true—that she was some kind of psychopath, dealing with a psychotic episode and dual identities?

ONE NIGHT TO KILL

Of course, she knew Valentina existed, but the boundaries had been clear-cut. They had kept out of each other's lives. To have Valentina intrude the way she had on those few days was too much to think about.

I have places to go, Izzy. Places to be, Valentina crooned.

Isabella closed her eyes and drew a breath. "No, you don't. Not now, anyway. Wait until the usual time. I need to work in peace."

She waited for Valentina to respond and was pleased that no voice answered her. She reached for a book on the lower shelf of the trolley and was about to put it on the bookshelf when a voice spoke from behind her.

"Who are you talking to?"

Isabella whirled, launching the book in the direction of the voice. It was a heavy tome, easily six hundred pages in length with a leather-bound spine. The book flew at the man, his arms flailing to block it as he cried out in pain.

"Jesus Christ, Bradley," Isabella admonished. "What the hell are you doing?"

Bradley rubbed his elbow, then picked up the book. He eased the bent pages straight and closed the volume. "Jesus Christ? Didn't have you down as the religious type."

"What are you..." Isabella started, then realized what Bradley was implying. "It's a reflex. I'm not religious. It's just..."

Bradley nodded and smiled. "I know."

"What are you doing here?" Isabella looked around to make sure that he was alone. "How the hell did you get in here?"

Bradley shrugged one shoulder. "I worked here for years, Bella. You think I didn't learn a few secrets along the way?" He picked up a book and placed it on the shelf. "The question is: what are *you* still doing here? The other guys clocked out over an hour ago. It's dark outside, for God's sake."

"Now who's religious?" Isabella returned. After a moment, she deflated. "It's Naomi…this job. I have to work through the list before I can leave."

Bradley gave an understanding nod. "Need some help?"

Isabella considered turning him down. In truth, she liked the quiet and the solitude. However, she wondered whether Valentina would let her appreciate the silence as time wore on in the after-hours.

"Sure," Isabella replied at last.

They set about working through the list together, Bradley speeding through the tasks that he used to do for a living but now was no longer obligated to do. Isabella glanced his way as she zig-zagged through the aisles and found him at the computer, an appreciative grin on her face. She wondered why Naomi would ever have let him go in the first place. He was a great employee. He merely made a few genuine mistakes.

On one instance of passing Mission Control, Bradley glanced up and waved Isabella over. The cart squeaked as she wheeled it to the desk. "Question for you." Bradley pointed at the screen. "Who *were* you talking to when I surprised you?" He looked up, impressed by his misdirection.

Isabella rolled her eyes. "Why so curious?" she teased.

Bradley waved an arm to indicate the library. "I want to know if there's a target on my back or if someone dangerous is looming around that I should know about. You hang out with questionable sorts."

Isabella cocked an eyebrow. "I hardly hang out with anyone. If anything, I'm spending more time with you than I care to admit."

"Exactly," Bradley agreed. "Questionable sorts."

Isabella laughed, a heaviness falling off her shoulders as she did. She hadn't known how much she needed to have some company tonight, but she did. She waved his comments away and returned to the shelves with a fully restocked cart.

The library had many rooms, all of them alarming in size. As Isabella navigated the aisles that created a labyrinth of Grecian proportions for those unfamiliar with its layout, she wound up thinking, marveling at the architecture and wondering about her life. Her mind drifted to Kit, then to Valentina and their deal to remain on the island until Valentina could fix him—whatever that looked like. She wondered about her new role at the library. Not for the first time, she yearned for more. She longed for adventure, but in a civilian way—a world unruled by Valentina and her experiences.

As if summoned by her thoughts, Valentina spoke up in her mind. *You're wasting time.*

Isabella put a hand to her temple, mid-crouch. She gripped a book in her other hand as she placed it on the lower shelf. "I'm not wasting time. I'm doing my job. You know, the thing that gives us an alibi and ensures that *you* don't get caught."

For a moment, her head was silent. The darkness cuddled her, long shadows cast by the aisles, not that Isabella needed light to see her way around the library.

Isabella resumed, presuming that Valentina was gone again. A moment later, she learned that wasn't true. *I have a job to do. Places to go. People to see. Time is coming up.*

Isabella shook her head. "I won't be much longer."

You have half a dump bin to empty.

"Bradley is helping," Isabella muttered and glanced around to ensure that he wasn't nearby and watching her again.

Even with his help, it's going to take you another couple of hours. Pick up the pace, girl. This one's important.

Isabella rolled her eyes and stood straight. She rested her head on the cool surface of a nearby shelf and closed her eyes. "You've said that before. What is it this time? Another excuse to bang a quick buck doing some back alley dealings?"

Valentina laughed, the sound echoing in her head. *Not this time. This time it's for Kit.*

Isabella's stomach panged as if someone had stretched elastic and snapped it on her insides. She missed Kit more than anything, but she often wondered whether she had mourned his passing. In the beginning, things had looked hopeful, and Valentina had let her in on Kit's progress, but as time wore on, progress had slowed—halted, even. She had begun to doubt whether any of this would ever truly be over.

"What is it?" Isabella asked.

Valentina paused, then replied, *You know I can't tell you. It would jeopardize everything. If you knew, you'd be open to torture, to interrogation. We draw a line, and we keep it.*

"Then fuck off," Isabella replied, a little too loudly. She glanced around, shrinking into the darkness. "Leave me alone," she whispered.

She waited for a reply that never came. Satisfied that Valentina had listened, she reached for the next book on the trolley. This time, her hand moved faster than she'd planned. She rapidly grabbed the book and placed it in the gap on the shelf. Her arm and body jerked as she did as if someone with invisible strings was controlling her like a marionette.

"What are you doing?" she hissed.

If you have *to get your work done, let me help*, Valentina replied.

Isabella was about to protest when Valentina wrenched control of her limbs from her. The library shrank into darkness, her consciousness viewing everything as if through a murky bus window. She tried to move her arms and legs, but nothing happened, even though her body moved.

What are you doing! she tried to cry but discovered that her lips wouldn't obey, and she was only a thought in her head.

Valentina worked quickly, speeding the cart around the library.

The wheel squeaked angrily, upset to receive so much action, but Valentina was tired of waiting. She had things to do, and this late-night work Isabella was doing conflicted with her mission.

She gritted her teeth, doing her best to block out Isabella's protests inside her head. Isabella was strong, but she was tired, and Valentina had used that moment to press her advantage.

Valentina snaked her way through the aisles at a rapid pace, tossing books onto the shelves until the cart was near empty. The knowledge Isabella had acquired over time came to her without conscious thought, and the job hurried along.

When the cart was empty, Valentina slowed. She made her way toward Mission Control and found Bradley standing at the computer with his eyes fixed on the diminishing stack of papers beside him. He looked up as Valentina approached, a warm smile on his face. "Making great time, boss. Don't you worry, we'll have you out of here in a jiffy."

Valentina stuttered, unsure how Isabella might address this man. She settled with, "Great."

"You okay?" Bradley raised an eyebrow. "You look like you've seen a ghost."

Valentina busied herself with taking the last of the books from the dump bin and filling the trolley. She avoided meeting his eyes, leaning over the large plastic bucket to hide her face from view.

When she stood, Bradley was staring at her over the counter. "Bella?"

"Hmm?" Valentina replied, doing her best to emulate Isabella's posture and not give the game away.

"I'm here for you," Bradley stated with sincerity.

Valentina nodded. "I know."

Bradley looked down awkwardly, "Thought it bore reminding."

Valentina nodded again, then turned. She hurried into the aisles and ducked into the darkness, a sheen of sweat on her forehead. She knew that she was the master of infiltration and disguise, but pretending to be someone else entirely? That was a brand-new game to play.

Valentina sped around the aisles and completed the last of the returns. The clock struck seven as she neared Mission Control once more. Isabella was wrestling inside her, her heart was racing, and Bradley was waiting with Isabella's coat and bag ready to hand to her.

Valentina peered around the corner. "He's a cutie."

Isabella groaned. *Don't even think about it.*

"Why not?" Valentina whispered. "What harm could it do? You need to relax sometimes, y'know?"

Me?

Before Isabella could say another word, she strutted toward Bradley. She fixed her gaze on him as Isabella protested inside her head. On a couple of occasions, Isabella managed to jerk Valentina's body to the side and slow her progress, giving Bradley the strange view of a woman moving as if between fits of slow motion and fast forward.

Don't you dare!

Bradley laughed. "It really has been a long night, hasn't it?"

Valentina neared. She felt as though she was walking through tar.

Bradley cocked his head. "Is this supposed to be some kind of performance art? Honestly, just a 'thank you' would work for me—"

Valentina gave one last push of effort and fell into Bradley. He held out his arms to catch her, and their lips bumped together. Bradley let out a surprised grunt as Valentina kissed him, one hand cupping the back of his head.

Isabella protested, cursing in Valentina's head. Valentina kissed him a little longer, then lips still pressed to Bradley's, relinquished control. She chuckled as she receded into Isabella's consciousness, allowing the meek librarian to take over.

Isabella's blood ran cold. Not because Valentina had hijacked her body and put her in a precarious situation, but because her senses were on fire as she emerged from the depths of her mind. The kiss was nice. His lips were soft and warm. His touch was tender.

She choked, startled, then leaned into the kiss. His hand was on her waist, and a cologne she didn't recognize filled her nostrils.

Then she pushed back.

Bradley looked up as if startled from a dream. He glanced at Isabella, one finger unconsciously trailing his lip as he cleared his throat and stood straight. "Well. That was unexpected."

Isabella didn't know what to say. She folded her arms and glanced at his feet.

"Bella? Are you…" he started.

Isabella grabbed her coat. She shrugged her arms into the sleeves, then grabbed her bag. "Come on, let's get out of here," she instructed, fiddling with the keys and leading the way toward the side door.

Bradley grabbed his items and followed in silence. He didn't speak until they were outside, standing under the night sky as the city bustled past. "Bella…I know you're under a lot of pressure with work and your sleepwalking and all that jazz. But, just know, that was nice for me."

Isabella rubbed one arm. "Me too," she replied, meaning it, but hating the fact that she did. When was the last time someone had touched her like that? When was the last time she'd been intimate with a man in any way that hadn't involved the other half of her psyche taking charge? She conjured an image of the man she'd met in the strange rooms and compared him to Bradley. Bradley was younger. He was cleaner. His stubble was lighter, and his smile reflected an innocence that had been long gone in the older man's.

Still, she couldn't allow this to continue. She knew that to be true. Those she cared about got hurt. There was no question about that. Kit almost died because of her.

Bradley studied Isabella, trying to read her thoughts. He looked up and down the street, then sighed. "How about we grab a coffee, eh? You can thank me for helping you with a cup of java. Deal?"

Isabella liked the sound of this, but someone was shouting in the back of her head, a manipulative woman who had taken advantage of her station and now wanted to get away so she could take complete control of Isabella's body.

She was about to reject the invitation when she grinned and replied, "Sure. I'd love to."

Valentina protested as they walked down the street. Isabella answered in her thoughts, *That's what you get for playing with fire, girl. You make me kiss a guy, and I can make you wait a little longer to play.*

CHAPTER SEVEN

Isabella's coffee date was cute, but God did it drag on.

Valentina knew she'd overstepped her boundaries. She couldn't help it, a chance to be mischievous had presented itself, and Valentina took it. That didn't mean she didn't regret it afterward, but at least, for a moment, Isabella was happy.

Valentina jumped the short distance between the roofs, not glancing down at the sixty-foot drop into the alley's darkness. She blamed herself for Isabella not being able to enjoy her life, and why wouldn't she? In the beginning, it had all been fun to play both sides and stretch and flex her muscles, discovering her abilities as a moonlighting mercenary.

For years, Isabella had sacrificed her happiness for simplicity. Valentina might be focused, determined, and bullish in her approach, but that didn't mean she didn't have a heart. That didn't mean she wanted to see Isabella suffer.

She vaulted over a ventilation shaft as the city rolled by beneath her. At the end of a long block, she swung down toward the fire escape, descending to street level. She landed softly in an alley, crouching to absorb the jump's impact.

A homeless woman lay sprawled across a series of trash bags

nearby, her mouth open as she snored loudly. Nearby, a rat pecked at the plastic, pulling it like pinched skin until it popped. Garbage leaked out. The woman's midriff deflated beneath it, but she didn't wake. The rat disappeared into the bag, and three of its brethren joined the feast.

Valentina advanced on the woman and tucked a hundred-dollar bill into the waistband of her pants. *Why is it that only strippers can earn good money with their bodies?* She strode to the mouth of the alley and glanced out at the quiet street.

It was long after midnight, and the city activity had tempered to a low boil. She checked her surroundings, ensuring she had emerged near East and Third, and was happy to see that she had. She stepped out into the street. A couple of pairs of eyes looked her way—mostly a gathering of men under the influence admiring her curves—but Valentina put distance between herself and their wolf whistles as she homed in on the Dustbox.

For those not in the know, the Dustbox might have been difficult to find. Valentina, however, had come across this venue before when looking for a target. As she stared down the stone steps toward the metal door securing the way inside, her mind flashed back to that moment. The smell had been awful. The atmosphere sad and miserable. She promised herself she would never revisit this place unless she truly had to.

Which she did right now. She had to do this for Kit.

She took her time descending the stairs, then rapped her knuckles on the door. The sound echoed and, for a long moment, it seemed that no one would answer.

A letterbox slot opened. Eyes looked up at her. The grimy face of the person behind was silent.

Valentina crouched slightly, meeting the eye level. "May I come in?"

The letterbox slammed shut. Valentina waited patiently as sounds of shuffling and hissed conversations came from behind the door.

The letterbox opened. A hand poked through, a message scribbled on the palm.

"$"

Valentina narrowed her eyes. "How much?"

The letterbox slammed shut again. There was more hissed conversation. The letterbox opened, and another hand shot out with more scribbles on the palm.

"$1,000"

Valentina scoffed. "You have to be kidding me."

A gruff voice replied, "Tough shit. No cash. No entry."

The hand began to withdraw, but not before Valentina grabbed a finger.

A yelp of pain came from inside.

"Let him go!" the voice called.

"Let me inside," Valentina replied firmly.

The man shrieked as Valentina tugged the finger toward her. She could feel the bone threatening to dislocate. "Ooowww!"

The gruff voice tried to negotiate. "Fine! Fine. Not a thousand dollars. Okay? But you have to give us something."

Valentina rolled her eyes. She drew a switchblade from her pocket and pressed the sharp tip to the end of the finger. Although she only applied a little pressure, the man squealed, a small drop of blood appearing as the skin broke.

"A hundred dollars!" the gruff voice called, hard to hear over the sound of the man's squeals. Behind her, a few passersby glanced down the stairs then hurried on their way, eager to forget what they'd seen.

Valentina removed the knife and pocketed it. She held the finger a moment longer before shoving it away. The hand retracted quickly, disappearing into the darkness.

Valentina took a hundred-dollar bill from her pocket and fed it through the letterbox. "Okay, now let me in."

The gruff voice laughed. "Stupid bitch. You gave us the money. Why would we let you in now—"

Valentina reached through the letterbox and managed to grab a fistful of clothing. She pulled hard, hearing the sound of a man mash against the door, his cheeks pressed against the metal.

She flicked open her blade once more and pressed it to the man's body. He flailed in her arms, but she held firmly. He begged her to let him go, for the gruff man to give her what she wanted. Locks clicked, and the door swung open, Valentina still holding the man. The streetlights revealed him as a strange-looking figure. Easily the height of an eight-year-old, but with the face of a much older man, he flailed and begged for freedom. Valentina held his gaze a moment, burning her image into him before finally releasing her hold.

The man dropped to the floor and landed on his knees. He crawled back into the darkness without pause, leaving the gruff man sitting on an old wooden bar stool. This man was larger, with folds beneath his chin. His salt and pepper stubble was uneven, and a thick cigar hung from between his lips. One eyelid was bruised purple and half-closed. He appeared unfazed by Valentina's appearance. "Welcome back to hell."

Valentina nodded acknowledgment, then set off inside.

The way ahead was dark, lit only by the weak glow of the remaining overhead bulbs that worked. The smell was thick, and the air was heavy. It reached into her throat with grimy fingers until it forced her to tie a mask around her mouth and nose. The floors were bare concrete, caked in dust that Valentina questioned whether it was safe for her to inhale. The last time she'd entered this facility, it had taken half a day to flush the second-hand residue from her system.

Bodies were scattered everywhere. Not dead ones, thank goodness. These people slumped against walls, on the floor, and draped the stairs. Their arms were mixtures of scars, and they'd painted their faces white. She stepped over a dozen or so before taking a right into the first available room.

Streetlight filtered through tiny windows embedded near the

top of the building, looking out at street level. The windows were thick with grime, allowing only a little light inside. Beds and tables were crowded with addicts, all sleeping and huddled together for warmth. A few of them were naked. Valentina left the room without a word.

Where would Deng leave the answer to the riddle? That was the real question she was facing. Based on her last visit here, she knew that the Dustbox spread out in all directions beneath the city for at least a block. At any time, there could be one hundred to one thousand addicts feeding their habits and losing themselves to their addictions down here. Valentina heard the sounds of love-making in a distant room. She shuddered, feeling cold despite the cloying atmosphere.

After fifteen minutes of searching, she heard voices down the hall. These were the first lucid ones she'd heard since the fat cat at the entry and were nothing like the addicts grumbling their prayers and talking to Valentina as she passed, weakly clawing at her legs.

She made her way to the voices, finding a room without a door opening up to her right. A projector shone a film that filled the entire wall as a dozen or so men and women sat on a beaten couch and talked among one another.

Valentina leaned against the wall. There was a dark stain in the corner, and some dark lumps, too. The men and women laughed, ribbons of smoke filtering from the joint they passed around the room. Compared to the rest of the withered and frail addicts, these guys looked well-fed.

"...ink-heads don't know what they're doing," a woman admonished with a shake of her head. She had dark skin and several gold chains around her neck. Her eyes were black, and her arms were as thick as her head. She looked as if she'd struggle to get out of the divot she'd carved for herself in the couch. "That shit is dangerous. I keep telling people, stick to what they know.

Don't go around trying shit that no one knows what it does. The classics, y'know? That's where it's at."

A lean white man with a row of gold teeth chewed his lip. "Don't fuck with the formula. The big bucks come from the steady hands. Ain't that the truth?"

The dozen nodded in agreement.

An athletic woman with an arm covered in scars and braided blonde hair sat forward, tapping ash from a cigarette onto the floor. "Still, times move on, fellas. Can't grow stale in this climate. They may not have worked out all the kinks right now, but give it time. They reckon ink is gonna be bigger than crack."

A couple of those gathered shot her a look.

"You been trying that ink shit?" a muscular man with a gleaming bald head asked. The TV showed a man, not too dissimilar in disposition, walking away from an explosion. "Didn't have you down as an inker."

The woman shrugged. "Tried it. Not for me. Gotta test your products, don'tcha?"

"Bullshit," the large woman replied. "Get the clients hooked. That's all you gotta do. Sell the poison, don't consume the poison." She took a long drag of the joint, then passed it on. "That's how you build longevity in this business."

Valentina watched, fascinated, as they talked. This was how the scum of the city looked, those who sourced the weak-willed, vulnerable, and desperate into the dark side, only to siphon out every last dollar they could as they rotted and killed themselves from the inside out. Anger boiled inside her, but she knew that it wasn't her job now to take these guys down. She was well within her rights, being on private property, but would it bring her closer to her goal?

Valentina stepped out from her hiding place. Still, no one noticed her as conversation died and eyes drifted to the screen.

Valentina cleared her throat.

The lean man noticed her first. He bit his lip and eyed her up

and down, one hand straying to adjust his crotch. "Damn, hey girl."

Valentina took a step closer. The muscular man noticed her, too, straightening in his chair and looking her way. "Damn. Who ordered the POA?"

"POA?" Valentina asked.

The blonde-haired woman waved a hand absently, eyes fixed on the film. "Piece of ass."

Valentina blushed, eyes glancing down. "Aw, thanks boys."

The lean man stood. He was even skinnier at his full height, his cheeks gaunt and his clothes hanging off him like adult clothes on a toddler. He took a step toward Valentina. "Hey, baby. You paid for, or do we figure out something afterward?" He licked his lip, finger tracing toward his belly button.

Valentina's stomach turned, but she held her composure.

The muscular man was up on his feet next. He leaped over the back of the couch to step in front of the lean man. He shoulder-checked him back, teeth biting into his lip. "You want a real man, don'tcha baby? A real tough piece of meat to show you a good time." He grabbed his crotch, then looked over his shoulder. "Whoever ordered this ho outdone themselves this time. She's in a league far beyond what we normally get in this shithole."

The large woman rolled her eyes. "Ain't none of us order this ho. You think we got the dollar to pay for a bitch like that?" She bit her lip. "Even I know that she outta my league. Whatcha doing here, sweet stuff? Wanna powder that nose with some pixie dust?"

Valentina looked past the beefy guy and his lean friend. She connected with the large woman and walked toward her, leaving a wide berth around the gentlemen who followed her with mesmerized stares. "I was hoping to speak to some people around this place, find out some information."

"All the information you need is right here, baby," the lean man declared, following with a haughty laugh. He raised a hand, waiting for a high-five from the beefy guy, but was left disappointed.

The blonde woman held up a see-through plastic bag filled with white powder. "You want information? It's all just a sniff away, girl. Premium white, rock-bottom prices. Nah mean?"

Valentina looked at the hallway, where a pair of legs poked out from around the corner. *Rock-bottom indeed.*

Valentina kept her head held high. "You guys had many dealings with Deng Zenim?"

"Deng?" the large woman replied as the two men started circling Valentina like sharks. A few of the others in the room watched with interest that faded in and out, sometimes watching Valentina, other times turning back to the film. "Name don't ring no bell. You wanna give us more than that, honey?"

"Tynamo Inc.?" Valentina nudged. "Rumor has it she left something around here. A mark of some kind."

"Only mark left 'round here is skid marks," a man with pale skin and fiery auburn hair replied, his laugh belting around the room.

Valentina couldn't understand how people lived like this. The scent was working its way down her throat despite her mask, and she was beginning to go light-headed from the marijuana fumes.

The men closed in on Valentina. Occasionally she caught their eyes scanning her up and down, a hungry look in their eyes. "Will you gentlemen stop, please. You're making me sick."

"We know the cure to that," the lean man replied. He moved in closer. Valentina punched him in the crotch, eyes fixed on the large woman. The man buckled over and exhaled, hands covering his crotch as he collapsed to the floor in pain.

The beefy man's nostrils flared. He made to grab Valentina's arm, but she pulled it away, twisting to leave a beat between them both. "Don't even think about it, sir. I'm warning you."

The larger woman laughed, a hearty sound that seemed strange in a place so depressing. "That girl got you both owned!

Dammit Stevie, you ain't got nothing on that bitch. She could knock you twenty ways to the side in less time than it takes to blink an eye."

Valentina readied herself, muscles tensing. She'd been in a thousand situations like this and knew that the minute someone threatened a guy's manhood, he'd try to prove his point.

Sure enough, the beefy man stepped toward her, hand reaching out to grab a fistful of hair. Valentina ducked under his arm, then jabbed three fingers into the soft tissue around his elbow. He grunted as she followed through with a quick jab into his armpit. Her fingers felt the moist, hairy skin of his pit.

The man tilted to the side as a shockwave of pain rocked through him. He winced, looking for Valentina, who had worked her way behind him. She jammed a foot into the back of his knee as she took hold of *his* wrist. She twisted around his back, forcing him to the ground. He resisted, and he was strong, but technique prevailed as his cheek kissed the concrete and a cloud of dust mushroomed into the room.

Valentina held his thumb at an odd angle, testing its flexibility. "Are you quite done with your dick-measuring contest?"

The man grumbled.

Valentina squeezed. The man groaned. "Answer me."

The man nodded, defeat and annoyance in his eyes. "Yes. I'm done, girl. I'm done. Damn."

Valentina held his thumb a moment longer for good measure. When she was at last satisfied, she released him and stood straight. She dusted herself down as several of the men and women in the room started to clap.

"Good show," the large woman announced. "Damn good show. Girl, you got something about you, don't you." She held out the joint to Valentina. "Come, join us. We'll see what we can do for you."

Valentina politely declined. "Just the information, if you can. Anything on Tynamo or Deng Zenim."

The woman thought, eyes searching around the room then glancing at the others. "Sorry, nothing comes to mind. Don't mean there ain't nothing, though. Place like this is full of mysteries. Each room is its own *Twilight Zone*. People come. People go. Ain't no such thing as a day or a week here. It all blurs into one. Y'know?"

Valentina nodded although she didn't know. "Is there anyone around here who could—"

The ringing in her ears stopped her mid-sentence as the shot blasted nearby. Valentina felt the wake of the bullet pass, the lead stopping in the concrete wall and leaving a few small spider-like cracks. Valentina turned in the direction the shot had come from and found the lean man on his feet, a shaky arm extended and holding a Magnum in front of him.

He gave a weak laugh, a drunken look on his face, then pulled the trigger again.

CHAPTER EIGHT

Valentina's heart leaped into her mouth. She ducked. The bullet passed over her head.

Someone shouted, only one person. The others seemed unperturbed.

Valentina charged forward and planted her shoulder in the man's stomach. A gust of air flew between his lips as he crashed to the floor. Valentina straddled him, raising a boot to tread on the crook of his arm that was holding the Magnum.

He roared, trying to sit up. Valentina threw a haymaker at his face. Spit flew out of his mouth. She pressed down with her boot until his grip loosened, then went for the Magnum.

A hand gripped her collar and lifted her. For a moment, Valentina was suspended in the air, flailing as she kicked in all directions. Her boot caught the beefy man in the chest, but he didn't let go. Instead, he reared back and threw her across the room.

Valentina soared several feet until the wall stopped her trajectory. She held out her hands and used her feet to kick off the wall and absorb some of the shock. When she landed on her feet and turned, the beefy man had a strange mix of impressed and annoyed on his face. "No more fucking around." He lowered his head and charged like a bull.

Valentina ran at him. When they were about to collide, she skidded, allowing herself to sweep between his legs and slide along the dusty floor. Her boot caught the lean man in the face and knocked him unconscious. When she stood, she met the gaze of the larger lady who sat and watched the action happen, then glanced over her shoulder and fired the Magnum at the beefy man.

His mouth fell open as the bullet found his shin. He crumpled where he stood, hands shooting to the wound as he rolled around on the floor in pain.

Valentina pointed the Magnum directly at the lean man's face. His gaunt cheeks were sunken and hollow, and his lips parted slightly to allow for the gentle snoring. She could take him out right now, and why wouldn't she? The man had tried to kill her—twice! Still, something held her back.

Instead, she stomped on his arm hard enough to hear the satisfying crack of bone.

When she was satisfied, she tossed the Magnum into the far corner of the room, then turned back to the others gathered around.

The larger woman was standing. Valentina had no idea when she got up or how. She looked even bigger now that she was up, her ass easily five times that of an average woman. She walked with it sticking out behind her, looking as if she was about to topple at any moment. She shuffled toward Valentina. "Come on, sugar. Let me show you around. Maybe we can help you get that information you're so desperate to acquire."

Valentina cast a final glance over her shoulder as they left the room. The others returned to their smoking and film party while beefy and lean remained on the floor.

The larger woman chuckled as they descended through the dim light. "You got some moves on you, girl. I tell you, if I was ten years younger, I'd be moving like you were. Tenth dan in my martial arts squadron, that was me." She laughed again, a throaty sound. "Not now. No sirree. In case you didn't know, I'm a little over the legal weight limit." She patted her stomach and chuckled.

Valentina offered a weak grin in return. The woman huffed as she stepped over the countless bodies, high and in another realm of consciousness. "You don't believe me, do you?"

Valentina considered this, knowing that she needed to be careful in her response to discover what she was after. She opted for silence.

"Ooo, I'm telling you," the woman went on. "Before I got the ol' diabetes, I was your size, sweetie. Smaller, even. Can you believe that?"

Valentina felt like the woman was angling for a response she couldn't give.

The woman stopped and turned to face her. On the ground was a young lad with a beaming smile on his face, eyes dilated, body grimy and thin. The woman followed Valentina's gaze. "Circle of life, honey. Way it is. Dealers don't take drugs—or don't take too many nohow. Would be a good way to lose weight, but instead, I get fat off their coin. Not my fault if they addicted. Supply and demand. There's someone in every profession bene-fiting from the weak. This happens to be my arena."

Valentina gave an understanding nod.

"I've considered it," the woman added, voice lowering to a murmur. "Almost had the needle in my skin. Felt its teeth. Turned out I was too coward. I seen too much. Know the strug-gles they fight. Figure I'd be heavy and proud than skinny and dead, y'know?"

Valentina chewed her lip. "It's a nasty business."

"Ain't that the truth…" She waited a moment, almost as if she could sense that Valentina needed to get her fill and process what she was seeing. A few moments later, she placed a hand on

Valentina's shoulder. "Come on, girl. I'll show you to Drake. He may know something more about what you be needing. Drake knows things, y'know?"

They twisted through the labyrinth. Sometimes they walked down a short set of stairs. Other times they climbed. They took lefts and rights, made their way through doors until there seemed no end to the eternal maze of the Dustbox. She lost all sense of direction, and eventually, there were no more windows to the outside world. Finally, the woman stopped outside a set of double doors. She paused, then knocked three times.

A call came muffled through the wood.

"You ready, honey?" the woman asked.

Valentina nodded.

She pulled the doors open wide, and a strange thing happened. Cool, clean air rushed out toward her, blowing away all the dirt and debris she had endured. Light flooded her senses, cast by a series of chandeliers on a ceiling that was almost double Valentina's height. In the center of the room was a fire pit, surrounded by a circle of large cushions where a couple of figures lay. In the far corner of the room, a man in an aggressively loud jumpsuit was busy pouring himself a drink.

"Tanisha," the man called as if welcoming an old friend. "How you doing, darling?" He wandered over with a bottle of rum in one hand. He kissed her on either cheek. "Rare I see you over this way. You got a problem in the lower decks?"

"Nah," Tanisha replied. "Brought you a present." She scanned Valentina theatrically. When the man's eyes lit up, she quickly added, "I'm playing, Drake. She a snake. You play with her, and you're gonna get bit. Trust me."

The man slunk over to Valentina and took her hand. He kissed the back of it and gave her a sly smirk. "My dear, what a delight to have a beautiful rose bloom in the middle of our hovel."

"Hi," Valentina replied flatly.

"I must admit," he continued, "you find me embarrassed. A

woman of your beauty to have to seek us out here, in the depths of hell. It is something that no man of my stature wishes to place on such a cherry blossom."

Valentina rolled her eyes. "All right, Jack. Let's get one thing straight. I'm no cherry blossom, okay? You don't have to pave the way for me or provide some kind of elaborate setup to make me feel comfortable. I've seen horrors your eyes wouldn't believe—initiated some myself. So, enough of the princess talk and address me as I am, someone who has the capacity to kill you if you so much as look at me incorrectly."

For a moment the room was quiet. Valentina noticed Drake's confident expression falter for a millisecond before he composed himself. Drake clapped his hands and laughed. "I love it. I *love* it! Come in, dear. Come in." He ushered her inside, wrapping an arm around her shoulder. "What is it that you seek? You must have something in mind if you've made your way into the center of the Dustbox? Not a lot of people make it here so...lucid. So composed. Clearly not a consumer of product, so maybe... a buyer?"

Valentina shrugged his arm off her. She looked behind, surprised to find that Tanisha was gone, leaving Valentina alone with this lunatic. "I don't want your powder, your blow, your glass, your ink."

At the mention of "ink," Drake placed a hand on his chest and gasped. "Don't you *dare* slander our good name by bringing that...that...*shit* in here. Ink is for the classless, the desperate. Ink has no standing in today's world. It's a fad. Something that'll disappear in a few years. Our product... That's the winner. That's what will stand the test of time."

Valentina ran a hand through her hair. "Sure. Sure..."

Drake allowed himself to fall into a nearby chair. He looked up at her, a boyish expression on his face. "So if it's not the product, what brings you to our humble corner of Atlantica? I have to admit that I'm at a loss to offer anything outside of our usual selection."

"Tynamo," Valentina announced. A couple of heads turned her way. "Deng Zenim and Tynamo Inc. Names that ring a bell for you?"

Drake sank deep into thought. "Tynamo? That's the rich bitch out in the rural, right? I saw something about her in the paper last week. Some chaos at her festival. Am I remembering that correctly? Smoke bombs and fleeing festival-goers and parade floats?"

Valentina's mind cast back to the thick of it all. She thought of the bow of the ship, a chance encounter with Dick Chambers gone wrong as she ended up staging the saving of Deng's life.

"That's right," Valentina replied. "I have reason to believe that something was left here, or a mark was made in the Dustbox. Have you any idea of what I might be talking about?"

Drake thought a long while, his face twisted as if the very notion of remembering pained him. He drank a swig straight from the bottle of rum, then called over his shoulder. "Ladies! Any idea what this one's talking about? Tynamo? Zenim?"

"Golden dragon crest?" a half-dressed woman lounging on a cushion called. "That's the logo, right?"

Valentina's ears pricked up.

A man lying across from her raised his head. "The shadow lady? Her? The weird one?"

A balding man sitting at a table in the corner piped up. "I don't care how weird she was. She bought enough of our stash to last us weeks. Good customers come with heavy pockets and leave with empty ones."

Valentina questioned further. "Shadow lady? What was she doing here? Did she tell you what she was after?" She tried to imagine Deng strolling into a pit like this and purchasing experimental drugs. It didn't seem like her, but then again, how well did she truly know the woman?

The man waved a hand, eyes half-closed. In front of him, a collection of conical glasses held liquids of strange colors. One held a vibrant orange powder that reminded Valentina of spices her mother used in her cooking. She had a sneaking suspicion that it wasn't, though. "Left a package. A parcel, even. Something that we were supposed to look after. This was weeks ago, you understand."

"Where is the package?" Valentina asked.

"Why do you want to know?" the man replied.

Drake's calm façade broke as he snapped, "What right do you have to question a lady?" He composed himself and ran a hand over his head. "Especially a lady as pretty as this one."

Valentina placed a hand on his shoulder. "Calm down, Romeo. I'm not going to give you your pleasures today."

"So, a timeframe?" Drake smirked.

"Nor tomorrow," Valentina specified. "Nor the next day, nor ever, for that matter."

Drake chuckled. "We'll see." He clapped his hands twice, and a door at the far end of the room opened. A woman with her hair tangled into nests and skeletally thin arms peered around the corner.

"Yes, sir," she answered, voice cracked and dry.

"Fetch the parcel," Drake ordered. "Our guest has come to claim what is hers."

"I thought you didn't know who Deng was?" Valentina asked.

Drake laughed as if Valentina had asked the stupidest question in the world. "Please. I may not remember names, but I remember bodies." He drank her in, licking his lips. He leaned closer, near enough to warm her lobe with his breath. "She was a wild ride. I'll give you that. Knew her way around a man's body. Had her crying out in ecstasy until the early mornings, lost in a whirlwind blitz of euphoria and passion. You don't know the lengths I'm capable of."

Valentina gave a small nod and whispered, "You don't know my limits, either."

"I'd love to learn," Drake replied.

Valentina remained still as the door opened again and the thin girl appeared carrying a lockbox in her hands, the size of a large loaf of bread. The item was heavy, evidenced by her shaking arms.

She placed the box on the floor in front of Drake and waited. Drake glanced at her with disgust. "What are you waiting for? Get!"

The girl flinched, then scurried away, closing the door behind her as she exited the room. For a moment, the overwhelming stink of the Dustbox made its way into the room and tickled Valentina's nostrils. She wasn't prepared to go back out there. Not so soon.

"What is it?" Valentina stared down at the box.

"We've yet to determine," Drake replied. "It'll take a man larger than me to open that box. Believe me. I've tried."

Valentina crouched, examining the box closely. The outside was smooth metal, and brush painted in rouge. There were scratches and marks and meager dents where people had tried to tamper with the box and open it. A small lock clasped the lid closed, and residue of gunpowder still stained the front.

"You tried to shoot it open?" Valentina probed.

Drake's eyes widened, startled that she was so observant. "We exhausted all the other methods first."

More alarming than the gunpowder residue littering its surface was the black stripe that encircled the box. One inch wide and almost perfectly black apart from a series of green flashing lights that illuminated as Valentina's hand touched the lid.

The Cyclops.

Valentina's breath caught. She could swear the lights hadn't been there a moment ago. Now, here they were, activated and looking at her. She could imagine the strip sending its signals back to Tynamo HQ and Deng Zenim watching her from some screen with a smirk on her face.

Clearly, this was a new occurrence for those in the room, too.

"What did you do?" one of the women asked.

The man at the table echoed this.

"Nothing," Valentina replied although clearly, that wasn't true. She learned closer to where she'd touched, looking for something she might have triggered, but from what she could see, she only touched a metal surface.

Drake crouched beside her. He picked up the box in both hands and brought the Cyclops to his face. "There are letters and numbers in the strip. What does it mean?"

Valentina was about to answer, thinking of ways to dodge the truth when Drake cried out. He threw the box as something flashed at his fingertips. "Fucker! It shocked me."

The others in the room rose to their feet, staring down with curiosity at the box. Valentina remained crouched, head cocked at the item.

Drake glared at the man who had been lying on the cushions. "You fuckers. You told me it was inactive. Couldn't be opened and meant nothing. Impenetrable, you said. A piece of shit."

"Boss, I—" the man tried to argue.

"It fucking shocked me!" Without hesitation, Drake drew a pistol from his side and unleashed the magazine's contents at the box. Metal on metal *clanged*. Those in the room covered their ears and threw themselves to the floor. The bullets ricocheted off the container and flew in all directions. One even shattered a conical glass and spilled its contents over the table and the floor.

Valentina shrunk down, then moved behind Drake. Finally, she grabbed his wrist and wrestled the gun from him. He resisted, but she was quicker and took him by surprise.

"What the hell are you doing?" Drake roared, frenzied into a sudden panic. "Get your hands off me!"

Valentina twisted Drake's arm behind his back. Two of the women rose, pistols now in their hands. Valentina could only assume the pair had hidden them beneath the cushions. They aimed at Valentina.

"Tell your women to put the guns down," she ordered.

Drake grumbled. Valentina heard something *click* behind her.

"Now," she commanded.

Drake grinned. "You're surrounded. What chance do you think you have?"

Valentina whispered, "You really don't want the answer to that question."

One of the women barked, "Let him go!"

Valentina looked over her shoulder, and the man at the table was also aiming his gun at her. She growled and was about to let him go when a strange thing occurred.

The box started leaking smoke.

CHAPTER NINE

Valentina held her grip on Drake.

"What have you done?" he asked, fear laced in his words. The room filled with smoke, the other man and women going foggy and disappearing.

"It's not me," Valentina declared, loud enough that the others should hear her. "I haven't done anything."

"Shoot her!" Drake commanded. "Shoot her!"

A shot fired, missing by feet. A voice followed, "I can't see anything. What if I hit you?"

Valentina took that moment to move. She gave a final, decisive twist of Drake's arm, then rolled toward the box. It was difficult to make out in the cloud, but she found it, lifted it off the floor, then held it to her chest. She moved out of the line of fire as Drake shouted incoherently in the madness. Valentina crossed to a quiet corner of the room as smoke funneled out of the box. She couldn't understand why or how this had happened, but she knew that she could use it to her advantage.

The thick smoke wasn't toxic, and that was something. She had encountered various types of explosives like this before and had been on the receiving end of a few that nearly hospitalized her because of their toxic effects. This one was harmless although it filled her eyes, mouth, and nose and made it difficult to breathe. She searched the box for some kind of off switch, looking for any way to block the smoke and return to some kind of normality. People cried out, running around the room. Drake shouted his efforts to find Valentina.

She held the box close to her face, barely able to see the Cyclops strip around the box. Something green flashed and drew her attention. She leaned closer and made out a sentence that filled her with curiosity.

Game on, Valentina. Good luck getting out.

Valentina's heart sank as the smoke stopped pouring out of the lockbox. Not only because she knew the cloud would soon clear and she had a limited amount of time before they would come for her, but because the box was humming in her hands and was now actively sucking the smoke back inside.

It was a strange sensation watching the smoke disappear in reverse. The space around her turned thick with dark smoke as it all funneled toward her. Drake and his team shouted to aim toward the sound of humming. Valentina stood stationary, unsure of what else to do at that moment. A bullet fired nearby, dangerously close to where she stood.

She moved out of the trajectory, but they were still aiming their shots to the humming. Valentina knew that she couldn't let the item go, but she had to. If she wanted to live, she needed to move away from the object drawing the enemies.

She dropped the box on the floor. The metal clattered. The humming continued as the smoke thinned in the room. She found what she was after in her pocket and looped it around the box. Satisfied and narrowly avoiding another bullet, she ducked away and ran for the door.

The nearest one, as far as she could remember, was where the skeletal girl had disappeared. She found the rich red double doors, then booted one open. The mechanism broke, and wood chipped off the door. Valentina could now see the others as clear as day as the box absorbed the last of the smoke.

Drake leered at her.

"For what it's worth," Valentina continued. "None of that was my fault, and I didn't trigger any of it."

Drake's face told her all she needed to know. He didn't believe her. She glanced to her left and saw one of the women bleeding out on the cushion, a casualty of the chaos.

Drake pointed at Valentina. "You'll pay for this, bitch."

Valentina held up her hands. "Again, not my fault." She nodded to the box. "At least I'm letting you keep it. Doesn't that mean something?"

Three guns pointed her way. She was pushing her luck.

Drake was momentarily confused by this, which was exactly what she wanted. If Valentina had triggered the box, why wouldn't she take it with her? Clearly, the box was of value, so why the sudden switch?

Drake held up a hand, pausing the others from further action. The other woman breathed heavily, her perfectly manicured façade shaken, eyes dark as she tried not to look at her friend on the floor. Drake kept his eyes fixed on Valentina as he moved toward the box, taking his time to cross the room. When he reached the container, he crouched, not once removing his gaze from Valentina's.

"What games are you playing?" Drake asked. "All of this effort for a box, and still you don't want to take it with you?"

Valentina shrugged. She held up a hand, a small device planted in the center of her palm. As she twisted her palm in either direction, the light winked off a thin sliver of wire that ran from her hand across the floor. "Guess it depends who's pulling the *strings*."

She thumbed the button and gripped the device. The thin cable went taut, then tugged the box toward her. It zipped across the room, lifting into the air as she stepped back through the door and caught it in her arms. Without looking back, she ran out of the confines of the well-ventilated room and back into the depressing corridors of the Dustbox.

Their shouts rang from behind. Valentina took a turn, eager to shake them off her tail. Ahead of her, addicts staggered around the halls like zombies. Some were in groups, passing around their latest fixes. They were all too late to look up in time as Valentina ran by them.

Drake's men and women gave chase, but Valentina soon lost herself in the passages of the Dustbox. Their cries and yells faded into nothingness when she ran down a series of stairs and entered a deeper pit of darkness than she had previously experienced. Here the air was cleaner, but the light was non-existent. Valentina blindly held a hand in front of her, taking her time to walk along the dark passage. She dug into her pocket and withdrew a pair of glasses, which she slid onto her face. The world lit up around her in strange shades of green and black as she tapped a button.

She was in a corridor. This one was, thankfully, absent of addicts but was also painfully bare. She paused for a moment, listening to the events taking place above, but nothing came down here with her. There was a chill that prickled her flesh and the taste of something strange on her tongue.

She followed the hallway.

She could have turned, of course. She could have retraced her steps and snuck back, but Valentina's vice had always been her curiosity, and now that it had its hooks in her, she submitted to its will.

The corridor stretched before her. She took her time, taking large breaths to recover from the sudden outburst above. The box was heavy in the crook of her arm, the Cyclops occasionally emitting its strange green glow, watching her as she progressed. She almost wanted to set it down and leave it here while she explored, now that she knew not to trust the box to help her.

Whoever was controlling its contents—and she had a pretty good idea who that could be—she knew better than to let down her guard.

Eventually, the corridor led to a series of empty rooms on either side. They were similar to the abandoned ones above, although no one had touched these in years. Work surfaces were bare, apart from a few plastic pots that had cracked as the plants inside strained in their efforts to live. Now they were wilted, black, and crumbling into dust. A little farther ahead, the corridor turned right, and at this junction, Valentina spotted a dull pulsing glow.

She slowed further, willing the box in her arms to behave. She peered around the corner, and the hallway opened, the glow broadening into a room lit entirely in ultraviolet rays. Marijuana plants, full and bushy, grew in long rows under the special lights. Someone walked around the aisles, although Valentina couldn't see who it was from this angle.

What she did know was that they were enjoying their product.

Valentina snuck ahead, ducking beneath a row of plants. She could hear the electricity powering the room, a faint buzzing from the lights. The person in the room stopped, and for a moment Valentina thought they'd spotted her until she faintly heard the tinny sound of music filtered through cheap headphones.

She parted the leaves of the bushes above, her mind going back to her spying in the gardens within Deng's compound, communicating with a gardener who turned out to be yet another spy. *Is the city crawling with spies, now? Are the soldiers of fortune simply minions for wealthier men and women?*

The man started humming, which helped Valentina. At least now she knew where he was and could track him. She spotted the back of his head and noticed a set of broad shoulders, the light picking up the definition of his well-toned muscles. He wore a white tank top that was dark with sweat, and there were green stains up and down his muscular arms.

The symbol of a sun rising over a crest of waves was shaved into the back of the man's head.

Valentina chuckled and stood.

She stared at the man, arms folded until he turned. He was busy twisting the head of one of the largest joints Valentina had ever seen when he spotted her. He didn't flinch, merely glanced up, spotted her, then looked back down at the spliff.

He turned back to the table where Valentina now saw dozens of paper bags stacked neatly on top of one another. "Not even a hello?"

Valentina was silent, a grin on her face.

The man turned back to her. "You going to answer me?"

She tapped her ears.

The man removed his headphones and asked again. "Three years and no calls, yet I don't even get a hello from you? Not even after all this time?"

Valentina chuckled and rested one hand on the countertop. Leaves tickled her chin. "Sure. Because it's high on my agenda to share acquaintances with a convicted felon." She tutted. "How you been, Jonny?"

Jonny massaged the back of his neck, then spread his arms wide. "How do you think I've been? Look at me. I'm on top of the world, baby. Got myself a steady job. Working in an arena that I'm passionate about like mama always told me to do. I'm living like a king." He lit the joint, then offered Valentina a drag.

"No thanks. I'll skip this one."

Jonny shrugged. "Suit yourself." He exhaled smoke into the room. "What brings you to this neck of the woods? Wouldn't picture someone of your caliber finding her way into a place like this." He reconsidered. "Actually, this is exactly the type of shit hole place you'd find yourself."

Valentina looked out from under her brows. "You just said you're living like a king. Does a king rule in a shit hole?"

He waved a hand, resting his back against the table behind him. "You know what I mean. I get the good end of the deal here. All the weed I can smoke, and none of the responsibilities of those aboveground. I'm guessing you didn't come through the front door, but if you had, you might have seen the state of things up there. Bodies all over the place. Like a mortuary for those waiting to fall the final few inches into the abyss." He clicked his tongue. "Damn shame if you ask me. Still, they pay well. Gotta learn to separate the humanity from the business."

"Read that in a fortune cookie?" Valentina probed Jonny where he was sore.

"That shit is behind me," he replied coolly. "I served my time. I paid my dues."

Valentina thought back to the raid at Xing Ping's Cantonese restaurant. Her employer had sent her in to send a message to the youngest son of the Ping dynasty. Then everything had erupted at once. AJS cars pulled up, flooding the street in red and blue. Jonny, one of the matriarch's guards, had been armed and shot at Valentina as she tried to escape. Valentina took offense to this maneuver, and after some play, she fed him to the AJS patrol.

Valentina escaped unimpeded.

"That was chaos," she stated.

Jonny inhaled from the joint, ignoring her statement. He grabbed a bag and threw it toward her. "For old times' sake?"

Valentina caught the bag without issue, then tossed it back. "Not for me. I'm clean."

"Me too," he stated without a hint of irony. He folded his arms and narrowed his eyes at her. "So, really. What are you doing down here? What trouble are you causing in the Dustbox HQ?"

"You didn't hear the gunshots?" Valentina asked knowingly.

Jonny pointed at his headphones.

"Nice. What are you listening to?"

"Bob Marley. Who else? The man who preaches peace and love above all things."

Valentina let out a soft laugh. "You've changed your tune."

Jonny nodded. "I'm saying."

Something moved at the far end of the long room, and Jonny and Valentina turned to face it. Valentina ducked slightly while Jonny simply waved. "That's me clocking out for the night, girl. Great having the chance to catch up. You're looking good."

"Yeah, you too," Valentina admitted. "Much more mass than when we last met."

"I'm telling you," Jonny explained, "I'm living straight. Working out, bringing in the dollar. Shit holes like this may be a wank stain on the soggy mattress of the world, but even the darkest pits can make the dullest lights seem bright." He saluted. "See you around, kid."

Valentina raised an eyebrow as Jonny headed in the opposite direction from where she had come.

"Hold on," Valentina asked. "Where are you going?"

"Back entrance," Jonny replied. He muttered something to a petite woman with dreadlocks and a baggy t-shirt as she passed. "No point passing through the shit pit to get in and out. Those fuckers take one look at me, and they'll be clawing at my gonads for some product. You feel me?"

Valentina nodded. "Mind if I join?"

"Free country, ain't it?" Jonny stated. He glanced at the box in her arm. "What's that?"

"Nothing." Valentina offered no further explanation.

Jonny shrugged, then walked ahead without looking back. Valentina followed a few steps back as he led her through a series of smaller rooms filled with bags of different substances. Finally, they ascended a set of stairs that led out a storm door in a back alley.

Valentina thanked Jonny, then headed off in the opposite direction.

CHAPTER TEN

Deng Zenim sat back in the comfort of her chair and chuckled to herself.

On the panel of monitors that surrounded her, she could see more than the world closest to her, more than her compound. She could see the parts of the city that she wished to, places where the Cyclops technology was installed, carefully embedded into the firmware that some of her dunderheaded clients purchased and implemented.

The Cyclops was a piece of pride for Deng. A sophisticated piece of technology that had no end. It was infinite, and that was all that Deng wanted. That was all that anyone wanted—access to the limitless.

She swirled a glass of chianti, the glare of the monitors drawing her attention as she swiveled and looked around the city. In one monitor was her attorney's home, the Cyclops firmware built into his security system that tracked his entire home. He was worth a lot of money, and Deng had never trusted lawyers. At least this way she could keep an eye on him. She had discovered he was unfaithful in his marriage. What other boundaries would he break for simple pleasures?

On another screen was the mayor's bedroom. He'd called one of her technicians to install antivirus software onto his devices, and Deng's staff had lovingly up-sold him to a whole new system. A computer with a high-res webcam built into the dark bezel around the screen. He didn't know he had it there. Now Deng had her eyes embedded in his quarters.

Now, the box…

That was a whole new ball game for Deng. The metal container was a feat of engineering that she hadn't thought to try before. A box of tricks to be controlled remotely, fitted with a power source that self-generated, and technology that could overcome the obstacle of building materials blocking signals. Ever tried to get Wi-Fi while riding the elevator? All of these obstacles she had conquered, and here it was in action.

She rested securely in the crook of Valentina's arm. She could see the city through the Cyclops system, buzzing past her. A city that she dared not enter unless necessary. A metropolis littered with enemies and dangers, and now here she was, watching it pass through the eyes of her toy.

Valentina had done well to escape. Archie should be impressed. Deng certainly was. What would Archie think of her little plan? What would he make of the gift that she had bequeathed Valentina, forcing the Red Countess to enter the filthy depths of a world that Deng wouldn't entertain the idea of stepping foot inside? She supposed she would find out soon enough. After all, the Cyclops could see everything.

She laughed, her lips stained dark from the wine. On another monitor, her guards wrestled with an infiltrator. Next to that, her team performed their bioengineering experiments on a patient who had yet to give their consent but was sliced and diced.

It was good to be on top. It was good to look down at the puppets and mess with the strings. With great power came great entertainment…

The game was only beginning.

Deng buzzed through the intercom. A voice answered, "Yes, your greatness."

"Set her free." Deng released the button.

She returned her attention to the monitor. *That's right, Countess. Let's see how you fare against my little foot soldier. Maybe that's a trap you won't be able to escape.*

CHAPTER ELEVEN

It was nearing morning by the time Valentina arrived at Archie's compound.

The sun was cresting, highlighting the edges of the clouds and casting them into a soft array of oranges and peaches. Valentina could feel Isabella stirring in the back of her consciousness and knew she didn't have long to finish for the night.

The journey had been trickier than usual, crossing the city with the prize beneath her arm. She'd removed her jacket and blocked the view of the Cyclops, ensuring that the camera feed couldn't track her routes and methods—paths which few others in the city understood or knew—until she was almost there.

She went through the front door, feeling secure in the knowledge that Archie would want to see her and knowing that climbing while carrying this box would be a bitch of a mission.

Archie was sitting at his desk when Valentina burst through the door. She had learned long ago that knocking gave the power to the other, and in this relationship, she needed Archie to remember who he was dealing with.

He barely glanced up from the tablet on his desk. "Come in, why don't you?"

Valentina smirked, taking the box and placing it on the desk. "Your prize. Straight from the pits of hell."

Archie's nose wrinkled as the smell of the Dustbox that had clung to Valentina's clothing made its way around the room. "You smell like a pig that shit itself and rolled around in its feces. Where the hell have you been?"

Valentina clicked her tongue. "You know where I've been."

"I've never been there myself." Archie returned his glance to his tablet. "Maybe I'll visit sometime."

"I wouldn't," Valentina advised.

"Good to know," he replied.

Valentina sat across the desk and helped herself to a bottle of red. She drank straight from the neck of the bottle, the wine staining her lips a deeper shade of crimson.

"That's poisoned," Archie muttered.

Valentina raised an eyebrow. They exchanged a glance. "If it's poisoned, why are your lips stained with the stuff? Why is the lid uncorked? Why are there a couple of drops on the collar of your shirt?"

Archie examined himself. "I'm impressed. Quite the eye for detail."

Valentina seethed. She had delivered this present to Archie, and he wasn't paying the slightest bit of attention. It was all a game. The screen showed the paused code, with the lines that had led Valentina to the Dustbox in the first place flashing. If he didn't care, he wouldn't still have the window open.

Nope. It was all mind games—Valentina versus Archie Fontana.

Valentina was certain that she would win.

Eventually, Archie turned off the tablet and looked at the box under Valentina's jacket. "So this is it?"

Valentina nodded.

"And what is it?" he asked.

Valentina removed her jacket to reveal the lockbox. Its faces were smooth, and the black line that linked around the box winked with green light.

Archie's face fell. He removed his jacket and threw it over the box. "Are you insane?"

Valentina shrugged. "Some may suggest."

"That thing is watching if it's uncovered." He stood, balancing his fingertips on the desk as his gaze studied the object lumped beneath his jacket. "It's probably listening, too. You brought that bitch's tools into my house?"

Valentina waved in negation. "Relax, Archie. Knowing that woman as little as I do, she's probably got her software worming into your system." She nodded at the screen. "You're unlocking her AI. You think if she wanted to be in your business, she wouldn't be in there?"

Archie turned off the monitor. Valentina didn't feel the need to point out he hadn't also turned off the computer. That was the equivalent of drawing the blinds when the doors were unlocked and open.

Archie sat in his chair. He sipped his drink, brow creased. "What is it?"

Valentina shrugged. "Whatever it is, it's clever." She went on to tell him about Drake's electrocution and fogging the central hub of the Dustbox.

"So she can control it remotely?" Archie asked.

"Seems that way," Valentina replied. She chuckled.

Archie looked at her. "What's so funny?"

Valentina thought of a wizard named Rincewind and his adventures with a treasure chest running on human legs. "Unless this thing sprouts mechanical legs and starts running around this room, nothing."

Archie looked confused but chose not to follow up on that one. He leaned closer to the box and raised the corner of his jacket. Bit by bit, he lifted until he'd fully exposed the box. He glanced around as if determining whether any classified information was in sight, then allowed himself to relax. He peered at the black stripe, then rubbed a finger along the lens. Valentina half-expected him to jump back as a jolt of electricity leaked out, but that didn't happen.

"Sophisticated," Archie admired. "Such definition in such a small package."

"I've been there," Valentina commented, kicking her boots onto the desk and taking the wine in her hand.

Archie ignored the comment. "What is the lockbox for?" He rotated it on the desk, examining its surfaces. "I don't have the key."

"That's the puzzle," Valentina replied flatly. "I've delivered the goods. Now it's your turn to play. Deng set up the treasure hunt for you. You can't hold me on the leash to help you cheat past all the riddles."

Archie sat in his chair and drew the box closer to him. His eyes narrowed, he scrutinized the box all over. Clearly dissatisfied, he turned the monitor on and studied the code on the screen. Eventually, he shook his head. "No. You're wrong."

"Rarely," Valentina replied.

"In this instance," Archie stated. "Never in a thousand years would I know how to answer this question. I wouldn't even know where to find the Dustbox. I've never heard of that place." He turned to face her. "No. This game isn't for me, is it? This game is for you." A smug expression appeared on his face. "Son of a bitch. She's a clever one."

Valentina sat forward. "What are you saying?"

"I'm saying that she's studied you," Archie replied. "It's no secret that she wants to recruit you for her side. I imagine she tried to pull you over to the dark side when you encountered her at Tynamo, am I correct?"

Valentina remained quiet.

"Your silence speaks volumes." Archie let a small chuckle escape. "No. Deng wants you on her side but knows that's not going to happen. You know as well as I do that your services can't be bought." He covered the box again.

"No, they can be blackmailed," Valentina replied, an edge to her voice.

Archie met her eyes, an intensity burning behind his pupils. "What did you say?"

Valentina held his gaze, the temptation to drink another measure of wine too great. She glugged from the bottle then placed it back on the desk.

Archie's voice was low in his reply. "Blackmail? How dare you. I'm working my staff to the ground, bending the realities of what is possible in modern medicine, trialing, making progress, shattering everything known about the human body to resurrect him from the brink. Do you know the amount of time I've invested in this project? The amount of money? The number of risks I've assumed in skirting the truth of what we've undertaken so that I can wheedle out a nugget of new information from the leading professionals of today? We've made *great* strides in Kit's progress. We've kept him sustained and alive for years, well past when he should have survived, and you're going to accuse me of blackmail?"

Valentina's cheeks flushed. The anger came without thought, and she wished she could hold it back. "I'm just saying that it feels a little convenient how long this process is taking. He's been with you for years, and the last sign of progress I saw was a blip on a monitor. Meanwhile, you have me out in the streets, doing your bidding, acquiring jewels for your associates, undergoing tasks and quests without real pay, all for the sake of...What? Another blip on the radar a few weeks later?"

Archie sat back in his chair. The air was thick with tension. He rubbed his chin, then waved dismissively. "Fine. Then you can consider our agreement terminated."

Valentina's breath caught. It was tiny, but it was there. She held his gaze, lips peeling into a snarl. She knew he had her hook, line, and sinker, but she didn't want to admit it. She leaned on the desk, closing the distance between them as the wine made her head woozy. She drew her pistol and aimed it at his chest. His gaze strayed, then returned. "I'm going to ask this one time, and one time only," Valentina started. "No bullshit. No golden tongue speech. A simple yes or no question. Can you fix him?"

"I *am* fixing—" he began before the bullet ripped past his head and sent pages flying from the books on the shelves.

"One. Word." Valentina's nostrils flared.

Archie took a composing breath. "Yes."

Valentina waited a moment, taking some satisfaction from the fear he was struggling to hide. He knew she was dangerous, and that mattered for something.

"Good," Valentina replied quietly. "Good." She rose to her feet and dragged the box toward her. She uncovered it and examined the outside while Archie sat in silent fascination. The black stripe twinkled with green lights, and Valentina knew that somewhere Deng was watching her. She leaned closer, turning the box to the light to inspect its surface. The faintest of marks caught her attention. A square was outlined on the lid of the box, only a nanometer in its embossment. Valentina leaned closer, and something thrummed inside the box. A moment later the outline of a pair of lips appeared in the center of the square.

"What the..." Archie breathed.

Valentina kissed the lid of the box, feeling the chill of the metal beneath her lips. Her imprint matched with the image to near-exact proportions. Something inside *hissed*. Soft steam emerged from the box as a crease appeared around the sides, above where the lock dangled.

Valentina took the box in her hands and raised the lid.

The inside lit up, flooded with bright LED bulbs embedded in the container. A perfectly crimson velvet pillow lined the inside, and on the bed itself was a gold medallion with "A$$" embossed on the front.

Archie leaned over the lid to see what was inside. Valentina picked up the medallion and examined it. She flipped it over and found an inscription on the back.

"How does it feel," the inscription read, "to know that I have just made you kiss my ass?"

Valentina smirked. Deng had a sense of humor. That was new information to her. She continued reading. "Perform division using repeated subtraction. Remainder. Quotient. Unluck."

Archie raised an eyebrow. "Do you have an idea what she's talking about?"

"My guess is that the bitch is feeling her power trip," Valentina replied. "But she's not putting in a great deal of effort into the quizzes. The hunt is the challenge. Sending me to the human version of a kitty litter tray to extract a lockbox fitted with gadgets and gizmos all to get me to answer a question I learned the answer to when I was thirteen? It all seems a bit tame to me."

She leaned down toward the black stripe on the box, leveling her eyes and shaking her head. "Hey, Deng. I know you can hear me, so how about you make this something of a challenge next time, huh? All of this, for what? A number that someone could extract from pure guesswork if they wanted to? Up your game, bitch. I'm coming for you."

She laughed and sat back before covering the box with her jacket again.

"What is it?" Archie asked. "What's the answer?"

Valentina rolled her eyes as she reached for the last of the wine. "Remainer is one. Quotient is negative three. Likely you're not going to want to put in the negative because the answer is 'unlucky.'" She held the medallion to Archie and thumbed the word. "The answer is thirteen."

Archie tentatively turned to his computer and typed in thirteen. The screen flashed green as more lines of code were unlocked and scrolled down from the point where they'd stopped before.

He shook his head, chuckling. "You're a smart woman, Val."

"Don't forget it," she warned, her face turning serious.

They both watched as the screen crawled and the code unlocked. Valentina saw passages of code that were standard in most scriptwriting software and some which were new to her eyes. The coding was sophisticated, written by someone who knew their way around this kind of arena with their eyes closed.

Eventually, the code settled on a passage scripted in red lettering.

"<DJPP&TMOC2001>"

Valentina frowned.

"Another easy one for you?" Archie asked.

She leaned closer to the monitor, reading through the strange sequence of letters and numbers. "I'm going to imagine that 2001 *could* be the year of something important. That's assuming that the four figures aren't randomly generated from a four-digit generation program." She shook her head, noticing the light beginning to filter through the glass in the ceiling above. "I have to go."

Archie grabbed her wrist as she made to leave. Valentina ripped it out of his grasp without a problem.

"You know the answer?" Archie asked hopefully.

"No." Valentina shrugged on her coat. "What I do know is that this is *your* problem to solve, and I have other places I need to be."

"No visit with Kit this time?" Archie grinned as Valentina froze. She checked her watch. "Not today, Fontana. Keep a close eye on him as always. I'll see you tonight."

She made her way out the door, leaving Archie flummoxed and a little angry as he narrowed his eyes at the screen and drank from a glass of whiskey.

CHAPTER TWELVE

The stale taste of wine coated her mouth. Isabella smacked her lips as she sat at the edge of the bed and looked out over the city.

Under the sun's blinding gaze, the fog had receded to nearly unnoticeable quantities. It shimmered in the distance, a vague haze that softened the edges of her vision and cast the city into a dreamy glow.

Or maybe that was the unfounded hangover she was feeling.

The buildings rose around her, yet through the gaps in between, she could see farther than she had been able to for years. Rarely did the veil retreat so far. Rarely was she afforded a glance at the city where she lived—the city where she was bound.

In the distance, the lands rose into the wild mountain ranges of the heart of the island. Forests covered the side of the rocky terrain, filled with life and wonder that, even now, several decades after the island's founding, were still being discovered. It seemed almost a weekly thing that a keen researcher claimed a new species of frog or dragonfly, bird, or marsupial.

She often thought about the wilderness and about the history that could lie in the heart of the foliage somewhere. Throughout her years on the island she had heard of explorers entering the jungles and never returning, tales of ghosts and relics and runes from the founding days of Atlantica, way before the island had been claimed by humans—if "claimed" could be the word they used. Even now, seventy percent of the island was untamed. There were many places for secrets to hide, more than only in the city.

Isabella stretched and brewed herself a coffee. She drank it eagerly, waiting for the kick to get her started. It was her day off today—her first day off since her stint with Valentina at the helm —and she had only a few plans to keep her occupied. She needed the rest. She wanted to refill her well and have a chance to wind down.

Her first venture into the city took her to a café by the coast. She'd hailed the driverless cab and let it take her wherever it chose. The café was beautiful, a construction of perfect reds and pearly whites in a candy cane pattern around the building. An awning stretched over an outdoor dining area where Isabella took her seat among the modest morning crowd and bought herself another coffee. The hum of people talking caressed her ear, complemented by the gentle lapping of the ocean waves. The fog stayed at bay, and for the first time in years, Isabella caught a glimpse of the grand scale of the ocean. It shimmered and glistened beneath the sun's rays. Seagulls whirled overhead, pelicans sat on the rocks by the shore, and a few Atlanticans strode the beach or lay on their towels.

Isabella drew a few deep breaths, listening to the conversations nearby. At the table across from her, two women discussed the latest episode of a podcast that Isabella was only aware of in passing. The Gloria Hayworth Show was a beacon for entrepreneurial women looking to create a business through digital commerce. Her show broadcast tips on mindset, marketing, and business, and she had become something of a local icon over the past three years of serving her crowd.

Her fame was also largely helped by the fact that Gloria had survived an attempted kidnapping and accidentally uncovered a major drug ring that the AJS had been looking into for half a decade.

Opportunity was the pacemaker to all great careers.

At another nearby table, an elderly man sat staring at her, eyes vacant. Isabella wondered if he was creepy or blind. She chose the latter and turned away so she wouldn't have to look at him directly.

When she finished her coffee, Isabella walked along the long path that snaked around the coast, eventually making her way onto the beach. The sand was golden and soft on her bare feet as she carried her shoes, and the salt air stung her eyes. A smile grew on her face as she allowed herself a chance to slow down and push work and Valentina and Bradley far from her mind.

Until something hit her in the back of the head.

Isabella groaned, hand rubbing where the object had struck. She turned and found a round plastic disc on the sand by her feet.

"Sorry!" a masculine voice exclaimed. Even from afar, she could hear the smile in his words as a man jogged up to her, topless and glistening from lotion. He'd combed back his wavy, beach-blond hair, and Isabella had to refrain from staring at the offensively colorful pattern of his board shorts. "My bad," he added, pulling to a stop.

Isabella glanced down at the frisbee. "Didn't realize that grown-ups still played with toys." There was a smirk on her face although her head still hurt.

"Total accident," the man continued. "Bodega gets a little carried away, and when the wind dies, his throw can go for miles." He held out a hand. "Myles."

"I'm sorry, did you break?" Isabella asked.

The man laughed, his pearly whites flashing in his mouth. "Nah. My name is Myles. Pleased to meet you."

Isabella tentatively took the hand, surprised by Myles' grip. "Hey."

"This is the part where you say your name," Myles added. Behind him, Bodega cupped his hands and hollered something that turned unintelligible in the distance between them.

"Isabella," she replied. Her pain started to abate. She reached for the frisbee and handed it to Myles. "Have a good day, I guess."

"Yeah," Myles replied, hesitant. "See you around."

Isabella turned to leave, the smell of freshly cooked donuts coming to her from a stand in the distance. She wasn't sure if her mouth was salivating for the food or Myles.

"Wait," Myles called. Isabella spun. "You can play if you want? Two's company, but three's a party."

"Three's a crowd," Isabella clarified.

Myles smiled, his abs rippling in the sunlight. "Not at my parties."

Isabella grinned, then waved. "Nice to meet you, Myles. See you around."

"Yeah," Myles added. "I hope so."

She could feel his eyes on her for a while before he returned to his game. Isabella smiled, a warm sensation in her stomach as she tried to remember the last time someone who wasn't a colleague or an attendee of the library had hit on her. When she turned, Myles was far in the distance, but she couldn't help but feel as though someone was watching her.

She turned to the recesses between the buildings, the only places where the shadows sat and thought she saw someone looking her way. Only, when she focused her gaze, it had disappeared.

Isabella spent the rest of the afternoon touring the city and visiting the places she had meant to go for some time. She visited the Artreux Museum of Art. She went inside the world-famous Stephenson Music shop, filled to the brim with grand pianos, gleaming clarinets, cellos, basses, guitars, and every instrument you could think of. She passed the fountains near Bon Vivant Valley and stopped for gelato in Atlantica's international cuisine district. By the time she arrived at Porter's Steak House at six o'clock, the sun was starting to dip and the city falling dark. Her thirst for culture was satisfied, and she smiled when Bradley approached the table. He sat across from her.

"Hey." He beamed.

"Hi," she replied, feeling a little flustered.

The server attended to them instantly, explaining the mechanics of the restaurant even though Isabella knew this method by heart. The edges of the glass table lit up with a digital menu. Isabella dragged her finger along the rotating carousel of menu items to pacify the server into understanding that she knew how it worked before he left them in peace.

Bradley jabbed a finger at his screen. "Mine's not working."

Isabella looked up to find a playful smile on his face. "Behave."

He chuckled.

Isabella found a thick-cut steak that looked appealing. The image showed the hunk of meat dripping with gravy surrounded by a bed of mashed potato and peas. "That'll do."

Bradley glanced over. "That'll do? That'd feed an army."

"I'm an army of one. I thought you knew that." Isabella was surprised to find herself smiling. She was in a good mood after the day she'd had. Who knew that all she needed was some time away from the job and all the stresses that came with it? She stared across at Bradley and thought of Myles and the way her belly had flipped at the attention.

Did she desire that from a man?

"It all looks too good to choose," Bradley stated. "Honestly. You'll have to choose for me."

"I won't." Isabella smirked.

"Okay." Bradley thought. "Pick a number."

"Three seventy-two."

He laughed. "Between one and four."

"Oh." Isabella tapped her chin and glanced at Bradley's menu. He rushed to cover the items with his arms. "Number three."

ONE NIGHT TO KILL

Bradley's nose wrinkled. "You couldn't have said four?"

"Okay, then. Four." Isabella rose higher, trying to see over his arms.

"No, no." Bradley sighed. "I'm a man of my word." He tapped the screen, and a sound confirmed his order. He tapped his phone to the table, and the sound of change falling into a pocket rang. He then tapped his phone on Isabella's side before she could confirm her payment.

Isabella frowned.

"What's the problem?" Bradley asked.

Isabella looked at him levelly. "I thought you were broke."

Bradley looked down coyly. "Yeah...about that..."

Before he could say another word, a server appeared with a glass of white wine for Bradley and a tumbler of whiskey for Isabella. "Anything else for the lady and gentleman?"

Bradley raised a palm. "No thanks. We're sorted."

"Very good, sir." The server zigzagged between the packed tables, beelining for the bar where another set of drinks were ready to serve.

"You were saying?" Isabella nudged.

Bradley grinned. "Oh, yeah. So, it seems that I have a job."

Isabella beamed. "That's amazing, Bradley. Well done. That's awesome." She skirted the table and hugged him. When she returned to her chair, she asked, "Who with? What are you doing?"

Bradley chuckled. "Well...I can't say too much about it at the moment. It's quite a private job in the city. One of these 'need-to-know' places, you know?"

Isabella understood perfectly. Although many companies in Atlantica were public about their trade dealings, there was a percentage of the city that traded their stock mostly on private properties. This kept them out of sight of the AJS and allowed them to deal in the shadier industries, namely drugs, arms trade, solicitation, and trafficking, to name a few.

111

Isabella's face melted into concern. "You're working for the dark markets?"

"No." Bradley waved that off, blowing the comment away as if Isabella was asking if he'd just shot someone. "Nothing like that. It's…" He looked at the ceiling, trying to find a way to explain. "It's a good job with good pay, and I can do it with ease." He reached across the table and took Isabella's hands. "It's not dangerous, I swear. It's just private, is all."

Isabella retracted her hands and placed them beneath the table.

Bradley gave her an intense look. "I thought you'd be pleased for me. I'm making money again. With a little work, I won't have to live across the hall from you anymore. I can leave you to whatever it is you do in secret in that place."

Isabella glanced down, finding a stray red hair on her sleeve. She absently plucked it and let it drop to the floor. When she looked up, Bradley was searching her face, waiting for an answer.

"That's good then," she replied.

Bradley's lips thinned. He sat back in his chair as the server brought their meals to the table. Isabella was always impressed by how quickly the food was prepared and cooked in Atlantica. She didn't understand the secret to efficient service, knowing how long it took her to cook at home.

They tucked into their meals in a mutual quiet as the place chattered around them. Bradley worked his way through his rib eye with peppercorn sauce, occasionally throwing a glance Isabella's way. She could tell he had something to say, but he wouldn't come out with it. On the same token, neither would she.

She wasn't even sure what her problem was. Was it that she had kissed Bradley—well, *Valentina* had kissed Bradley—and now he genuinely thought he might have a chance? Was it because part of her wished *she* could make a go of something with someone, and Bradley was the first person to appear on her radar? Was it that she was concerned for Bradley as a friend and didn't want him to run off into some back alley dealings with a mafia crime lord, finding himself bobbing around in the ocean as he slept with the fishes three weeks into his new job?

Isabella was conflicted. The shine from her day was beginning to fade. Even the succulent juices of the steak did little to lift her spirits. She ate the meal down to the bone, then pushed the plate aside. She drained the remaining whiskey and stared at Bradley, whose sullen face looked set to fall into the remains of his food.

The server walked past, glancing their way. Isabella waited for him to pass. "Bradley."

Bradley glanced up.

"I..." Isabella halted.

You what? Say it, Bella. Say what's on your mind. You can't, can you? Because your mind isn't yours. It belongs to someone else.

"You kissed me," Bradley replied flatly, filling the void of silence Isabella had left.

Isabella gave a subtle nod, eyes drifting down.

"You invited me here," Bradley continued. "You said we should talk."

Isabella nodded again. "I'm sorry, Bradley. I don't know how to explain it."

"I didn't even think anything more was going to happen," Bradley interrupted. "All I knew was that I wanted to hang out with you and share the good news. If something else happened, great. We're supposed to be friends, Bella. Could you do that, at least?"

Isabella gazed out across the tables, hoping no one was looking her way.

"Bella?" Bradley insisted.

Isabella drew a long breath, then met Bradley's gaze. "I don't know what to tell you, Bradley. I'm a complicated person with complicated emotions and feelings. I wanted to have fun here, too, but... The idea of you working for some black market trades dealer is laughable."

Bradley raised an eyebrow. "Laughable—"

"Any idiot off the street can make money as a henchman," Isabella continued before Bradley could speak again. "Anyone can become a footnote in someone else's story and make a killing dodging the law. You know why so many don't? Because they get shot in their first few weeks of service. You'll either die a hero or live long enough to become the villain."

Bradley held up a hand. "Is that a Batman line—"

"All I'm saying," Isabella stated, "is that you're better than that. I know you. I know what you're capable of. You're better than becoming some rich fuck's goon."

Her eyes sparkled with a sheen of tears along her bottom lids. She wasn't sure where this emotion was coming from. All she knew was that Bradley was the closest thing to a friend in this city, and the idea of seeing him take a job as someone's lackey hurt her on some visceral level.

At the sight of her tears, Bradley softened. He moved around the table and sat beside her. She rested her head on his shoulder. He rested his head on her head.

They were quiet for some time. The server passed half a dozen times, looking to grab the plates but unsure if they had finished. His impatience showed in his strut.

Eventually, Bradley lifted his head and looked down at Isabella. "Bella, I care about you."

"I care about you, too."

Then she kissed him. Again. His lips were as inviting as she remembered, the musk of his cologne washing over her. This time Valentina was absent, and it was all her. It was all Isabella's choice, and it was terrifying and exciting all at once.

The restaurant fell away. The music died, and at that moment, Isabella felt free for the first time in years. When was the last time she had made a personal choice for her, without thinking of the consequences? All this time she had been protecting

Valentina, but Valentina had pushed her to this point. Valentina had initiated the first kiss, and now this was the second.

Her thoughts drifted to the city, to the ocean, to the beach, to Myles and a smile crept across her lips. Not because she wanted to be with Myles in any way, but because he represented the carefree nature of those who lived on Atlantica. Those who weren't bound to endless nights of mercenary work and years of hidden identities. Everything she wanted to be hit her with a frisbee earlier that day, and she was determined to claim that for herself. One way or another, she would begin to live the life she'd always wanted.

Bradley pulled away. Isabella's mouth was impossibly dry. She glanced at the table, afraid to meet his eyes. She wondered if Valentina was watching her right now, would she be judging her for how coy she was being? How differently might Valentina handle this kind of situation?

By getting into bed with the whiskey-soaked man with dark hair, I presume.

"That was nice," Bradley whispered.

Isabella nodded.

"Are you quite finished, sir and madam?" the server asked, impatience in his words.

Bradley and Isabella laughed. They told him they were and he collected their plates. Once he was out of sight, they rested their foreheads together and talked. They talked about Bradley's job and his options, about Isabella's day, and the other men and women in the restaurant.

Still, as much as he tried to turn the conversation, they never got onto the topic of Isabella's personal life.

Funny, that.

CHAPTER THIRTEEN

Valentina sat four stories above street level, one leg dangling over the lip of the rooftop.

The neons glowed brightly below. Crowds spilled out of the thumping clubs into the cordoned-off smoking areas. Large bouncers with crossed arms stood nearby, keeping an eye over the rowdy drunks as women in too-short clothing and men in suits that were far too expensive for drinking in chatted, laughed, flirted, and sang.

It was a whole different life to Valentina. She couldn't understand it. She'd never been one of those for as long as she could remember. Her life had always been solitude, running the rooftops, collecting the cash, and doing what others wouldn't. That was her MO. That was her life. The ants down below wasted their lives away, drinking into oblivion and fucking without reserve. Who knew what deadly diseases they risked transmitting or what kind of mess they were getting into with the people they chose to fuck? There was an epidemic of cheating husbands and wives, and Valentina knew that money allowed that to happen. She had worked for enough clients to know that the right price could send the pain away and buy the silence of those involved.

The smell of freshly cooked pizza rose into the sky. The fog had thinned a lot, allowing Valentina her clearest glimpse at the moon in some time. If she strained, she was almost certain she could see the stars beyond the veil. She could never be sure, though.

Valentina closed her eyes and rested back on her hands. She was frustrated that she had solved Archie's riddle. Not because she didn't want to help him, but because now she couldn't get the next one out of her head. She saw the letters floating in the darkness behind her eyelids.

DJPP&TMOC2001.

She separated them, forcing them to float before her. She rearranged them, looking for ways they could turn into another word that might make some sense. There was only one vowel, which was an issue, but something might appear.

Down below, the music thudded. A song played that Valentina hadn't heard in years. The crowd agreed too, the lot of them screaming with joy and singing out loud as they sang along.

2001? That has *to be the year.*

"The year of what?" Valentina asked out loud, jaw clenching. "The year of acronyms that make no sense? Goddamn you, Deng. Goddamn you."

The sound of boots on gravel reached Valentina's ears. She remained facing forward, not wanting to alert the newcomer to the fact she knew they were there. Not that they could think they'd ever sneak up on the great Red Countess. What was their plan? To hurl her off the rooftop and into the street? Four stories high might give her a chance at survival. If she landed on any of the clubbers down below, and the odds were high that she would, they'd likely die before she did. It was a loser's bet.

She hoped they weren't a loser.

A figure appeared beside her. She sat on the rooftop's edge

and kicked her leg over the lip, assuming the same position as Valentina.

The shadow of a smile appeared on Valentina's face. "I thought you'd have learned your lesson by now."

Gabby Torres looked down at the people below. "I'm not here to fight, Val. I'm not here to start a war."

"Probably for the best. You know you could never win. I think I proved that the other day."

Gabby glanced at her with resignation, then turned away. "You could have let me have that one."

"You know that's not true."

Gabby sat back and looked at the sky. "Moon's beautiful tonight."

"Moon's beautiful every night," Valentina corrected. "Just because you can't see something doesn't mean it loses its sparkle. There is a beautiful world beyond what we will ever see. Something doesn't have to be visible to be admired." She nodded at Gabby. "You should know that."

Gabby smiled a genuine smile. "It's one of the first things you ever taught me."

The music below reached its crescendo, met with a chorus of chanting, "Do you really like it? Is it, is it wicked?"

"We're lovin' it!" came the repeated chorus from the crowd before the DJ switched the song into another thumping monstrosity that hurt Valentina's ears.

Gabby watched her closely, studying her face. "You wish you could be down there with them?"

Valentina's lip curled. She shook her head as her eyes stayed fixed on a young woman leaning over the railing and throwing up, much to the chagrin of the nearby bouncers. "No. I wish I could understand them. The life of a...a 'normal' is so far beyond my understanding. I've tried to get my head around it, but it doesn't make sense to me. How is this what people look forward to? Numbing themselves from toxins and expelling their guts into the street while a DJ plays music at a volume that should be labeled dangerous to their health?"

A flashing image of Dick Chambers' liquor cabinet sprang to mind.

Gabby chuckled. "You sound like my mom." She followed Valentina's gaze. "Some people have nothing to strive for, Val. Before you picked me up—before you taught me the way, this was all there could have been for me. Have you ever been for a night out in Madrid? It's one of the greatest you can have. Delicious men with rippling abs and low-buttoned shirts. Margaritas in delicately shaped glasses. Dancing surrounded by friends…"

"You sound like I took you from something you loved," Valentina murmured.

Gabby gave a thoughtful nod. "You did, in a way. Still, I've never looked back. You gave me something more meaningful than I could ever have asked for. When you found me in that gutter, sprawled out in the rain and almost choking on my vomit, you saved me. You showed me another path, one that was just as intoxicating as any amount of booze and liquor." She drew a long breath and looked up at the moon. "It's amazing how far we've come. How one encounter can switch your entire life and change your direction." She laughed to herself. "I honestly believed that you were gone, Val. When you hopped on a plane and disappeared from Spain, I thought that was it. No more Red Countess. The journey was over. Then I saw you on the news, a story larger than what the *Atlantica Gazette* could write. You were world-famous. A blurry picture caught on the front of every magazine and newspaper page in the world. The Red Countess: caught at last?"

Valentina smiled, remembering it well. It had been the closest she'd ever been to capture, a chase gone wrong. At the height of her notoriety, every journalist in Atlantica had been hot on the lookout for the Red Countess, and it had become almost impossible to get anywhere without being spotted.

Valentina loved the challenge at the time. She saw fame as an opportunity to test her skills. To embrace the obstacle and see how far she could push herself. She took risks, performed her duties, and rolled in the money.

Still, not everything could always go to plan. Archie had been furious with her at the time, and his face turned red as he hollered at her to be more careful. She put their entire operation in danger, the links being made to the Fontana Foundation by bright-eyed, snooping journalists. They thought they had her cornered in that alley. They never anticipated how fast Valentina could scale the walls and disappear, the blurring of a red leather jacket as she melted into the night.

She laid low after that. Archie fed her small jobs, and Valentina took others to keep herself occupied. Soon the city forgot about her although her fashion trends were picked up by the rich and the easily influenced in Bon Vivant Valley.

"You shouldn't have followed me here," Valentina commented at last. "You should've stayed where you were."

"Are you kidding?" Gabby retorted, a grin on her face. "Madrid became vanilla once I looked into what Atlantica had to offer. The prices were higher for services, the dangers more acute. Val, this is all we've ever dreamed of. A battleground to hone our skills and become the top of our profession. I love it here. The pay checks are *amazing, and* the system rigged to benefit *us.*"

Valentina side-eyed her.

"Think about it," Gabby continued, growing more excited as she spoke. "Half the time, I'm requested to deal with matters inside private residences. That means there are no repercussions to my actions. I can do what I want to achieve the goal, and I don't have to worry about what happens in the process. In Madrid, every job was a risk. Those flashing blues and reds haunt my nightmares, blaring and coloring every damn job I undertook. But here… Here the AJS can't do anything to stop us. It's a mercenary's dream."

Valentina wanted to disagree but remained silent. While it was easier to perform your duties and receive a pay packet, the risks were much higher, too. One wrong move and you were dead. One shot and nobody would be able to claim your body. She had stopped thinking of the city as public and private a long time ago and now saw the private residences as simply pockets of lawlessness. A Wild West contained within the boundaries of artificial ley lines and concrete walls.

Shouts rang from down below as a fight broke out. A plane engine roared overhead as the latest wave of Atlantica visitors descended on the island. In the distance, an AJS siren wailed.

"Who are you working for?" Valentina asked at last.

Gabby raised an eyebrow, thrown off by Valentina's sudden change of subject. "You know as well as I do that information is confidential."

"Honor among thieves," Valentina replied.

Gabby laughed. "There is none." She spun on the lip of the roof to face Valentina. "You tell me yours, and I'll tell you mine."

"I can't do that," Valentina replied firmly.

Gabby shook her head. "Typical Valentina Winters. Pushing the boundaries of others, yet unwilling to bend, herself. Do you know how much shit I got in for losing that diamond?"

"I can imagine. I've been there."

"No you haven't," Gabby replied knowingly. "You're Valentina Winters. You've never lost anything in your life, have you?"

Valentina's lips thinned at the thought of Kit laying motionless behind glass.

"Either way," Gabby continued, not noticing Valentina's slight change in posture, "all I know is that I'm hoping our paths don't cross in that way again at any time soon. Who knows what will happen the next time we come to blows."

"You had your chance," Valentina commented. "You could've

ended it all then and there, couldn't you? You could've shot me, had it finished, taken over the throne, but you didn't." Her eyes narrowed, filled with genuine curiosity. "Why?"

Gabby rose to her feet. She wiped the dirt from the rooftop on the top of her purple pants. "Honor among thieves."

"There is none," Valentina parroted.

Gabby shook her head, resigned. She glanced up at the moon. "That's always been your problem, Val. You've never been able to trust."

"And you can?" Valentina replied.

Gabby considered this. "I trusted you as a mentor, Val. I trusted you as a friend. If we ever came to blows and our guns were talking for us, I'd trust that yours remained as silent as mine."

Valentina turned away, her gaze drifting to the drunkards below. "Then that'll be your downfall."

Gabby remained behind only a moment longer before her boots crunched gravel and she was gone.

Valentina's phone vibrated. She took the call, then followed in Gabby's wake.

CHAPTER FOURTEEN

Gail Howser met Valentina on the corner of 46th.

She stood beneath the lamplight, cast in its ethereal glow. Her hair was greying, her body reminiscent of a melting pear. Despite her strange appearance, a charisma exuded from her before Valentina could make herself known. She was a woman of strength and power, so why had she called Valentina?

"Gail," Valentina remarked, appearing behind the old woman.

Most people would have jumped at her sudden appearance, but Gail merely turned. "Valentina." She checked her watch. "You're late."

"You never provided a time."

"No," Gail admitted. "Although I figured you'd be faster in your commute."

Valentina looked up at the rooftops. "Granted. Still, this city can be difficult to navigate."

Gail brought a cigarette to her lips. She started walking down the street, and Valentina joined her. "I appreciate you seeing me on such short notice," Gail offered. "I realize it has been some time since our last rendezvous, and you know that I wouldn't bother you unless there was something that required some attention."

"Your fella still playing you up?" Valentina asked. The last time she had seen Gail, the woman had considerably fewer wrinkles on her face. She hadn't limped either, and Gail had been in something of a domestic dispute with her then-husband.

Gail had paid Valentina for reconnaissance. The Red Countess had followed Lesley Garrison around the city, snapped photographs, and collected evidence of his illicit affairs. Lesley had brought Gail into the business over a decade ago, and the whole thing had gone messy. Gail paid good money to prove her husband's infidelity, and ultimately that evidence led to a very healthy settlement and a divorce, not only from her husband but from the business, too.

Not that Lesley made it easy for Valentina. It had taken her a few days to realize that Lesley was truly a master of disguise.

At first, she had thought he kept evading her. She'd follow him for some time, then lose him in the depths of an alley or entering the subway.

Yet, after some time she caught onto his disguises. He'd wear toupees and change his clothing. He'd add fake mustaches or beards to change his character for each woman he was seeing. All in all, Lesley did well, finding the time and energy to entertain one woman every day of the week.

When all came to light, Valentina also discovered that only a few of the affairs were consensual. Lesley had found enough dirt on three of the women that he had blackmailed them, and they wouldn't speak out about what information he had on them.

Ultimately, Valentina saved Gail's integrity while protecting vulnerable women under Lesley's control. For that, Valentina was glad to have at least made that little part of Atlantica just a little bit safer.

Now, as Gail rounded the corner and led Valentina through the city, she wondered what the issue could be.

"Nothing like that," Gail replied. "I'm on fella number six since that whole debacle with Lesley, don't you know. Keeps me on my toes. I keep them on their toes."

"Then what's the problem?" Valentina asked as they passed a kebab store and she got a whiff of the cooked meats inside. Her mouth salivated, but she resisted the urge to stop. "People don't call me when things are going well."

Gail chewed her lip. "Must be a horrible life."

"It has its perks," Valentina replied.

Gail lowered her head, then crossed the road when the little man lit green. "It's my current number. Dale. He's having an affair."

Valentina scoffed. "You know how to pick them. Need me to discover who he's cheating on you with?"

"No," Gail replied. "I know who he's cheating with."

Valentina raised her eyebrows. They stopped by the gated fence of Atlantica's oldest church as Gail turned to her.

"Who?" Valentina asked.

Gail laughed. "Me."

Valentina frowned.

"I'm the one he's cheating with," Gail replied. "He won't leave his wife. I've been trying to get him to leave that bint for six months, but he's having none of it."

Valentina put a hand to her forehead. "I'm sorry, you called for my services because you want me to make your man leave his wife to be with you?"

"I know it sounds stupid," Gail explained, moving closer to Valentina. "I'm desperate. I didn't know who else to call. You did such an amazing job last time, and you got me out of a tight spot. Please, you gotta help me here. There has to be something she's doing that can make him leave her. No one who's happy in their marriage has an affair, right?"

Valentina thought about this but admitted that she didn't have an answer. She wasn't the type to provide help with situations that so-called "normal" people went through. She'd never had a relationship like that. She'd never felt the need to.

She took a step back from the other woman and shook her head. "Sorry, Gail. I'm not into getting into this kind of shit for the sake of it. If you're being wronged in some way, fine. I'm here. I'll help, for old time's sake. If you're asking me to break up a marriage so you can have your hunk of meat, that's something you two will have to determine for yourselves."

Valentina turned to leave, frustrated and annoyed at having her time wasted. She stopped when Gail called, "I'll pay handsomely."

Valentina looked at the sky and composed herself. When she turned, she called, "I don't think you'll be able to match my price—"

"Thirty thousand dollars," Gail interrupted. From this distance, in the city's darkness and away from the streetlights, she looked tiny, insignificant.

Valentina exhaled and shook her head.

"I don't think so, Gail. I—" Valentina started.

"And a key!" Gail blurted before Valentina could finish.

Valentina cocked an eyebrow.

Gail closed the gap between them. Across the street, a group of shady figures strolled on with their heads bowed closely together as they walked away. "A key to the unimaginable. Something that has been sought after in this city for years. A key to the impossible."

Valentina tilted her head. "The impossible?"

Gail nodded eagerly. "It's a key to a hidden chamber. The unknown that dwells within this island. It's the key that can unlock it all. The one that can open Pandora's Box and unleash it all onto the island. There are those who would trade handsomely to acquire it, but I offer it to you. Just do this one thing in return."

Valentina sighed. "Show me."

Gail looked taken aback as if she hadn't expected Valentina to accept what she was presenting.

Gail took Valentina to her apartment. She lived on the third floor of a building that looked more like a giant glass bubble than a piece of architecture. The only thing that made it clear that people were living inside was the buttery filter of the lights and the drawn shades in people's apartments.

Gail's hands shook as she unlocked her door and led Valentina inside a luxury suite that spoke of money and success. Everything was spotless. The overhead lights glittered off glass and oak and gold. There was a faint smell of bleach in the air, and orchestral music automatically played as they entered the suite.

"Nice place," Valentina admired. She looked around but could see no evidence of this so-called private and sought-after object. Gail excused herself and disappeared into her bedroom. Valentina could make out the sounds of scanners and keypads before a metallic door opened and she withdrew something from the safe.

Gail returned and placed a velvet drawstring bag on the counter. She carefully pulled apart the opening, then dug her hand inside. She drew out a glass container with an object that Valentina wouldn't exactly describe as a key.

Gail looked at Valentina expectantly. Valentina leaned closer. There were runes carved into the side of the object, which looked a lot more like a sawn-off section of a child's musical recorder. Patterns and people were painted among the runes, and in the center of the key was a faint blue pulse.

Valentina reached for the object. Gail pulled it away.

"Do we have a deal?" Gail asked.

Valentina's lip curled. "You have to let me see the goods before I verify."

"You've seen them," Gail retorted. "You see with your eyes, not your hands."

Valentina grabbed the object and brought it toward her. She

removed the lid as Gail gasped and cursed, afraid to go too close to Valentina for fear of what she might do.

Valentina delicately removed the object from the glass case. She studied the pulsing blue through the slit in the center, recognizing it instantly as a fragment of an Atlanticore. She twirled it in her fingers, then sniffed the material and gently scratched a thumbnail along its body. After a few minutes of examination, she set the object down.

"The most valuable part of that is the Atlanticore," Valentina informed Gail. "The rest of it isn't worth shit. It's plaster cast. You try to unlock anything with that, and it'll dissolve in your hands."

Gail looked dejected. "No. You're wrong. That's a solid piece of artifact, that. I fought Lesley for that in the divorce. It was a gift from an old client, and I won it. Worth thousands, he told me. People were searching all over for him to find it."

Valentina shrugged. "You're going to trust the man who cheated on you?"

Gail's face dissolved as realization struck. "You're kidding me. Bastard! All these years and he's still pulling the wool over my eyes."

Valentina tapped her fingers on the counter. "You're right in some regards. There may be people out there who would kill to acquire an item like this. I suppose it all benefits the treasure hunters of Atlantica. Those who believe the myths and want to explore the legends." She picked up the object with considerably less delicacy than the first time she held it and laughed. "People believe the craziest shit in this place. The Atlanticore is great as a power source, but it's all finite. Once we harvest the island for the power, there won't be enough to go around. The power may be portrayed as limitless, but there's not enough to power the world. It'll take some time to realize that."

She threw the object to Gail, who caught it clumsily. "Still, you can probably find a use for that fragment of core. Maybe charge your phone or power your internet for a few decades with it. The rest of that shit is worthless."

She walked toward the door. Gail tried to call her back, but Valentina wasn't listening. She had far more important trails to tread. Far more important riddles to solve.

The treasure hunters could play their games, but Valentina's skills were better suited to the city. To solving the riddles of the AI and saving Kit's life over pursuing what she knew was a fruitless treasure hunt that the gullible city dwellers wasted their time with.

Or so she suspected.

She wasn't naive enough to completely disregard the truth.

CHAPTER FIFTEEN

The box sat silently in the center of the room.

The stripe around the center had been mostly black for some time. It hadn't watched Archie examine its contents and try to discover its mechanisms inside. It hadn't felt Archie pick up the container and throw it on the floor in an attempt to shatter its components and leak its secrets. It hadn't listened as he'd covered the box with a cloth and ran his nightly meetings, working until the early hours of the morning to keep his company running.

The box simply sat there, quiet and respectful. It might have been on Archie's mind, but Archie wasn't on its mind. Covered by a cloth, even if the box powered up and tried to see Archie, it wouldn't achieve this. Its operator would be blind to all in the office, as long as the cloth covered its eyes.

Or so Archie thought.

The black stripe blinked into life in a dazzling array of green stars. The entire perimeter of the box winked and glowed into life, lighting up the space beneath the cloth. No sound emerged as the box whirred into life and the internal cameras started their search.

The green lights ran a lap around the stripe, settling at last on a tiny fragment where the cloth didn't entirely cover the table. The opening couldn't have been more than a couple of millimeters wide, but it was enough to start its functions.

Rays emitted from the box, driven like sonar echoing around the room and back toward the box's receiver. It listened for Archie, spending a good ten minutes on active digestion of auditory information until it moved into action.

The bottom of the box shook as the metal surface twisted and revealed several motorized wheels. It moved forward, only an inch to begin with. The cloth tugged with it, resistance causing the progress to slow. The person controlling the cameras shifted to look behind, but it was impossible. The covering was too thick.

Another inch forward before the box edged over the table's lip. It could see the carpet now, dark maroon and stained with dark droplets that could have been wine or blood. Another inch and something in the room grunted.

The box stopped and retracted its wheels. With more room to operate its sonar, it sent out its signal and gained a clearer image. A light was on nearby, and now that it had broken more of its cover, it could make out the gentle snoring of the man in the room with it.

Archie was asleep. He was resting on the corner of the cloth.

The box juddered as it prepared its next sequence. It bided its time, ensuring that the man was fast asleep before taking the final leap.

It neared the edge. It was almost halfway over the lip. Its weight began to bear down. It tumbled through the air and flipped upside down. Hundreds of nanoscopic pockets filled with air, exploding from the box's lid like tiny bubbles of gum. The container hit the floor, its impact cushioned by the bubbles and the carpet. After a few seconds of listening, the bubbles expelled their air and shrank. The nano-pockets receded, and the box lay still.

The camera corrected itself, no longer upside down as it catered for the change. It explored the room, finding Archie's legs shadowed beneath the table. A smashed bottle of whiskey was on the floor beside him, the contents of the bottle growing sticky and dry. If the box could smell, it might have wrinkled its nose.

The wheels emerged on the bottom of the box. A grid-like pattern materialized in the surface as though hundreds of thousands of tiny operators were deploying the wheels of a strange-looking aircraft. From its sides, two long robotic arms emerged. The box looked insectoid as the arms pushed against the floor and angled so the container began to right itself.

It levered itself to a quiet standstill and waited.

After another few minutes, the box rumbled into life, rolling along the fine fibers of the carpet toward the bookcase. From down here, the world looked enormous. The bookshelves loomed like great statues, the books like breeze blocks of ancient knowledge.

Archie snored. The box stopped. It sent out a pulse toward the man who was now in plain sight and ran a quick detection of his vitals, taking a reading of heart rate, breathing rate, oxygen intake, and REM movement. Satisfied that deep sleep had resumed, the box closed the distance to the bookshelf.

When the box was directly underneath the right part of the bookshelf, a faint thrum of power came from inside. The box knew which book to trigger, having seen Archie grow complacent and open the door a few times that day to gain access to the other rooms. It might have been for a bathroom break or business means, but it didn't matter to the box. The device had one purpose only.

The lid of the box parted, revealing a small hole from which a drone the size of a coaster rose. The drone let out a faint buzzing noise as it rose into the air, slowly lifting itself to the height of the trigger book. Around the drone was a smaller version of the Cyclops system. The eyes were in place, and they were all one.

The drone reached the height of the book. It lined itself up, then shot a dart from its body. Trailing the dart was a coil of wire.

The dart penetrated the book's spine.

Archie shuffled.

The drone lowered itself slowly, finding its place perfectly into the box's top surface upon landing. The lid closed, leaving behind enough of a gap for the coil of wire to penetrate.

The box wound the coil. The line went taut. The book leaned on its base, triggering the bookshelf door to open.

It opened half an inch. The box moved to the gap and revealed its insect-like robotic arms once more. One limb reached inside the crack, then tilted until the opening grew larger. While the box manipulated the door, it cut the line to the book and coiled the remainder back inside.

Finally, with enough space to enter, the box drove through the gap and into the clinical corridor.

The walls were gleaming white, even in the dim glow of the emergency lighting. The box trucked dutifully onward, maintaining a steady pace as it searched for its destination. This next part was tricky, but it had prepared for the task at hand.

A service robot passed, its mechanisms astronomically loud compared to the little lockbox. It paused by the box only for a moment as a camera zoomed in on the object. It seemed to debate whether or not the thing was garbage until the box jolted, sending out a frequency that caused the robot to judder.

The robot returned to its factory position, the lights momentarily cutting out. A moment later, and the LEDs kicked back in, the robot's mechanisms whirring once more as it drove ahead and left the little box to its own devices.

The box trucked on.

As it journeyed forward, it constantly surveyed its surroundings. Tiny hums emitted from inside as a barrage of information was sent out from the little box, only to be received moments later. The Cyclops stripe processed heat signals, IR frequencies, sonar, and more as it searched for its target.

Above, the stars wheeled beyond the glass arch that spanned the corridor. Only the robot knew what Valentina had assumed but did not know for sure: that the glass was one-way, and from the outside would be seen as simply a thick silver wall bouncing the images of the sky back at it.

Another robot crossed ahead, leaving a slick gloss on the floor behind. The pungent smell of bleach would have overpowered human nostrils, but the box drove on, slipping only slightly on its moist surface. Once it cleared the slick area, it detected what it was after.

A signal bounced back. It was faint, but it was there. It honed its focus onto the door directly ahead, the signal growing stronger with every inch it grew closer. The box could almost feel its master's excitement behind the lens, but unfortunately, that person hadn't fitted the box with an AI that served its metal casing with feelings.

The door was close. The robot dutifully rolled on at its consistent pace. It levered out one of its long limbs, the mechanisms unfolding from several hinge points along its length as it snaked toward the lock panel...

Which was when a foot landed on its surface.

The robot fought against Archie's grasp as he tore at the metallic limb and pulled it away from the door.

"Goddamn son of a bitch!" he roared, appearing as a giant in the Cyclops camera. His foot rose in the air, then stomped on the lid of the box. The wheels tucked into the body, leaving almost no trace that anything was there. Archie picked it up and hurled it across the corridor, the arm hanging at an odd angle. A string of wires connected it to the machine, leaving a tiny hole exposed.

Archie's face was red. He drew his Ruger and aimed it at the box. He pulled the trigger until the magazine was empty, the bullets pinging off the metal and heading in all directions. Glass shattered from above, raining down on him, but he didn't seem to care. Viewed through the Cyclops, all anyone could see was rage.

Once the Ruger was empty, Archie stomped over to the box again. Glass crunched beneath his feet, and a chill wind blew through the corridor. The robots were obediently tidying the glass and clearing the floor. Archie picked up the box and held it beneath his arm as he stomped back toward his office. He was halfway there when something shocked him, and he dropped the box.

"Fucking bitch," he exclaimed. He knelt to where the box lay, its surface barely dented or affected, only a hole to break the near-flawless surface. He shook his head, jaw clenched. "That's how you're going to play it, huh?"

He disappeared, striding toward his office. When he returned, he was wearing unflattering yellow rubber gloves. "Let's see how you shock me while I'm wearing these," he stated as he closed the distance and approached once more.

Before he could get to the device, smoke erupted from the creases around the Cyclops. Despite this strange set of circumstances, Archie laughed, a loud, belly laugh. Hands appeared through the smog and picked the box up. Archie coughed but kept his grip, eventually bringing the container back to his desk in his office.

The box stared at Archie, gas still seeping from it. Archie still stared at the device, knowing that somehow the substances used to make the smoke would be finite. He wasn't taking his eyes off the box, now.

The game was over.

CHAPTER SIXTEEN

"DJPP&TMOC2001."

The riddle was killing Valentina. She sat in the hammock, rocking side to side in the chill night air as her mind ticked over and tried to solve the puzzle.

The hammock wasn't hers. It belonged to the wealthy couple who owned the Dominican Hotel. Here, thirty stories up and a stone's throw from the beach, Valentina could look out at the docks, listen to the gulls, and allow her mind to ponder. The balcony veered around with a pool nestled into the center. The inside of the apartment was dark, the temporary occupants presumably asleep or out. Valentina didn't mind. If they stirred and showed their faces, she'd be gone. They'd have no idea that she was ever there in the first place.

DJPP&TMOC.

She scrolled through her phone, searching in all of the obvious places first. That was something she'd picked up over her time in this industry. So many people thought that they were clever in hiding their information, but most forgot to check the obvious places first. It was amazing how many people she had nailed because of a fourth-page Google result when they'd spent most of their time removing their presence from the dark web.

She typed in the acronym, and nothing of use showed up. A few articles in Japanese, some listing for "Reef Carbonate Budgets & Symbiodiniaceae diversity in..." something or other, another result for some brand of Bluetooth device.

Nothing seemed to link to Deng or the AI. At first, she suspected that maybe the Bluetooth device could be a link, but when she investigated the website, she received an error notice in return.

There was no information she could dive into farther down the page.

DJPP&TMOC 2001.

Something niggled the back of her head. Something that told her the answer was within reach and that she should know this. She, of all people, should know where to look. Why else would Deng set up this riddle for her? Why else would she drag Valentina into the epicenter of all this fuckery?

"2001..." Valentina thought back. That was twenty-six years ago. She would have been four at the time. Not the most useful age to draw from your experience and solve a mystery.

The millennium bug had passed. She remembered that much, at least. Her father had regaled her with tales of the horrors of the millennium bug and all the pain and heartache people thought it would bring. Would that be a part of it?

Probably not. Otherwise, it would be 2000 in the clue.

"Shit." Valentina ran her fingers through her crimson hair, then turned to stare over the coastline. Silhouettes of young couples walked along the beach, the moon finally fading behind the thickening veil. Somewhere in the distance, clubs thumped their music, the drumbeats and melodies clashing harshly. People on this side of the island wouldn't mind too much about the music, the glass thick enough to drown it all out. Valentina closed her eyes and listened intently. Music had always unlocked things for her, and she felt that it might do that now.

DJPP&TMOC2001.

Valentina clenched her fists in frustration. The hammock swung lazily in the breeze. She searched through her phone for a little longer, getting to a point where she reached a blank. Her head hurt. She had no leads. Her anger began to eat her from the inside.

She glanced across the pool to the large glass doors that led inside the apartment. A light clicked on, and two silhouettes came into sight, naked and writhing in the king-sized bed. Their bodies glistened with sweat. Although Valentina couldn't hear them, it seemed they were having a great time.

Her loins ached.

Valentina sighed and pocketed her phone. She vaulted over the balcony rail and climbed down the side of the building.

Dick Chambers stared into the mirror as he brushed his teeth.

White foam lathered between his lips. His eyelids were heavy and looked bruised. A thick mat of dark curls covered his exposed torso as he brushed and cleaned away the day he'd had.

It was always something in this city. Private investigation wasn't the glamorous trip that people suspected it might be. Jobs could be arduous, and they could be long, even if they did pay well. There were fresh bruises on his ribs from the mess after last night's poker game, and he wondered if a day would ever come when he didn't crave bourbon and a smoke.

The stamped-out cigarette in the living room and its ribbon of fading smoke told a different story.

He still smelled of her. Her perfume lingered in the weaving of his hair despite the long, warm shower he'd taken. There wasn't a great deal of joy in the sex with Marissa Leymon, but it was something to pass the time. She wanted to thank him for his help, and he wanted to let her. There were no laws against that kind of reckless frivolity as far as he knew.

Throughout the evening, his mind had strayed to Valentina Winters. He wondered where she was and if she would ever come back. She had disappeared on him before. A mystery so deep that even the great Dick Chambers couldn't solve it. For years his mind found a way to remind him of her presence, and there was a time where he truly believed her dead or gone.

Until recently. Until he had put his life and hers at risk by getting too close to her work.

He didn't feel good about it after. It was a reckless move, but one that he felt he needed to take at the time. Valentina had helped him endlessly in a recent case of great magnitude, and he wanted to return the favor somehow. She seemed to need it. Dick had skills that Val didn't. Although Val had considerably more skills than Dick.

The most prominent difference was Dick's overwhelming moral conscience. Dick didn't mind doing bad things if he knew he was going to be helping good people.

Valentina took money for glory. That was an entirely different ethical code.

Dick sighed, then spat the toothpaste into the basin. He hated to think that his feelings for Valentina might be deeper than skin, but he couldn't get her out of his head. Not only was she beautiful, talented, and dangerous, but she had moves and could do things he had never experienced before. They both gave it their all in the bedroom, and their rendezvous were times that he held onto, often resurfacing in vivid Technicolor when another woman leaped on his body and started her work.

He opened the medicine cabinet and put his toothbrush back. He picked up a bottle of moisturizer that Doug had bought him a week ago, not quite knowing whether it was a joke or not. The lines on his face had deepened over his time in Atlantica, but he knew he would never get back to his baby-faced prime. He uncapped the bottle and poured a small amount of the white liquid into his palms. He sniffed it, detecting notes of scents he couldn't identify.

He touched a dab to his cheek, about to scrub around the bags beneath his eyes when she spoke. "Not the first time I've caught you with your hands and face covered in white."

Dick closed the cabinet and looked in the mirror. Valentina rested against the door jamb, a grin on her face painted in bright red lipstick. Dick returned his attention to rubbing in the lotion. "It won't be the last, either."

"You getting worried about your old age, Dick?" Valentina asked. "Some women like the distinguished look on a man. Makes them feel like their daddies are coddling them. Gives them a chance to experience the love they were missing as children."

Dick dabbed some more on his face, not sure how he felt about the whole procedure, but feeling like at this point he had to commit. The cream was soft and smooth, and it left his skin feeling strangely tacky after. "Is that your whole deal? Sleep with an older man to overcome your daddy issues?"

Valentina turned away, the smile still on her face. "Not for me. I had all the love my daddy could give."

"Do you still see much of him?" Dick knew that he was pushing Valentina's rules on personal boundaries. Still, since he had assumed her missing or gone for the last few weeks, he figured he might as well go for broke.

Valentina's face hardened a touch. She stepped into the bathroom and folded her arms. "You look good, Dick." Her eyes strayed down his torso, taking in the litter of scars, bruises, and cuts that covered his body. It was the same any day of the week, his body a canvas of ever-shifting injuries and marks of his successes. He had grown used to them by now. Each one told a story. Some stories he could forget, others he wished he could, but the gunshots, knife wounds, and broken bones would never fully heal.

"So do you." Dick applied the last of the lotion to his face. "You always do."

"You always know what to say," Valentina remarked, moving closer to Dick to wrap her arms around his waist. Her fingers laced around his belly button before drifting toward the bulge at the front of his pajama pants.

Before she could get there, Dick took her arms and gently eased them away. He turned to face her, thankful he had brushed away the booze from his breath given their proximity. Valentina smelled as good as ever, a perfume he had never been able to detect on any other woman.

"Problem?" Valentina asked, that coy grin on her face as she eyed his lips.

Dick resisted her advance. He slipped past her and walked toward the door. He scratched the back of his neck. "No problem," he informed her, knowing that he was lying. "I just…I'm tired, is all."

Valentina let out a soft sigh. "Don't tell me the great Dick Chambers is upset that I was gone longer than he wanted."

Dick cocked his head. "I don't want to have this conversation."

He left Valentina in the bathroom as he made his way to the living room and poured himself a glass of water. First, he had to find a clean glass that didn't have the residue of liquor.

Valentina was sitting on his couch before he realized she had entered the room. It stunned him how quietly she could move, how quickly she could slip through the shadows and appear without him realizing. "You're sore. I get that."

Dick leaned against the counter. His face scrunched up as he considered his words carefully. He wasn't bound to Valentina, nor she to him. He didn't need a girlfriend, and he knew that she didn't need a boyfriend, either. Whatever their arrangement was, they'd built it on sudden drop-ins and hazy nights of passion.

So what was his problem?

He thought he'd possibly, finally, figured it out.

"I'm not sore," Dick replied softly. The living room was gloomy, only faintly lit by the sheen of silver from the moon and the streetlights outside. A glow came from the bathroom. "I just… I completely get that there's nothing to be gained by us engaging in anything similar to a 'conventional' relationship."

"So, what's the problem?" Valentina asked. Did Dick detect a hint of knowing in her eyes? Did he see a vulnerability in there that he'd never seen before?

"You left," Dick replied simply. "You left. Again. Without a word."

Valentina offered a weak smile. "It's what I do. It's what I'm best at."

"I know," Dick continued. "Believe me, out of everyone you've met, I know better than anyone. I admire it. I respect it. It's what makes you who you are. It's what gives you that edge."

Valentina sat forward. "Then what's the problem?"

"I don't know," Dick stated. He stared at the window, eyes drawn to silhouettes moving in the apartments across the street, a group of young twenty-somethings partying into the early hours of the morning. He wondered what it would be like to live a life as carefree as theirs. At that age, Dick was in the thick of his military journey, exploring the possibilities of leaving and getting out. He never had those years.

Valentina crossed to Dick and leaned one hand on the counter beside them. "Our arrangement is our arrangement. I'm not obligated to you, and you're not obligated to me."

Dick squared his gaze to Valentina, her pupils like dark, hypnotic abysses. "Do you know how rare it is for a PI to surrender his power?"

Valentina smirked. She hooked a finger into the waistband of his pants and teased around his hip. "Is that what this is about?

Power?" She nodded to the bedroom. "I know you like it when you're powerless in there."

Dick looked down, only slightly annoyed by his body's reaction to her touch. He took her wrist and eased it away. "In most power dynamics there's at least a see-saw effect. One has some power. The other has more. But…I don't have any. I'm powerless against you. The cards are all in your favor."

Valentina stepped closer, pressing her crotch against Dick's. She whispered in his ear. "Again, what's the problem?"

Dick closed his eyes, his logic going foggy. "This is *too* one-sided. Let me have some way to contact you. Give me a line into your life."

Valentina tensed up. Her breath hitched. She pulled away, still close enough that their breath mingled in the air. "Is that what you want?"

Dick nodded.

"You *need* that?" Valentina asked.

Dick nodded again. "I guess I do. Not to bombard you with messages or to get clingy, or in any way be a boyfriend-type of yours. But something that evens the keel and levels the playing field."

"And if I don't?" Worry showed in her eyes—an emotion that Dick had never glimpsed from her.

Dick shrugged. "I guess I'll take what I can get." He kissed Valentina deeply, sensually, using their tongues to do their speaking for them. Their bodies pressed against each other as if they could merge into the same being. They spun, they threw each other, they writhed beneath the sheets.

The whole time, they never spoke a word.

Dick snored soundly beside Valentina. Her breathing had caught up with her, and her heart had slowed.

She turned onto her side, propping her head up with her hand. She was naked, only loosely wrapped in Dick's sheets. The smell of sex hung in the air, though there was something else on her mind that she couldn't quite allay.

Dick's request had been a heavy one, one that she was still processing as she silently rose and dressed. Her eyes had acclimated to the dark, and even in the middle of the night she could see the sharp angles of his face, his lips slightly parted, his bare ass hanging out of the sheets.

She tore a page from a nearby notepad and scribbled her number on it.

She stood for some time, the paper shaking in her hand.

She drew a long breath and laid the paper on the nightstand.

Her eyes caught Dick's CD collection. An eclectic mix of long-forgotten songs. An album caught her eye. A tune came to her mind, thumping in the night air as she lay on a hammock.

She left, her heart racing once more.

CHAPTER SEVENTEEN

Sixteen messages.

Archie had left sixteen messages for Valentina. She thumbed through them all, a strange array of incomplete sentences as he ranted and raved about something that didn't make sense. Clearly, he was trying not to overtly say what had happened while using some strange code that Valentina didn't understand.

The only word to catch Valentina's eye was "infiltrate," but even then she had no context. As she worked through the messages and listened to the voicemails, she thought of Dick lying fast asleep. She had done the right thing, hadn't she? Archie had her number, for God's sake. Surely she could trust Dick.

Trust...

She glanced out the window of the driverless cab, watching the city whir by, wondering what trust meant to someone like Valentina. Gabby trusted her, but Gabby shouldn't. Dick trusted her, but he shouldn't. Archie trusted her...

Kit trusted me.

She absently thanked the vehicle as she exited onto the sidewalk outside Archie's compound. The cab drove on, oblivious to the gratitude.

Valentina liked the compound in the early hours of the morning. She had once visited during the day and found the place overrun by staff milling around like a hive of bees. She liked the quiet. She operated best in the empty and the desolate.

Archie opened the door on the first knock.

He looked tired—haggard and disturbed. There were creases in his brow, and his eyes were wild. He took Valentina by the wrist and pulled her in. He was successful, but only because she allowed it.

"What?" Valentina asked before her eyes found the box in the center of the room. It lay still on the rug, its flawless body dented, covered in scorch marks, and with one long, strange limb protruding from its body like the flailing arm of a dying bug. "I see you've had some fun."

"That bitch," Archie exclaimed, slamming the door closed. He marched around the room. "That fucking bitch."

Valentina cocked her head. She crouched to one knee, examining the lockbox. "What happened?"

"Thinks she can fuck with me like this, does she?" Archie continued. "Thinks she can send her droids in to fuck with my industry. I'll show her, I'll…"

"*Archie!*" Valentina cried, snapping Archie from his whirlpool of anger.

Archie turned to face her, brow low, eyes dark.

"Context, please," Valentina demanded.

Archie nodded with one finger pointing at the lockbox. "That box is more than it appears. It's an android of some kind. Operated remotely. Hers. A fucking scout droid."

Valentina raised her finger. "It's not an android."

Archie looked at her incredulously. "What?"

"An android is a robot that has taken on a human appearance," Valentina explained. "This is a machine. Maybe a robot, at a stretch, but not an android."

Archie picked up a glass and brought it to his lips. He found it empty, so he poured himself a healthy measure and tried again. "You're getting pedantic over semantics when that fucking monstrosity tried to infiltrate my compound?"

He explained to Valentina what had happened, how he had been sleeping when something disturbed him, and how he had awoken to find the box driving itself down the secure corridor and reaching to unlock the door. His expression emphasized which door as he finished.

Valentina brushed her hand over the robot's surface. It was smooth to the touch, an impressive piece of machinery if it could truly do the things that Archie was saying it was capable of. The only fault in its surface she could see was the hole where the broken limb extended. She assumed the Cyclops stripe was powered down since no green lights flashed around its body. For all intents and purposes, the machine was dead.

"Why would she want to go to Kit's room?" Valentina asked.

Archie's jaw clenched. The drink shook in his hand. "Because the bitch knows there's something up."

"Which bitch?" Valentina asked.

Archie gave her a level look as if to say, "you know who."

Valentina nodded.

Archie shook his head angrily. "The bitch is a snake. I don't know why so many people call her a dragon when it's clear that she's a different reptile entirely. Dragons you can see coming for miles. 'Enter the dragon.' That's the phrase people use to announce them, right? There's no secrecy or subtlety to a dragon, but a snake...a snake can creep up on you without you realizing. That's Deng. The snake of Atlantica."

Valentina paused a moment, pondering Archie's words. Something struck her that she couldn't quite comprehend. "How would she know that something is awry? Why would she be trying to infiltrate your place?"

Archie scoffed. "Why wouldn't she? It's all games with these rich assholes. Atlantica is full of us—I mean, them. We all hold our secrets, and we all try to gather intel from the others. You think this is the first time I've encountered a situation like this?"

"You seem underprepared for when they do," Valentina replied.

Archie took a long sip.

Valentina continued. "So Deng knows that something is up, and she's trying to pull the information. This is about me again, isn't it? She wants me. She wants to find out the truth so she can leverage me into her service?"

Archie considered this. Valentina noticed the flush in his cheeks and the subtle eye shift as he replied. "She's oblivious. She knows nothing. Can't know anything."

Valentina's gaze lingered a moment on Archie before examining the robot once more. "It is a powerful piece of tech—" She stood, eyes narrowing as she focused on Archie. "Say that again."

Archie raised an eyebrow. "Say what?"

"The dragon thing," Valentina clarified. "You said something about Deng being the dragon."

Archie waved a hand, a tired expression on his face. "Oh, come on, Val."

"No." Valentina stood firm. "Say it again."

Archie submitted. "You can see dragons from miles away. They can't exactly hide from the public view."

"Not that," Valentina replied. "The next bit. What people say."

"What?" Archie squinted in thought. "Enter the dragon?"

Valentina heard it then, a wave of clarity washing over her. Her mind took her to the hammock, rocking on the stretch of fabric with a view of the ocean under the moonlight. The bassy thump of music below. She heard the same song on the rooftop edge in her conversation with Gabby. Dick's CD collection—which, why would *anyone* still collect CDs in this day and age?—and a particular album calling to her.

She ran to the computer and jogged the mouse to awaken the

screen. The length of code remained, the flashing red digits asking for the code, the clue still lingering there.

"**<DJPP&TMOC2001>**"

Valentina typed in the code with a grin on her face.

The computer beeped. Archie came around the side to watch. He staggered a little under the influence as he finished his glass. He fixed his gaze on the computer, eyes wide in fascination.

The red turned to green. One by one the code continued to write, letters climbing their way around the monitor. Valentina shook her head in disbelief as the code wrote itself before their eyes for a good few minutes before finally reaching the next red checkpoint.

Valentina studied the lines, her brain processing what was before her. She gave a soft snort. "You're right, Archie. She's after me. Every part of this is designed for Valentina Winters."

Archie's brow creased. "What do you mean? What was the code?"

Valentina sat in the chair, eyes fixed to the monitor, studying the next red lines. "Enter the dragon…that was the key. DJPP&TMOC2001."

"I'm not following you," Archie replied.

"DJPP. 'Enter the dragon.'" Valentina laughed. "It's so stupid it's laughable."

Archie's impatience grew. "What? What are you talking about?"

Valentina sat back in the chair. "There was a song in 2001 that went viral—y'know, before viral was a thing on social media. The song was *Do You Really Like It?* by DJ Pied Piper and the Master of Ceremonies. Get it? DJPP&TMOC2001?"

Archie struggled to process this. "So what has all of that got to do with dragons?"

"'Enter the dragon' was the first phrase sung in the song," Valentina informed him. "It was the starting three lyrics of that song. Deng is *the* dragon, so the message is clear. The message is there."

"What's the message?" Archie struggled with accepting that Valentina was able to figure all of this out.

Valentina nodded toward the screen. "The message is there. Plain and simple."

Archie drew closer to the screen. He squinted at the red lettering, taking a moment to absorb what he was seeing. The red letters blinked, no longer written in strange code or any kind of riddles, but declaring their message boldly for them both to read.

"Execute command: GAME ON."

Archie glanced at Valentina, then slowly typed in "GAME ON."

The computer *dinged*. The green lettering started to warp and morph on the screen, flying around as if caught in a digital tornado. They scrambled, wove, and navigated the black spaces until they settled into the shape of a smiling face. The face winked, then continued to morph, forming the shape of a large winged dragon that flew across the screen, breathing flames of green letters at the bottom of the monitor. The dragon disappeared from view, then returned a moment later, streaming toward them both, growing larger. When the green letters encompassed the entire screen, letters dripped and melted down its surface.

A single message remained in the digital residue.

"Good luck."

As they both stared at the screen, a hissing sound drew their attention to the carpet. The robot juddered. A delicate spray of mist expelled from its growing crease above the Cyclops stripe. The lid opened, and in the center of the box was a single USB drive, isolated and embedded on a velvet cushion.

Valentina shook her head in disbelief. How could the box contain so many secrets?

She moved before Archie could, taking the USB stick and

ONE NIGHT TO KILL

plugging it into the computer. The screen dissolved into the start-up process and, a moment later, a program filled the screen. A welcome message popped up on a digital scroll.

Congratulations.

You have passed the riddles and unlocked the secrets of the DominaFIX Intelligence. This program is worlds beyond any software that currently runs on the world's machines. It is smart. It is cunning. DominaFIX is to be used with great caution and in conjunction with collaboration to ensure the efficacy and moral progression of this software's survival.

You will, no doubt, be tempted to hit the ground running. Familiarize yourself with the program. Come to terms with the power that you hold in your hands. Communicate with me your intentions for the software and any developments made. I am curious to understand its workings in capacities other than those for which I have intended.

Consider yourself a beta tester.

A well-chosen beta tester.

May this serve you well in your purpose.

Long may he live.

The scroll was signed by Deng and undersigned by "The Dragon." Valentina raced through the message, bubbles of caution popping in her stomach. Archie was a slower reader. His eyes widened as he reached the end of the message and tried to close the pop-up.

Valentina had read the message. She knew the tone for what it meant. She turned her gaze to Archie. "You knew this was all a game? You and Deng are working together?"

Archie turned up his nose, realizing that he couldn't deny it any longer. He laced his fingers behind his back and nodded. "Yes. In a sense, at least."

Valentina stood and grabbed Archie by the collar. She shoved him back toward the books, slamming his body into the hard shelving. Some of the books wobbled dangerously close to the edges, and a few fell to the floor. "You best get speaking, asshole."

Despite himself, Archie smiled. He moved his hands to Valentina's as he attempted to peel her fingers away. She held him fast.

"Val," he cooed, trying to soothe things over. "You should know better than anyone else that life in Atlantica is never as it seems."

Valentina shoved him again. He grunted. Another book fell. "Get talking, asshole," Valentina demanded.

Archie sighed. "Let me go."

Valentina lowered her hands, refusing to move from where she stood.

Archie patted himself down. "Life is a game, Valentina. Atlantica is no different. Do you think it's easy to keep ourselves entertained? To maintain the excitement of working our way up the ladders once we end up on top of it all? No. Life gets dull." He stepped away, walking toward the robot. "We have a communion, those of us with the wealth to pull the strings. We have our methods of keeping each other on our toes, trying to outdo our peers, and come up with new ways to test ourselves. It's how the great minds advance. Consider this a game of chess, multiplied to epic proportions, and with live, moving figures."

"So, I'm only a pawn?" Valentina asked. "All of your men are pieces to be lost and discarded in the service of the greater good."

Archie considered this, his face hardening. "Yes."

Valentina raised her hand to hit him. He raised a finger and stopped her. "Not in the sense that you're thinking."

Valentina growled. "No more riddles!"

Archie sighed. "So aggressive."

Archie staggered as Valentina threw a punch that connected with his cheek. He growled in return. "Fine!" he exclaimed. "Fine. If that's how you want to play it." He moved his hand to his cheek and manipulated his jaw to check that she hadn't broken it. "Damn good punch."

Valentina gave him a warning look.

Archie rolled his eyes. "The truth is that you are not only a pawn, Val. What we have here is true. My ultimate priority is protecting Kit and ensuring that he makes a recovery. However, sometimes in war, there has to be peace—subsidence of animosity for the sake of fighting a common enemy. Deng knew about your raid because she was made aware that I needed help. She welcomed you into the belly of the beast where you proved your worth as a talented individual." He spat on the floor, the saliva a soft shade of pink. "Deng wanted to test you. She needed to know that we were serious about our acquisition of the artificial intelligence. It was all true, you know. The fact that this AI could have the power to rework the human mind, to forge new connections, and repair what's broken. What is lying on that computer system may very well be the key to unlocking it all. It may be the key to Kit's recovery."

Valentina's heart raced. "How the hell am I supposed to trust you?"

"You read it, didn't you?" Archie asked. "Long may he live? That was your brother. Deng is aware of the fact we're in this game to heal the unhealable. She knows that this will serve a greater good."

Valentina blinked, trying to comprehend it all. "So, Deng knows about Kit and me? That's impossible. She asked me to join her in her facility. She said to ask you what you knew about it all."

"She knows that something binds us," Archie admitted. "She doesn't know the what. She knows that you're talented, and she wanted to see those talents in action. What she doesn't know is that Kit is related to you."

Not to me, Valentina thought but held back on correcting Archie.

"Deng is a woman of intelligence," Archie continued, eyes fixed on the robot. "She is a woman of many skills and a woman of superior intellect. I didn't want to admit it to you, but I reached a dead end. It forced me to call in assistance. We, the rich of Atlantica, speak in our code, and we call for aid only when we seek to serve the betterment of society."

Valentina turned to the computer. "So, you're telling me that you can fix Kit? You're telling me that the answer is in that software?"

Archie smiled, the humor not reaching his eyes. "Yes. That's the hope."

"What have you promised in return? I've met enough people of your types to know that no trade is complete without the stakes of a bargain."

Archie drank from the neck of the bottle, wobbling a little as he stood. Valentina hadn't realized how glazed over his eyes were. How long had he been drinking?

"To share the software," Archie replied. "To perform our experiments and report the findings back to Deng." He nodded at the USB. "That stick is the only one of its kind, the cargo inside so secretive that even Deng refuses to make a copy. She's placed a lot of trust in us to make this happen. And it's all for you. I hope you understand that."

Valentina's eyes flashed to the robot, her skin crawling at the fact that they might have forgotten that Deng could be listening. The Cyclops stripe was black as onyx.

Archie opened his mouth to speak. Valentina hushed him, nodding toward the robot.

"Oh, relax," Archie replied. "That thing is destroyed. It hasn't powered up or moved in hours." He hiccupped, then continued, swaying as he grinned and leaned toward Valentina, "What she doesn't understand is that she's not going to get her software back." He let out a dark laugh, then returned to his seat. His fingers found the keyboard as he left Valentina looking down at the robot.

She studied it for a long time before finally demanding that Archie show her to Kit. It was growing light outside, and she needed to get going soon. It wasn't until they'd both left the office that a small green light glinted on the Cyclops stripe, and a tiny hum sounded as the machine powered up again.

CHAPTER EIGHTEEN

Kit filled Isabella's dreams.

A clouded montage of images of Kit and Isabella playing in the park swallowed her dreams. One moment they were laughing, running in the sunshine, and playing on the park's apparatus. The next, they were sitting by the lake and throwing bread to the ducks. Kit was smiling, as he always did. Two years younger than Isabella, she had always felt protective of her baby brother. Their parents were often busy with work—not that she ever understood what they did for a living—and it was up to Isabella to help Kit learn how to survive. Their nanny, an elderly woman named Charlotte who was the biggest softy in the world and didn't understand or agree with the common benefits of discipline, was no example to follow. Even at a young age, Isabella knew that she had a role in Kit's development.

Isabella threw bread to the ducks, laughing as they came nearby and pecked at her shoes. Kit stood cautiously behind her, hiding away from the waterfowl.

"No need to hide, silly." Isabella chuckled. "They're not going to hurt you. They only want the bread. See?"

She threw another chunk of the stale roll, and the birds flocked toward it. A few geese joined, honking as they fought for the morsel.

Kit peeked out from behind. "There's so many of them."

Isabella nodded. "There always will be. As long as you have me beside you, no one's going to hurt you. You know that, right?"

Kit gave a tentative nod.

Isabella smiled and offered her pinky. "Pinky swear on it. Your big sister will be here for you, okay?"

Kit came out from behind Isabella. He hooked his pinky into hers, and they shook. A duck came nearby, stretching its long neck to Kit's ankles. He froze. Isabella waved a hand. "Shoo!" The duck ran back, afraid to get too close.

"Point proved." She grinned happily.

She handed Kit a piece of bread. He threw it, then laughed as the birds flocked toward it.

"There we go!" Isabella declared. "Great job."

The dream shifted. The lake and the birds melted to reveal a fifteen-year-old Kit and a seventeen-year-old Isabella. Only, it wasn't Isabella staring at Kit from behind the bushes. It was Valentina.

Kit sat on the bench outside their house, the rain sheeting over him. His hair was limp and soaked, and the torrent worked hard to mask his tears. Valentina watched him, using the foliage as cover. Even at seventeen, her persona had been developing. Her parents put it down to sleepwalking, but back then, Isabella knew that something was amiss. Something was wrong. Why else would she wake up covered in twigs, mud, bruises, and scratches?

Why else would the papers report that low-grade criminals were being found most mornings taped to a lamppost with a confession tucked into their waistbands?

Valentina composed herself before walking up the pathway into the house. Her hands dug into the pockets of her father's

MICHAEL ANDERLE

leather jacket. It would be this leather jacket that Isabella's father was wearing the day he mysteriously disappeared, only a few months later. "What's up, Kitty-kat?"

Kit glanced up, confusion on his face. Valentina was silhouetted from the streetlight behind, but even if she wasn't, there was something amiss in her eyes. A hardness that Kit hadn't seen in his sister before.

"It's Kylie," he replied at last. "She broke up with me."

Valentina resisted rolling her eyes. She thought about what Isabella might do in this situation, aware that she needed to keep up the façade. She sat beside him and wrapped an arm over his shoulder. The movement was stilted and felt unnatural, but Kit didn't detect anything strange. He fell into her arms and sat there crying for half an hour before she finally managed to coax him inside.

As he stood at the bottom of the stairs, drenched and shaking, he offered a weak grin. "I guess you can't protect me from everything, huh?"

Valentina nodded, not quite sure what he meant. "Yeah. I guess I can't."

He offered nothing else before he trundled upstairs to strip out of his clothes, dry off, and sleep.

Isabella watched all of this in her dream, unaware until now of that exchange. The only memory she had of Kit's heartache was a brief "Thank you" the next morning before Kit headed out to school. She never asked him what he meant. She only discovered Kit and Kylie weren't together anymore based on his Facebook relationship status and posts over the next week

She rolled in her dream, pulling the sheets tight about her. Her face creased at the strange memory, surfacing after all these years like a sunrise after a storm. When she finally awoke, she sat for a long time, staring out the window, her mind filled with thoughts of Kit and concerns for Valentina.

Something happened last night.

Something significant in his healing process.

She just didn't know what.

It was rare that Isabella ever gained a glimpse into the life of Valentina, and that dream haunted her.

She wasn't sure that it *was* real. All she knew was that it *felt* real. As she continued her dayshift at the library, constantly put on her toes as Naomi threw jobs at her and tested her, pulling her in all directions, she couldn't fight the feeling in the back of her mind that something important was happening.

On a few occasions during the day, Isabella found herself in a quiet moment in the belly of the library, not a soul in sight. In those moments, she closed her eyes and reached out to Valentina, trying to coax her from her subconscious to ask the questions she felt she needed to ask. On each occasion, she failed to get anything from her. She supposed it shouldn't surprise her. Recent events notwithstanding, Valentina slept when Isabella was awake and vice-versa.

The day blurred by, and before she knew it, she was out in the rain. She popped open her umbrella, rounded the corner, and found Bradley standing there with a bouquet in his hand.

He grinned weakly. "Jill laughed at me. She said I shouldn't wait for you. Was I wrong?"

"Why would Jill..." Isabella started before she remembered the encounter with Jill earlier that day. Jill had spent far too long processing paperwork that would have taken Isabella minutes. After a glance of disdain from Naomi, Isabella ended up speaking harshly to Jill, words that Jill couldn't handle. Jill went tight-lipped and kept her head down for the rest of the day.

"No," Isabella continued. "You weren't wrong."

She took the flowers and offered Bradley a kiss on the cheek. She was exhausted, her mind circling the dream she'd had the night before, and she hadn't prepared for this. Was this what it was like to be in a relationship with someone? To have them pop out on you like stalkers in an alleyway?

Not that she considered them in a relationship. As far as she was concerned, they were having fun. She and Bradley hadn't declared that they were dating or that anything was indeed happening.

Bradley asked about her day, and Isabella opened up, exposing everything. Bradley knew the staff, so there was little to explain or hold back on. He took her to a waffle house two blocks from her apartment, and there they ate mountains of sweet treats, whipped cream, and syrups.

Bradley told Isabella all about his new job, cautious initially but opening up more as Isabella remained quiet about the nature of his work. He had spent the day standing guard outside a Victorian Gothic building on Lemon Street for half the day, and for the rest of it, he merely had to monitor security footage of the place in the comfort of the warm guard room.

Isabella raised an eyebrow. "So you're on guard detail?"

Bradley shrugged, his mouth full of waffle. When he swallowed, he announced, "I don't know. I don't think so. It's an interesting setup they have there. I'm not supposed to talk about it."

Isabella fixed her gaze on Bradley.

"Fine." Bradley leaned in closer. "From what I can gather, the Italian family that owns the joint are dealing in high-grade jewelry. Diamonds, zirconias, rubies, opals, that kind of stuff."

"Zirconias aren't high-grade," Isabella corrected.

Bradley turned up his lip. "You get what I mean. From what I can gather, there's hardly anything dodgy about it. No drugs involved, no trafficking, nothing in the way of serious criminal problems. I'm only protection in case people get wind of their stash."

"Is their stash legally acquired?" Isabella asked earnestly.

Bradley shrugged. "The hell should I know? I'm new."

"So how do you know you can trust them?" Isabella replied.

Bradley thought about this, then changed the subject. "You have sauce on your cheek."

Isabella moved to rub it away, but Bradley beat her to it, sitting beside her and stroking her cheek. He leaned in and kissed her lips. "You taste sweet."

Isabella looked down, stroking a lock of hair behind her ear. "Thanks? I guess."

They ate until their stomachs hurt, and Valentina began to wake. Isabella could feel her inside her mind somewhere, an uncomfortable parasite that demanded attention. She went with Bradley to the apartment building, and when they reached the hall that separated the two apartments, they stood awkwardly for a moment.

"I like you," Bradley announced.

Isabella stared into his eyes, unsure what to say.

Bradley sensed her hesitation. "Do you like me?"

"Of course I do."

"Not like that," Bradley stated. "You know what I mean."

Isabella drew a long breath. "I don't know. I mean… This is all so new to me. I don't know how to…"

Her words stopped when his mouth met hers. His fingers tangled in her hair. His kiss was urgent, laced with passion. She reached up on her toes, eyes closing as she sank into the kiss.

He cupped her cheeks as he removed his lips from hers. "Ball's in your court, Carter."

He turned away, entering his apartment a moment later, only pausing long enough to catch her eye before he disappeared.

Isabella's breath came in rapid pulses. She stood in the hallway a long while before finally retiring to her room. Valentina's voice came from far away, so far that she couldn't make out the words. When she turned the stereo to Beethoven, a smile was on her face.

There was also a smile on the face of the man who watched the alley to the rear of the apartment building. The same smile that had been on his face the whole way there.

CHAPTER NINETEEN

Valentina patted herself down, removing the wrinkles and creases from her outfit. Beethoven played softly in the background, the little metamorphosis room bright with light. She studied herself in the mirror, taking in every curve, every detail. Tonight was going to be fun.

Or so she thought.

She made her way into the chill night air, folding her body as she emerged through a window at the side of the building. The apartments had ledges for house plants and flower arrangements, but most of the residents left them bare, not having the time or wherewithal to bother with house plants when there were more important things to do in the city. For Valentina, they made terrific ladders.

She had only stepped down one story when she heard the sounds of disturbance from above: a loud banging on a door and the shouts of a woman.

Stirred by intrigue, Valentina pulled herself up a story and scaled the side of the building. From this distance, a drop to ground level would kill her, but she wasn't worried about that. She was confident in her abilities, and she proved it with ease.

She stopped by the window on the other edge of the building. She peeked through the murky glass and saw three AJS officers standing in the hallway and crowding a door to an apartment.

Bradley's apartment!

Valentina watched closely, unsure how they had found their way to this floor. In all her years of residence here, not once had anyone made their way up to the "abandoned" floor. Now she had three AJS officers there to visit a man who had only moved in a little over a week ago.

They knocked on the door again, fists thumping against the wood. The door wobbled in its frame. She wondered why Bradley wasn't answering and what he could be hiding. He should answer the door for them, even though he technically didn't need to. They were inquiring at a rented property, and therefore the rules didn't apply.

Still, courtesy was courtesy. What did Bradley have to hide?

Valentina studied the three officers. A tall dark woman, an athletic man, and an average woman with dark hair and eyes that drew attention. Valentina had seen those eyes before, on a few occasions, now. It was no wonder that she worried that Dick Chambers had a romantic relationship with Terra Kris. She was beautiful. As much as he denied affection toward her, Valentina always doubted it.

She thought back to the last time she had seen Terra Kris close up. It had been during the Dragon Boat Festival, surrounded by the aftermath of the chaos Valentina had wrought in the belly of Deng's festival float.

What the hell was she doing here?

They muttered among themselves before checking that the coast was clear. Satisfied, Terra banged on the door again. "We'll give you one more chance, sir."

No answer.

Terra nodded at the door handle. "Technically, that's hanging over property lines. The handle itself is encroaching on public territory." She glanced at her comrades who shook their heads, but their grins egged her on. "Stand back."

Terra took a step back, too. She raised a leg high, her form accentuated by the shimmering blue AJS uniforms, complete with the beehive pattern that contained the patented nano-protection that kept the officers safe. Tiny pockets of Kevlar that were lightweight and activated only in the event of an emergency. She slammed her heel down on the handle, and it tore away from the door.

The door swung open.

Valentina watched in fascination, knowing that she had places to be but unable to turn away. What would Bradley say or do when they entered his room? Was he asleep and oblivious to it all?

Terra pushed the door open, the three officers remaining behind the threshold. Terra whispered something to her colleague, and a moment later the tall woman activated a set of glasses that broadcast a holographic display. She put a finger to her ear and announced, "Dispatch, this is unit two-four-one. We're reporting a possible homicide on the upper east block…"

Valentina's grip tightened, her knuckles going white. She angled her head but couldn't see in the room. What could they possibly mean a homicide in Bradley's room—*her* room?

Terra advanced into the apartment, much to the chagrin of the other two, who began examining the nearby areas. Valentina knew it was only a matter of time before they knocked on her door and tried to extract information from anyone inside. The other two apartments on that floor were empty, but they didn't know that.

Valentina scowled. She scaled her way back toward the window she had exited through, her heart thumping in her throat.

What the hell was going on?

A knock came on the door. *Right on cue.*

Valentina opened the door, one fist rubbing her eye. She stretched and yawned. "Can I help you, officer?"

The athletic man stood proudly before her in his uniform. His eyes scanned Valentina, who now stood in a pair of loose-fitting pajama pants, and a white tank top. Her red wig was gone, replaced with ruffled dark hair as though she'd been sleeping, though her lipstick was still flawless.

The officer's badge read "Tweedy."

"Sorry to disturb you, ma'am," Officer Tweedy stated. "We've come across a disturbance in the apartment across from yours, and I wondered if you'd heard or seen anything of note over the past few hours."

Valentina poked her head around the corner, looking at the open door. She frowned. "No, I haven't heard a thing. Well, not until the thumping of you all at the door. What's happening? Is there anything I should be worried about?"

Tweedy examined her face, but Valentina was a great liar. "So, you haven't noticed anyone up here that shouldn't be? No arrivals from the stairs or elevator? No unusual sounds for this time of night?"

Valentina yawned again. "No, nothing at all."

"Do you know the resident in that apartment?" Tweedy asked. He took out a cell phone and tapped on the screen, taking notes of his conversation.

Valentina nodded, doing her best to maintain her Isabella persona. She came across brasher than Bella would, but all in all, it wasn't too bad. "Bradley Pepper. I used to work with him at the library. Is he okay? Has something happened in his apartment?"

Before Tweedy could react, Valentina shouldered past and strode across the hallway. She folded her arms around her shirt and stopped only when the taller officer held out a hand and ordered her to stop.

Valentina could see inside. The bed was unmade, and something stained the sheets. As the woman spoke to her and tried to move her back, she moved her head around, trying to see as much as possible.

The blood was everywhere. It was on the bed, the walls, and the carpet. Valentina's breath caught as she saw Terra shining a flashlight over the area, examining the scene while trying not to disturb the evidence.

The large woman shoved Valentina. "Ma'am, if you don't back up and let us do our job, we'll have to place you under arrest."

The words cut through to Valentina. Tweedy ran up, taking her other arm and helping. Valentina shook her head, snapping herself from her reverie. "I'm sorry, it's just... He's a friend of mine. God... Who'd do such a thing?"

She burst into tears. Hot, salty tracks stained her cheeks as she buried her face in her hands. Her shoulders shook with sobs, and Tweedy took pity on her, pulling her away from the scene. He brought her to her apartment and sat on the edge of the bed in the moonlit darkness, offering comfort.

His words didn't offer much. Valentina wasn't surprised that a hardened man of the law didn't know how to comfort a woman properly. He left after a short while, closing the door behind him. Valentina knew that soon there would be a forensics team, and they'd cordon off this place entirely. She needed to act fast.

Locking the door, she slunk away to her window. There was no time to change again, so she skirted the building barefoot, the breeze nipping at her skin and prickling it into gooseflesh.

She navigated to the window where she had seen the AJS officers. It took some skill to lower herself enough to duck beneath the window and not be seen by the officers in the hallway. Finally, she rounded the corner of the building and stopped by the window of Bradley's apartment.

She could make out Terra's voice as she spoke. "The damned thing's a mess. All this blood and not a single sign of a body. Who would do a thing like this?"

The tall officer's voice answered. "Many people. This ain't the first time I've seen something like this. Some people want to make a point. Spray blood on the walls in the same way that dogs piss on hydrants. Territory, y'know?"

Terra sighed. Valentina peeked and saw her silhouetted from the hall light. Her flashlight scanned the room, not that there was much to be found in the way of decoration.

"At least it's not shit," Terra replied. She crouched and raised the duvet at the side of the bed. "Hello…"

She reached down and grabbed the object on the floor. She pinched it between her fingers and held it up to her flashlight. A rainbow of colors sprayed as the diamond fragmented the light.

"A diamond?" Terra asked. "A funny object to leave behind, don't you think?"

The other woman drew closer. She accepted the diamond and held it up to her eye. "Damn. Not too shabby. You're right, though. Who leaves a diamond behind? It's not like it's a copper penny fallen out of someone's pocket, is it?"

Valentina frowned. Once again, she asked herself what the hell was happening. The diamonds gave her a lead, but she couldn't assume that Bradley was dead because there was no body. All that was left was blood.

Which meant that either he'd gone willingly and staged something strange or that he was dead, zipped up, and someone had thrown him into the river or the ocean.

One thing was for certain, though. Valentina wouldn't stop until she found out the truth.

CHAPTER TWENTY

Valentina didn't have time for this shit.

She was torn, pulled in two directions from two urgent situations. On the one hand, Bradley had been either taken or murdered. On the other, she wanted to investigate the code that she and Archie had unlocked—well, mostly her—and find out if there was more she could do to help. If the AI was truly as promising as he suggested, Kit could be back to full health in a few months, maybe even a couple of weeks.

She looked across Lemon Street at the huge Victorian Gothic building. Her lead from the diamond in Bradley's apartment had brought her here. Yellow brick stretched high into the sky where spires and towers decorated the building's many wings. Long strips of translucent glass obscured her view inside, a thick layer of dust or condensation fuzzing its clarity. Ornately carved decorations made up most of the outside, and a few gargoyles were scattered around. It could easily have been some kind of palace or extra wing of Hogwarts School of Witchcraft and Wizardry.

Across the road was a large arched front door. The front was black, with giant hinges to add to the grandeur. While no one stood guard outside, Valentina could make out the blinking light of a security camera fixed into the recesses of the brick.

Guess the front is out of bounds, then.

She looked up and down the street, checking for people watching. There was only a trickle of foot traffic, with half a dozen cars in sight. She dug her hands in the pockets of her jacket and pulled up her collar as she made her way down the street. She slipped into an alley and disappeared into the darkness.

The chatter of strangers came from ahead. A gentle glow of orange pulsed as Valentina rounded the corner and found four homeless vagrants gathered around an empty oil drum. Their clothes were torn and tattered, and the faint smell of whisky was in the air.

She thought of Dick Chambers.

As they focused on the flames, Valentina slipped by unnoticed. She didn't have to try. They weren't on the lookout for Atlantica's most infamous assassin.

When she faded from view, Valentina gripped the brickwork and began her ascent. The building she climbed was smooth and half the size of her target. It gained her enough vantage to look down at the homeless group and cast a sad eye. A part of her wished she could help them all, that she could invest her money in solving the million and one problems of the world. Still, it would never work. She had learned that well, that no matter how much people tried to fix the world, there would always be problems.

The rooftop was flat. She strode across it toward the neighboring high-rise side of the Gothic building and took advantage of its adjacent stone decorations. Each carving and nodule provided another place to dig in her toes and ascend. Before long, she came to a part of the Gothic building's roof that was slanted, with a large window that looked down into a dark, empty room.

Valentina studied the room, ensuring that there was no one present. Satisfied, she eased her fingers around the edges of the window and tried to pry it open. It didn't budge.

She dug into her pocket and drew out a device that appeared to be a suction cup connected to a small metal plumb by a length of thin silver cable.

Valentina pressed the suction cup to the glass, then unraveled the coil. She squeezed the metal plumb and a hot red light activated. She dragged the light in a circle, the line taut while maintaining her grip on the suction cup.

When the circle edges joined, the glass popped out in a perfectly round shape.

Valentina braced herself and grabbed the edge of the glass to stop it from falling to the floor. She carefully brought it to the rooftop and laid it against some tiles. She released the suction cup, pocketed the device, then set off a search scan on her phone, waiting to see if it picked up the use of any more technological equipment within the room.

The scan came back empty. Though, there were cameras in the next room over.

Valentina lowered herself inside.

She expected the room to smell of dust and time, having visited ancient buildings such as this over her years. However, what met her nostrils was the sterile scent of bleach. The building, while aged and weathered on the outside, was almost new inside. The walls were spotless, shelves and items of furniture were without a stain. She wondered what this room was used for and if she was in the right place.

Bradley mentioned this building. He said they dealt in jewelry.

Not one to let her guard down, Valentina snuck to the edge of the room and listened for activity. She was high up, probably about five or six floors at an estimate. The ceilings were high and grandiose, which made it more difficult to get a sense of altitude.

All the head honchos live on the higher floors. So why are things so quiet now?

Valentina stopped by the only door leading out of the room and pressed her ear against the cool wood. There was no disturbance outside that she could detect. She crouched to the lock before utilizing the lock picking equipment in her pocket. The lock *clicked* a moment later.

The hallway was dark. There were no portraits on the wall or decorations of any sort. A long runner carpet rolled down the center of the corridor, and Valentina counted eight rooms shooting off on either side. She raised her cell phone and activated the scan, finding two security cameras—one at either end of the hall.

She poked one eye around the corner and found the first camera. It was about thirty feet from where she stood. She ducked back into the room and navigated through a series of apps on her phone. She was confident that the camera's manufacturer was CamLox—a multi-million security firm born in Atlantica that provided much of the island's security tech, and one of Tynamo's primary rivals. She selected the options and hooked into the camera's wireless feed, granting herself access to the real-time video footage from the camera.

She grinned. *It pays to sleep your way into dark places.*

The security protocol was easy to compromise. Only the CamLox staff knew the patch that Valentina exploited. She knew that soon they would fix the hole, but she was glad they hadn't yet.

Great job, Tyrone. Always slow to the fix.

She tapped her cell screen, and the video feed froze. To make sure that it had, she eased her head around the corner and saw that the feed on her phone didn't pick up the movement. She repeated the process with the other camera, then stepped into the hall.

She walked on the rug, moving almost silently. She made her way toward the stairs, taking them two at a time as she advanced to the lower floors. The building was spooky with no real character or decoration or any kind of style to it. It was almost as if someone had built the place but hadn't done anything inside.

Was Bradley lying to me? Did he make up his job and the location where he was working?

No. Why would he do that?

Because he was trying to get a reaction from you? Because he wanted to seem like he was doing something good instead of wasting his days lying around in the apartment you let him stay in?

Valentina chewed her lip, her sensitive ears still not picking up any activity in the building. She rounded the corner to yet another empty hallway and deactivated yet another series of cameras. She stopped at the end of the corridor and listened before making her way down yet another set of stairs.

Her skin prickled as she neared the bottom of the stairs. A fresh draft of cool air wafted over her. She closed her eyes and felt its direction, determining that it came from one of the nearby doors. On the left, three doors in, the door was ajar. She eased herself to its edge and waited, breathless.

Silence met her from inside.

She nudged the door wide enough to peek through. The room was dark, a large suite complete with a four-poster bed. The floors were stone, and the far wall was more of the glass paneling that Valentina had witnessed from outside. A glass door was ajar, the large, floor-length curtains flowing gently in the breeze.

Valentina made her way to the open door. The air was refreshing. This place was freakishly sterile, and Valentina felt the leftover particles of bleach and cleaner on her skin like an unwanted parasite.

She slipped through the glass door onto a balcony with galvanized black railings. Below her was the city street. She could

MICHAEL ANDERLE

make out the area where she had been watching the building earlier.

It didn't make sense. What the hell was this place? She went back inside.

Valentina got her answer when the door closed gently behind her.

CHAPTER TWENTY-ONE

"You're certainly one for taking risks, aren't you, Valentina?"

Deng Zenim released her grip from the door handle, then laced her fingers behind her back. She was petite, not much larger than the height of a thirteen-year-old. She looked even smaller in the darkness that she stood in, and Valentina wondered why anyone would ever be so intimidated by such a woman.

"Speak for yourself," Valentina replied. She slipped her hands into her pockets, her fingers scanning the various items she carried, just in case. "After the shit that went down at your compound, I'm surprised you wouldn't bring backup with you the next time you sought me out."

Deng stared at her placidly, with little expression on her face. "Who says I haven't?"

Valentina grinned.

Deng stepped closer, stopping by the four-poster to leave space between them both. "You've picked the wrong location to scout. A place like this is dangerous, to say the least." She cast admiring eyes around the room's architecture. "A private residence in which jewel thieves and collectors while away their time, stewing in their fantasies of world domination? Nothing good can come of breaking and entering."

The tension was thick. Valentina remained silent, trying to work out what she'd stepped into. It wouldn't be the first time Deng had taken her by surprise.

"Did you know that all of this was once mine?" Deng asked.

Valentina shook her head.

Deng nodded, eyes scanning the room once more. "Not the only one I had, mind you. But one of mine, all the same. Real estate was a big boom in the inception of Atlantica. It was where all the big bucks came from. We drew up plans of impressive buildings, wanting to make Atlantica the metropolitan city of the world, a place where culture and place and time could mash into one beautiful mess. It's poetic." For the first time, a ghost of a smile traced her lips. "How I've missed this."

"So, what?" Valentina started. "You've lured me into a piece of real estate so you can show off your dominion in Atlantica?"

"No," Deng replied softly. "Not at all. Just coincidence, mostly. I had no intention of winding up back here tonight, not after learning what I know about the owners of this place now. You see, they bought the building from me half a decade ago, desperate to find a place to commit to their operations." She shook her head. "Hard to believe that more people don't invest in tech, but instead choose the easy route with fickle resources like jewels and drugs. At least in tech, there's progress. All that exists in drugs is a never-ending line of weak-willed civilians who soon grow out of pocket and out of time."

Valentina glanced at the building beside them, certain that she could see dark figures moving in the shadows, the glint of guns trained on her.

"What do you want then, Deng?" Valentina asked. "I'm afraid I'm out of time for a history lesson on the Zenim empire. I'm here for another purpose, and you're standing in the way."

"Yes..." Deng's eyes narrowed. "Your friend, correct?"

Valentina's jaw clenched.

Deng sat on the bed. She looked so small and fragile. From what she could see, Valentina was certain that she wasn't armed, either. How easy would it be to take her out then and there? To put a bullet in her head and end it all?

Deng contemplated a long moment. "Bradley Pepper, aged twenty-five. Formerly employed at the Atlantica Public Library, no criminal record, but several cautions from the AJS. Son of Larry Pepper and Mary-Beth Turnstall. Five feet, and ten inches in height, with a blood type of O rhesus negative."

Valentina's heart beat faster. "You've been spying on him?"

Deng half-shrugged. "It's easy when you know how."

"Where is he?"

"Ah, now we come to the crux of it."

Valentina ran forward. She pounced on Deng, knocking her back onto the bed. She grabbed Deng by the collar, raising the other fist, ready to punch her in the face. "Where is he!"

Deng's expression remained passive. Her gaze darted to the door. "I'd keep my voice down if I were you. They'll hear you, and you don't want that. I've done my part to distract them from the upper levels while you break in. Don't ruin all my hard work."

Valentina's brow creased. Somewhere outside and far away, she could have sworn she heard someone shouting.

Deng chuckled, a hollow laugh. She sat up, and Valentina let her. When Valentina turned to see what Deng was looking at, she saw several red dots on her chest.

Valentina scowled. "Talk."

Deng looked at her passively, as if they weren't talking under the threat of sniper fire. "I want my AI back," she stated simply.

Valentina raised an eyebrow, unprepared for the simplicity of that response. "What?"

"I want my AI back," Deng repeated. "Archie has broken the terms of our agreement. I want my technology back."

Valentina's hackles raised. "No."

"Yes." Deng's gaze fixed on Valentina.

Valentina scoffed. "We earned it, fair and square. You wanted to surrender the tech voluntarily, so now we have it. Archie is doing what he needs to with it under whatever fucked up conditions you two had for the games you played. You can have it when he's finished, I'm sure."

"No. I won't," Deng stated calmly. "You were there when he said it, weren't you? He's keeping it from us."

Valentina thought back to that moment, to the tipsy Archie and his slip of the tongue in front of the freakish robot. "You were watching?"

"We were listening," Deng confirmed. "We don't stop listening when the lights are off."

"Which is how you knew where I'd be in this building?" Valentina asked.

Deng nodded again. "Tynamo Inc. bought out CamLox three weeks ago. We're still in the final stages of the transition and announcing to the general public, but it's there. We are well on our way to owning the monopoly on Atlantica security. It's great for business. An entire security infrastructure built around our systems. Our self-serving economy on an endless loop."

Valentina frowned. "How is that possible? That sounds like a terrible idea."

"For all except us," Deng replied. "The city and the island have signed their approval allowing us to proceed. Not that the bureaucrats in government didn't try to stop us. Still, this island is built on the backbones of private business, so who are they to try and limit what we can accomplish? Even if they *did* vote against us, don't you think we'd find ways around that? Money can buy anything on this island, and I have a *lot* of it."

Valentina's blood boiled. "Where's Bradley?"

"In the basement," Deng replied as casually as if she was telling someone the time. "He made a schoolboy error on his first day, and his new employers are punishing him." She tutted and shook her head. "Revealing vital information on private business to a stranger in a waffle house...naughty, naughty."

Valentina swallowed. Isabella and Bradley had been discussing his job earlier that evening. Had they been listening? If they had been, it would've been because of Deng's systems.

"You did this to him?" Valentina replied.

"*You* did this," Deng replied. "I didn't make him squeal. I didn't ask questions. You did this."

Valentina didn't know how to reply. The jig was up. Deng knew her true identity. She knew who Isabella was talking to and where she lived. Deng had the keys into the heart of her life, and there was nothing she could do about it.

Or so she thought.

"It's a shame that your friend is so secretive," Deng pondered aloud. "Funny how similar she looks to you." She glanced up with a devilish look in her eye. "Although to acquire a name and further information has been difficult. Bradley's was easy. That man leaves his fingerprints everywhere he goes. Your 'friend'... now that's another story altogether."

Valentina grew tired of Deng's words. She stormed past her toward the door, pausing when the voices called loudly from somewhere below them.

Valentina looked back at Deng, surprised to find her sitting on the other side of the bed facing her. "I can give you everything you need, Valentina. Hear me out."

Valentina lingered a moment before softening her shoulders. "You want the AI. You can't have it. Fair is fair, and Archie needs it." She couldn't say more than that, as much as she wanted to. Kit needed the software. Kit needed the help.

"Archie and I had a deal, Valentina," Deng stated. "Archie is planning to go back on it. I can't allow that."

"Well, take it up with him, then," Valentina replied. "I'm done being the pawn between you two. I'm not a plaything for rich idiots to enjoy. I'm Valentina fucking Winters, and I could kill you while you sleep."

Deng smirked, the first break of genuine pleasure Valentina had seen in her eyes. "You'll need me before the end."

Valentina narrowed her eyes. "We'll see about that."

She marched over to the door, pausing with her hand on the knob. When she turned back to the bed, Deng was gone.

So that's how it feels, Valentina thought.

CHAPTER TWENTY-TWO

Valentina held her breath as she briskly walked along the hallway.

She could hear the activity now, several voices murmuring and laughing and talking as they made their way up the stairs. Valentina stayed close to the wall, wondering what her best path downstairs would be. Deng told her that Bradley was in the basement. She had no idea what they'd be doing to him down there, but basements weren't the places for birthday parties and bar mitzvahs. If experience had taught her anything, it was that time would not be on her side if she wanted to see him alive again.

Shit.

She paused near the top of the stairs. Light came from below, and silhouettes of figures approached the bottom of the stairs. She looked around, deciding to enter the nearest doorway. She eased it shut behind her.

The door locked from the inside. She nudged it into place, then waited by the entry. Footsteps *clicked* loudly on the stairs as the crowd arrived. She listened, trying to catch distinct snippets of conversation, but couldn't hear them through the thick door. In the empty room behind her was a small window, and

Valentina was also wary that Deng could be watching her right now, her men and women fixed on her with their sniper sights.

The walls were closing in.

Valentina put a finger to her temple and massaged it. She needed to come up with a strategy, some way to distract everyone so that she could escape. She couldn't fit out the window, and she couldn't head out into the throng. If she waited for the crowd to thin, it might be too late to save Bradley.

What to do...

Valentina ran through a list of options in her head. She examined the upper walls, looking for ventilation systems or other entrances that could provide some leverage, but nothing came to her.

The voices laughed outside. Something banged on the door. Valentina stepped back, ready to fight her way out if she needed to. She couldn't count their number, but she'd give it a damned good go. She'd been in similar situations before, surrounded by enemies, able to slip quietly away in some, and others...

In others...

The idea came to Valentina in a flash. She thumbed the number into her cell phone and made the call. There was enough noise outside that they shouldn't hear her voice, but still, she whispered.

Terra Kris switched off her motorcycle engine and lingered behind while the other officers walked the stairs into the AJS precinct. They paused by the door. She told them she'd catch up. She needed a minute.

Another day, another dead end.

She gritted her teeth, then tried to employ the techniques she'd read about online to deal with stress. *Breathe in. Breathe out.*

It was all that simple. The only way to calm down was to do the damned thing everyone did anyway.

The case had gotten to her. Yet another visit to a murder site they weren't allowed to legally access, yet another loophole she'd had to create to gain them entry and try to sniff out justice.

It was bullshit. How the hell was the AJS supposed to solve anything when they couldn't enter private properties without permission? The whole justice system was backward.

Then why are you still fighting for justice?

She shook her head, clearing the negative thoughts. If only they could have pursued the attacker. They found his DNA. They had samples of his hair, fingerprints, and blood. He was on their system, a man by the name of Harvey Vincent. A five-time felon and someone who should be permanently behind bars. They even had his goddamn address, but despite knocking on the door and requesting permission to enter, they had said no.

Shocker.

Terra growled, her fists clenched as she thought of the injustice of it all. Any other city in any other country around the world, and she could investigate further without reprimand. She could either grab a warrant or go rogue and not suffer any consequences quite as harsh as she would in Atlantica.

She had learned that the hard way.

She tapped her HUD on her glasses and examined the case again, Harvey's face grinning back at her as if he knew even when he had his picture taken that he'd have the upper hand.

Her cell phone rang.

"Hello?" she answered.

"Hey. It's me," the voice replied.

Terra checked the Caller ID. It provided no information. "I'm sorry, but who…"

"Valentina," Valentina replied. "I know you saw me earlier, and I saw you. I'm in a bit of a jam, and I could do with your help."

Terra contemplated this. She knew Valentina, but she didn't know her well. Her only encounters had been brief and through Dick Chambers, or in the thick of some chaos that had occurred down at the docks a few weeks back.

Terra checked that no one was eavesdropping. "You know this is a monitored line?"

"No. It's not," Valentina replied. "I've taken care of it."

Terra glanced at the information on her display, noticing a small red circle with a line through it in the top corner—offline mode.

"How is that—" she started.

"Not important," Valentina interrupted. "You're an AJS agent with a fire in her stomach to fight for what's right, aren't you?"

Terra told her she was.

"Must be pissed you can't track your guy that you discovered tonight?" There was a hint of enjoyment in Valentina's tone. "The blood in the apartment. Bet it's led you to another dead end, hasn't it?"

Terra frowned. "How do you know?"

"I'm in the building," Valentina replied. "Lemon Street. Gothic-style build. I'm there."

Terra glanced around her again, offering a friendly smile to a fellow officer who had just arrived back from being out in the field. Terra dismounted her bike and moved closer to the shadows of some nearby bushes. "What are you doing there? That's breaking and entering. You're going to get yourself killed. Do you know who you're dealing with?"

"No," Valentina admitted. "You're going to tell me, and you're going to help me bring him in."

"Bring him in?" Terra was flummoxed. "Since when did you care about seeing guys behind bars?"

There was a pause before Valentina replied. "Let me rephrase that. I'm going to gain you entry, and you're going to lock him up. I'm not getting involved in AJS business. I don't get paid enough for that shit."

"From what I hear you're better paid than me," Terra replied.

Valentina laughed. "You heard correctly. So are you in, or are you out?"

Terra grinned. "I'm in."

Valentina held her breath and pressed her ear against the door.

The steps were quieter, the bulk of the passing foot traffic dispersing around the building somewhere. It still didn't make sense to her. Of the few rooms she had entered, most were empty.

There were rooms you didn't see, weren't there?

Somehow Valentina had the impression that this place wasn't a residence for people to stay very long. She planned to obey that ethos.

Ensuring that the lock was firmly in place, she moved back into the room. The small window on the far wall was dirty, but she could dimly see through it and down into the streets below. She watched the cars hum past and wondered whether she was thin enough to smash the glass and slip outside.

Not without cutting your stomach, girl. Also, who are you kidding?

It was at least ten minutes or so before she saw the motorcycle speed past below. The lights weren't flashing, which was a good sign. That would buy her a little more time before the others became aware that she was there. The other cars followed, and Valentina smiled. If she could pull this off right, the whole operation would be a cinch.

Next stage: get downstairs.

CHAPTER TWENTY-THREE

Another ten minutes passed before Valentina felt safe enough to risk leaving the room.

The footsteps had faded a while ago, but the voices still lingered. Occasionally someone would walk up and down the hall, chatting with another.

The silence had lasted a full minute now, and that was enough for Valentina to ease open the lock and poke her head around the door. The hallway was empty. Adrenaline raced through her, and the hair on her arms stood on end. The familiar tingle of action pulsed through her and activated her senses. She was coiled and ready to strike if needed.

She had a funny suspicion that she'd need to.

She slipped out the door and kept close to the wall. The stairs curved around the corner, and she clung to the pivoting edge where the treads were narrowest. When the lower floor came into sight, she paused and assessed the situation.

Three people loitered ahead—a chunky man in a white sleeveless tank and slicked-back greasy hair that was a mottled mix of grey and black, and two women. The women appeared to be identical twins, except one wore her hair in a bob, while the other's hair flowed down her back to the waist of her pants.

Valentina looked past them to the stairs at the far end of the hall. She only had a few options, and she wanted to weigh them carefully. It was a choice between stealth and disruption.

She opted for stealth.

She took a small item from her pocket and laid it in the palm of her hand. It was the size of a large housefly. With her other, she opened an app on her phone and thumbed in the commands. A digital joystick appeared on the screen. Valentina moved the joystick in the directions she required and sent the small drone hovering into the air.

The drone flew across the hallway, emitting a gentle buzz as it cleared the trio's heads. Their conversation masked its passing as it zeroed in on the end of the hallway. Valentina studied the low-resolution feed from the drone's eye on her phone and saw many more people at the bottom of the stairs.

How many people are in this building?

Voices came from behind. Valentina knew she had to act fast. She pushed the joystick to its maximum reach in one direction, and the drone zoomed at the wall during a conversational lull. It made a popping sound as it hit the brick before falling to the floor.

The trio's heads all turned at once. They walked toward the sound.

Valentina tiptoed the remaining distance down the stairs. She opened the door to the nearest room and slipped inside. On her phone, she made out the trio's image through the drone's cracked lens. She pressed another button on the screen, and the drone sparked as it destroyed all residual data that could have linked the device back to her.

The world's smallest self-destruct button.

Valentina took a moment to pause and listen. The trio was alarmed, but at least they hadn't seen her. She moved the lock into place on the doorway behind her, then examined the room she had entered.

Only to find a woman staring back at her.

The woman was like something out of a Grecian myth. At least two feet taller than Valentina and five times as wide, she was a giant to behold. Her face was sunken in, and her skin looked as though made from stone. The confused look on her face was slowly melting to annoyance as Valentina drank her all in.

"Hello," Valentina offered casually.

"Hello?" The woman was more uncertain. Luckily she was quiet. "Have we met?"

Valentina shook her head.

"Oh." The woman put down the can of beer she was holding. The room was a mess compared to the others, with clothes strewn all over the place, crumbs on the floor, and packets decorating any spaces that might have been clear before. "Then what are you doing in my room?"

Valentina put her hands in her pockets and shrugged. "I'm afraid I don't have a good answer."

"Can you leave, please?" the woman asked, politely enough. Valentina could sense the tension growing, alarm appearing on the woman's features as her eyes darted to the door. Outside Valentina could make out the trio drawing attention to the drone they'd discovered.

"Not just yet."

The woman sighed. "Now."

"No." Valentina held her gaze.

"Fine." The woman cracked her knuckles and flexed her neck. "We'll have it your way, shall we?"

She slowly advanced on Valentina, looming over her and casting a shadow as large as a blimp. Clearly, this was a tactic that had worked in the past without a need for violence because the woman looked shocked when Valentina didn't budge an inch.

The woman paused, close enough that Valentina could smell

the stale scent of her sweat. There was something else, too. Was that weed she smelled on her clothes?

"Go," the woman insisted.

"No. I can't go out there."

"Why?"

Valentina shrugged again. "None of your business."

The woman rubbed her tired eyes, then extended a meaty paw down at Valentina, aiming for her collar. Valentina stepped back and avoided the swipe. Irritated, the woman clawed again, looking like a bear trying to grab a salmon from the raging river.

The annoyance reddened her cheeks. She let out a soft growl. "Enough games." She clenched her fingers into a fist and threw a punch at Valentina.

Valentina dodged the blow, the woman's fist narrowly avoiding colliding with the wall. Her step forward threw her off balance, and Valentina took a moment to step farther inside the room. She tried to navigate around the debris and trash, but it was impossible to miss. A chips packet caught on the heel of her shoe.

She had no time to pay attention to that as the woman turned, her expression thunderous, and advanced on her. "Get out of my room, you piece of shit." The giant had lost her placid demeanor when she realized she couldn't deal with the issue easily. Valentina checked her watch, then cast a glance at the window. The curtains were drawn. She needed to see outside.

As the woman came at her, Valentina launched two quick jabs —one to the stomach and another to the neck. The woman made a strange coughing noise as Valentina's fist connected. Her eyes flashed. She let out another growl as she sent a hook at Valentina.

Although the full blow didn't connect, Valentina felt some of its impact. The fist caught her in the side, narrowly avoiding her ribs and organs. She stepped back, stumbling to remain upright. There was a bed beside her, which she stepped on, evening out the height difference between the pair.

The woman scowled. Valentina bounced gently, then delivered a kick to the woman's face. Her head snapped back. Spit flew from her mouth. The giant stumbled into the bureau behind her, colliding with the drawers and making a louder crash than Valentina would have liked.

Those in the hall didn't miss it.

"Lissandra? Are you okay in there?" a voice called.

Why are they all so polite? What the hell is this place? Maybe Bradley was right, and these guys aren't all bad.

Tell that to him now.

Lissandra righted herself and was about to answer when Valentina kicked again. This time she snapped to the left, falling onto her stomach. Her face narrowly avoided crashing into the wooden floor. Valentina took the opportunity to jump down near the window. She peeled the curtains back and glanced outside.

The cars were parked at the curb, their lights off. Their tinted windows hid the people waiting inside.

A fist banged on the door. "Lissandra. Talk to me."

Lissandra lifted her head. "Intruder! There's an intruder in my room!"

Valentina watched as the door shook in its frame. The bodies barged against the wood from the other side. The corners creaked and began to splinter as the thuds continued.

Valentina knew that now was the time. She turned away from Lissandra's gleeful expression as she drew her pistol. She aimed it at the glass, straightening her arm to line her shot up at the AJS cars outside. She closed one eye, lining the sight up with her target. Her finger tensed on the trigger.

"What are you doing—" Lissandra started.

The shot fired and drowned out her words. Glass shattered and rained like daggers of frozen snow. The few people wandering outside screamed and shouted, fleeing in all directions with their hands raised over their heads. One of the AJS cruisers sank in one corner as the tire blew and the air expelled from inside.

The sirens activated. Their lights flashed. Car doors opened, and a fleet of officers ducked behind the vehicles, pistols at the ready, aiming their guns at the window that had shattered.

Valentina ducked as a handful of officers peeled away from the cruisers and crossed the road to the building's front door. She heard their calls for those inside to surrender and come out with their hands up.

The banging and thuds on the door stopped as alarmed voices rang out from inside. People ran up the stairs. Lissandra looked from Valentina to the door, then began to crawl.

Valentina kicked her once more in the face as she passed, leaving the giant snoring on the floor.

She had better places to be.

CHAPTER TWENTY-FOUR

Glass rained onto the street. Terra shook her head as a tire on the cruiser two cars in front burst and sank in one corner.

Not cool, bitch. Not cool. You're only supposed to break the seal of the building.

"The seal" was a concept that Terra had invented herself. It was a loophole that allowed her to gain access to private residences if she needed to. She didn't often utilize it herself, well, not as much as she used to, but it was the only way they could overcome Atlantica's ridiculous judicial protections on private residences.

Gunfights, drug-fueled parties, and trafficking could all happen within the boundaries of a private residence. In many cases on the island, it was encouraged. Why else would so many crime lords and corrupt move to this particular part of the world?

However, the moment that threshold was crossed, damaged, or broken, it was all fair game. The triggering of the bullet through the glass, violating "the seal" and crossing into public territory was enough to break that sacred barrier of protection. Civilian lives were now at stake.

Not that Valentina needed to pop the tire, though. That was poor sportsmanship on her side.

Terra climbed off her motorcycle and ducked behind the back of the nearest cruiser with three of her colleagues. She knew another shot wouldn't come straight away, but they trained to be prepared. After a minute of silence, she waved at them to follow her. She broke cover and raced across the road.

They flanked the doorway, splitting into two groups. There was a commotion inside. A couple of faces had appeared at the window, and Terra knew they had been alerted. She knocked on the door. "Atlantica Justice System. We're coming in."

"Like fuck you are!" came a gruff voice from inside. Wood splintered as a large hole appeared in the door.

Terra smirked. One bullet into public space was good. Two was a gold mine.

"Let's go then, bitches," she muttered as she slapped a small detonation device on the door. She waved the officers back. They turned away, hands to their ears as the device exploded, making short work of the lock and the door.

The door swung open. Gunfire rained from within. The noise was deafening, volleys of thunder. Terra and the officers stayed low and out of sight until the gunfire died. More voices cried. People fled. Footsteps ran from the scene.

Terra kept her back to the wall and eased to the door. She poked her head around the corner and found the entrance empty.

She nodded to the other officers. They covered her six.

Keeping her Glock trained in front of her, she advanced. She scanned the room in an arc, keeping an eye out for any sign of movement. Although the form-fitting AJS uniform was great protection from bullets, it did little to numb the pain of the actual impact. She had felt enough bullets graze or collide with her skin in her time. She didn't need to relive it.

Dark wood decorated the reception area, and the floors were stone. She could hear people running away, somewhere down the corridor that opened to her left. They must have run up the stairs since the place looked deserted.

That didn't mean it was.

She held up a hand to the officers behind her. They followed in her steps, covering the areas she couldn't, a flock of cops in blue. In front of Terra was a dark, polished counter. Behind that, a shadow moved.

Terra pointed her gun at the counter and advanced. The closer she drew, the more of him she could see. She coiled down, ready to dive to the floor if needed, but there was no need. She gained vantage over the counter and found the man quivering behind the desk.

Terra nodded at the others, telling them to continue their search as she dealt with the shaking mess before her. She aimed her gun at the crown of his head. "Hands on your head and stand straight. No arguing. No funny business."

The man laced his shaking hands behind his head and pushed himself to his feet. He was young, with a strip of wild, thin hair around his chin. He glanced at Terra, then turned away.

"What's your name, son?" She held the gun steady.

The man's lower lip trembled, and his breath came in uneven waves. "Ryder, ma'am."

"Ryder," Terra replied, narrowing her eyes at the young lad. He couldn't have been older than eighteen, yet the track marks on his arm showed that he was far beyond innocent in whatever operation they ran here. She glanced back down the corridor, where the sounds of footsteps were growing louder. She wondered if anyone had counted their number and if they were now forming a defensive strike, gathering their masses to flood out the handful of officers. "Ryder, I'm going to ask you a question, and you need to answer quick, got it?"

Ryder nodded.

Terra scowled, bringing the Glock closer. "I said, have you got that?"

"Yes. I've got it. I'm sorry."

"Where's Harvey?" Terra asked.

Ryder glanced at Terra with shimmering eyes as if he couldn't believe she'd had the audacity to ask the question.

"Where's Harvey!" Terra repeated, her patience thinning. Footsteps were growing even louder now. If she wasn't mistaken, they were running toward her. Time was short.

"I don't know!" Ryder finally replied. "I don't know. This is my first week, okay! I don't know shit. I was just trying to earn some holiday cash so I could fly to my parents in Mauritius. Please...please don't kill me."

Terra lowered the gun. Ryder caught his breath. Terra slapped him with the back of her hand. "You think the AJS is going to kill you? We're the good guys, kid. Remember that."

She spun at the alert from her colleague, who was now on one knee, pistol trained at the figure running toward them. She lined up her gun, looked down the sight, then held her breath.

There were many more of them behind.

Valentina heard the gunshots from downstairs, the sound echoing eagerly around the stone walls and floors.

She made her way into the hallway and broke into a sprint. She needed to get lower. Deng told her that Bradley was in the basement. How the hell did she get down to the basement?

She clattered down the stairs, ignoring the cries from those behind her who ran in the opposite direction. When she reached the bottom, her face hardened. More enemies were running at her, fleeing from the disruption at the doorway. Terra was serving her purpose, and Valentina was glad for the distraction. Only a few turned their head at the crimson stranger running toward them.

A shoulder connected with Valentina's, knocking her off-kilter. She regained her balance, slipping through the stream of people as she navigated to the next set of stairs. These she sped down, weaving around the crowds, narrowly avoiding further collisions. More alarms were raised. Voices rose, calling for the others to pay attention to Valentina as she sped away from them. A glance over her shoulder showed a crowd of enemies chasing her, disregarding their earlier flight from the AJS. The name "Harvey" was thrown around, along with snatches of phrases such as "Don't let her get to him."

Valentina hopped down the last two steps onto the first floor. A stone hallway led straight to the reception area, where a handful of figures in blue were dealing with someone behind a desk. Valentina paused, wondering how this was going to play out. As a rule, she never got within arm's reach of law enforcement if she could help it—or if she wasn't in disguise.

She narrowed her eyes, examining the space around her. A shadow caught her attention on her left.

"Grab her!" voices called from behind. There were heavy footsteps on the stairs and something that sounded like a gun cocking.

Valentina ran.

Her arms pumped at her side, her thighs burning from the explosion of momentum. She tore toward the AJS officers, eyes spotting Terra as she dealt with a cowering figure behind the desk. She closed the distance toward them, aware of the hammering footsteps behind her. A gunshot fired. Stone cracked. Dust rained. Valentina ducked.

The AJS officers lined up to return fire. An officer was on one knee, pistol trained directly at her. They called their threats and told her to stop. Neither she nor her pursuers paid attention.

The officer pulled the trigger. Valentina leaped sideways, darting toward the shadow she had seen, which revealed a passageway that led farther into the building. Her sudden movement surprised the throng, which continued toward the AJS for a few steps.

Someone shouted. Another shot fired. More shots rang. Metal ricocheted off the stone. Glass smashed. Men and women went down.

The sounds lessened as Valentina darted through the passageway, losing herself in the bends and turns that came her way. She guessed her direction, looking for any entry that could lead to a basement of some sort. There were no windows down this part, but several sconces lit up the stonework, emulating candlelight. Valentina turned a sharp right and shouldered into a woman whose skin was almost translucent. Her bones sounded hollow as she fell to the floor, and a gasp escaped her lips. Valentina fought for balance, then continued.

Around the next bend, she came across two men who had been slowly advancing in the direction of the gunshots. They had no weapons on them, and she wondered what use they'd be in the fight. They cocked their heads her way, eyebrows arching as she sprinted at them. She half-turned as she ran, intending to slip past them both until hands gripped her arm.

Valentina tugged, but the second set of hands gripped her. The men didn't know what they were doing, but they were right in thinking that Valentina shouldn't be down this way.

"Hold up, darling," one of the men stated. "Where do you think you're going?"

He eyed her hungrily, thoughts passing behind his eyes that Valentina could read without much effort. She'd seen it a thousand times before. Valentina kicked the man's shin. He growled, his grip slipping as he buckled to his knee. "Son of a bitch."

The other man's eyes widened. He was missing a tooth in his blackening gums, and he was long overdue a shave. He should have let go, but he didn't. That happened sometimes. Fear made fools of cowards.

Valentina chopped her hand into the crook of his elbow. The man kept his grip, his arm pulling him closer. Valentina's face was inches from his. "I'm sorry," she whispered, not meaning it as she slammed her head into his.

His grip relaxed, and she was off.

Her brief interlude had allowed a few of the scattered pursuers to catch up with her. She reached the end of a hallway and had no choice but to stop. On the right was a door, which she yanked open, almost pulling it off its hinges as she ducked inside. She closed it behind her, then looked for a light.

It was impossible to find one. The room was pitch black, with no source of natural or artificial light in sight. She used the flash on her cell phone to hunt on the walls but found nothing. She did find a latch to secure the door shut, as well as a set of stairs a short way ahead of her.

She padded quickly down the stairs, measuring her footfalls to soften the noise her shoes made on the stone. The sound of water dripping reached her, and the air took on a sudden chill. She had the strange feeling of entering some kind of underground cavern, with great rows of stalactites and stalagmites arranged like uneven teeth around her. She knew there were great caves beneath the island, although she had never had cause to explore them in her line of work. She'd seen pictures on the news, though. Glittering pools that seemed endlessly deep, ceilings that stood over a hundred feet high, holes in the ground with no definitive end.

Valentina shuddered and strode into the darkness, descending as fists pounded the wood and the door shook behind her.

Terra took the shot. The bullet ripped through the air and embedded in the thigh of a man who had almost closed his hands around Valentina. It was a tight shot as it was, so it was lucky that Valentina darted off to the side at that moment, disappearing into some recess of the building.

Terra hopped back, twisting as she tucked herself away behind the desk. There were at least twenty of them running behind Valentina although the AJS officer spotted a few following in the direction she had gone. The remainder continued the charge, their attention stolen by the shiny new enemies in blue.

Bullets bounced off the walls. Something crashed into the desk. Ryder yelped in fear and shrank behind the counter.

Terra glanced at the officers, each one taking position behind a pillar or door frame. Another round of shots fired and a couple of bodies hit the floor.

She peeked out from the counter, leading with her pistol, and shot the foot of a nearby attacker. The stone painted crimson. The man folded, shouting in pain as his gun slipped from his grasp. "We are officers of the law. Put down your weapons, now!"

The enemies were too far gone. They were a weird mixture of people in a strange array of clothing. Some wore exercise pants. Others wore leather, and some wore jeans. There seemed to be no rhyme or reason to their operation other than to attack the officers who had entered their domain. Terra pulled the trigger twice more, then ducked behind again as a volley of shots came her way.

One of the officers grunted as a bullet hit their side. The nanopocket Kevlar activated and sent the projectile in another direction, but the impact still winded her.

She looked at Terra. Terra offered her a nod as if to say, "You good?"

The officer waved a hand, then secured her grip on her pistol and returned to her duty.

The wave continued. Terra glanced out, trying to get a headcount on how many of the enemies had weapons. At a glance, she counted four, but she couldn't trust such a quick count.

The other officers communicated silently, throwing signals at Terra. Terra aimed at two of the four and incapacitated them, either shooting the gun directly from their hands or catching their arm and forcing their grip free. The other officers took care of the rest as Terra eased from cover, examining the remaining five who came at them, fists bared and ready.

"Very well," Terra mumbled as she holstered her pistol and advanced on the nearest to her. A woman, similar to Terra in build but with sunken cheeks and scraggly hair. She had a good punch though, and it would've hurt had it connected with Terra properly. Terra ducked her head to avoid the blow, then uppercut into the center of her stomach.

The woman wheezed and doubled over. A man came behind her and shoved the gasping woman out of the way as he aimed his punch at Terra's chest. Terra crossed her arms for the block, then stomped on his foot. As he grimaced, she sent a right hook at his cheek, bone connecting with bone. The man blinked stupidly, pink saliva dribbling down his chin. The woman rose and came for Terra again.

"Cover!" Terra called.

"We're kinda busy here," the nearest officer replied, engaged in fisticuffs with her woman.

As Terra avoided a blow from the woman, the man doubled down on his attack. His eyes flashed, irritated from the punch Terra had dealt him. His fist caught her in the side. Although she twisted away from the main blow, it knocked her sideways.

Utilizing the momentum of her twist, she spun behind the woman. Hooking her arms beneath the woman's armpits, she dropped her knee into the back of her legs and forced her to the floor. The woman complained as her face fell to the stone with nothing to cushion it. Terra caught her at the last minute, avoiding the blood splatter of her nose, then twisted her arm behind her back.

Taking the other arm, she brought them together at the small of her back. She drew handcuffs from her pocket and slapped them on the woman's wrists. They were strange in appearance, looking like a single metal loop. As she hit the wrist, the loop opened, and a coil unraveled as the loop split in two. As she worked the second loop onto the other wrist, a faint humming sounded as a small charge of electricity locked the handcuffs and secured them in place.

The woman howled in rage. The man grabbed the back of Terra's collar. His fingers hooked into her uniform, but the woman, at least, was no longer a nuisance, even if she was wriggling like a malformed insect.

The implacable grip lifted Terra to her feet. The man was strong and held her with one hand. With the other, he threw a punch at her stomach. Now that both her hands were free, Terra caught the man's fist and softened the blow. She yanked sharply to the side, then hooked her fingers around his thumb. She pulled the thumb back. The man grunted in pain but tried to fight through, taking the hand from her collar and threading his fingers through her hair. She bared her teeth as he yanked her head back, then grinned at him. A moment of confusion crossed his face before she lifted her foot and kicked his chin. His tongue caught between his teeth and red flecks sprayed the air. His fingers released her hair, but she kept hold of his thumb. As he shouted incomprehensibly, she twisted the thumb and hooked her leg around the back of his knees. He toppled backward, head thumping hard on the stone and knocking him unconscious. Before he could wake, she cuffed his hands.

She rose to her feet, taking lungfuls of air to steady her body. The other officers were cuffing their charges, and as Terra looked down the hallway, she saw the shapes of the others still trying to move, many of them in pain and dealing with their bullet wounds.

She fished out another set of handcuffs and advanced on the others. At a glance, only one of their number was in urgent need of medical attention. She began her work securing the area, curious as to what she would find as they hunted through the building and wondering where exactly Valentina had gone.

CHAPTER TWENTY-FIVE

Booming *thuds* rang down the stairs, each one a staccato beat of an impatient fist. Valentina tuned them out, knowing that it was useless to concentrate on what was behind when the way ahead could be fraught with danger.

It was dark down here, the cavernous chill working its way into her bones. The stairs rounded a corner and continued indefinitely, or so it seemed. The stone steps were wide, and after a short while, the walls fell away, and all there was were steps and darkness.

And voices.

They started as whispers and worked their way into mutters. It was difficult to gauge how many, given the echoing distortion that followed each syllable. Valentina blindly felt her way with her feet, slowing and testing each step now that there was no wall on either side of her. She wondered whether she was truly heading into a cave, and her suspicions were confirmed when a bright flare of orange light sparked in the distance.

At first, it had been nothing but a tiny ember framed by the entrance of a tunnel. The tunnel looked tiny, and it was only when a figure emerged that Valentina realized it was because it was some distance from her. A man appeared holding a flaming torch, and as the flame illuminated the area around him, Valentina distinguished the umber coloring of the rugged walls. Daggers of stone jutted up from the floors and grew down from the ceiling. The walls were uneven, with large areas in concave and convex formations. A pool over to her left caught the faint twinkling of the flame as the man strode toward the steps.

Valentina stopped and sat on the step. She swung her legs over the edge, realizing as the man grew closer just how far the distance to the ground truly was. She judged her angle and lowered herself until her fingers gripped the stone and she dangled over the chasm.

She was there for only a minute before the man ascended the steps while grumbling to himself. "The hell is going on up there? They know better than to disturb us when we're at work. Vincent's going to have their heads on pikes by the end of this shit. Better be a good explanation."

The man took the stairs with measured steps, and his eyes fixed ahead to where the booming sounds came from. He drew close to Valentina, the flame burning brightly and creating a glowing orb around him. Valentina held her breath and shrunk against the rock. As the light grew, she noticed an outcrop a few feet lower and gently eased herself down to try and remain out of sight. His steps were loud as he passed her. Fragments of rubble fell onto her face. She looked away and closed her eyes.

He paused right beside her.

Valentina looked up again, but the man was out of sight from her angle. She could only make out the flame and the top of his head. He was looking down. Valentina prepared herself to make a sudden move. If she grabbed his ankles, she could drag him down and into the depths. It would be a painful way to die, but at least it should be instant.

The man lowered to one knee, his form disappearing

completely. A bead of sweat trickled down Valentina's forehead and into her eye. The salt stung. She blinked it away.

She could make out the sounds of the man's huffing, as well as the dragging of cotton on cotton, amplified by the cavern's acoustics. Was he tying his shoelaces? She didn't know for sure.

Valentina pulled herself up slightly, trying to glimpse the man. As she did, he rose to his full height. She quickly lowered to her original position, her knee hitting the rock. She held back a slight grunt of pain.

The man's eyebrow raised. He rubbed his nose with the back of his hand and sniffed. He cast a cursory glance behind him at the entrance of the tunnel, then shrugged. The booms were louder than ever. "All right, all right," he complained. "I'm coming."

The man continued his walk with his head lowered as he trudged up the many stairs before him. Valentina waited until the man reached the place where the walls fell away. A few more seconds and he was out of sight.

She pulled herself up on the stairs once more, fingertips raw from clinging to the rough rock. She patted herself down—not that she could see much from the darkness that cloaked her—then continued.

She still trod carefully, but she quickened her pace. She had memorized the direction from the man's ascent and was thankful to know that there was only one bend to the right, approximately twenty-three steps down.

She found the bend, then assumed the straight. Above, a mangle of voices called over each other, mixed with the sound of metal on wood as the latch opened and the men spilled through the door.

Valentina quickened, finding the ground unexpectedly before her. She stumbled, recovered, then marched to the tunnel's entrance.

She glanced back over her shoulder and saw the flickering

orange of the torch as the man descended the stairs at an increased pace. Behind him, a handful of thugs followed, using the flashes from their cell phones to light the way.

Valentina darted into the tunnel, swallowed once again by darkness.

She moved slowly—she could only move slowly. What other choice did she have? She traced the walls with her hands, occasionally tripping over small chunks of rock. A gentle breeze came from ahead, which she followed, hoping it would lead her somewhere useful.

More voices came from ahead, but the sounds of running from behind soon drowned them out. Valentina pulled herself into what she believed to be a hollow within the wall and ducked out of sight. The tunnel grew lighter, and the umber rock came into view. Footsteps magnified around her until it sounded as though an army ran through the passage.

Valentina used the light that led the procession to her advantage, slipping farther into the crevice. The group sped by, each man and woman looking around for any sign of Valentina. They passed, none of them detecting the petite woman tucked away and hidden by the shadows.

The light faded.

Darkness smothered her.

With the memory of the tunnel burned into her retinas, Valentina followed the path that the others had gone. The echoes were still around her, and it was almost impossible to tell how far away these people were. She couldn't make out what the operation was down here, either. A staircase leading to an underground cavern? Tunnels heading to some unknown destination? She had seen strange things in Atlantica in her time, but this was one for the highlight reel.

Voices were raised. They were incoherent, each blending into the other as the tunnel warped them. After a short distance,

Valentina distinguished the tunnel's end as it opened into another chamber.

She drew closer, trying to understand what she saw.

The group of pursuers stood in the center, all shouting over one another. The man with the torch pleaded with them to be quiet as he tried to address a man sitting on the hood of a 1955 Corvette. Valentina had no idea how the man got the car down here, but the body gleamed, and the details sparkled. The only damage to the car was the missing windows, giving an unobstructed view inside to the piles of burlap sacks that bulged from the interior.

The man on the hood looked as though he could have belonged in a version of *Grease*. He'd slicked back his dark hair, and he sported a leather jacket with a white tee beneath. A cigarette hung from his lips with a ribbon of smoke curling into the cave.

He sat patiently, waiting for the rabble to stop bickering. When it seemed that wouldn't happen, he narrowed his eyes and drew a revolver from his pocket—a six-shot pistol that Valentina had seen in many a movie, complete with sandalwood grip.

He fired without mercy, taking out one of the group. The woman fell to the ground, hitting the stone with a loud *thwack*. The others instantly silenced, their heads turning to the man.

He scanned the sight on his revolver among them, one eye closed. The cave was cast in a pregnant silence as they waited for the next shot. Valentina spotted more men in the far reaches of the chamber and several magazine-cover women who lay at the back of the area on a bed of crimson blankets and sheets.

What the hell is this place?

"Enough of your shit," the man, who Valentina could only assume was Harvey Vincent, stated. His voice was breathy with a tinge of Italian in his words. "I ain't paying you a pretty buck to bicker like bitches. If there's a problem, you tell me what's going on. You be straight. I don't like embedding bodies with bullets, but goddamn it, I'll do it until I've got all of you straight, you hear me?"

Silence met his words.

"You hear me!" he roared, his words amplified by the cave.

A general round of nods came back with a few utterances of, "Sure. We hear you."

"Good." Harvey hopped neatly off the Corvette and advanced on the group. He walked a circle around them, examining the men and women, some of them visibly quaking under his gaze. "You bitches have one job right now, and that's to tell me what all the fucking fuss is about. Who's going to give it to me straight?"

The man holding the torch glanced at the man standing to his left—who had a pathetic rash of stubble on his face—as if to say, "Your turn."

The stubbled man puffed out his chest and announced, "You got intruders. AJS has broken through the front door, and we followed some red bitch down into these tunnels. Your operation is compromised."

They must have expected Harvey to blow his lid, but he took the news with a gentle calm as he nodded and chewed over his thoughts. "AJS, you say?"

"Five of them," the stubbled man replied. "At a glance."

Harvey's lips thinned. "Well, they're going to be sorry they broke in. Wait until the city hears about this. Every single one of those punks is going to find themselves out on their asses, and then it'll be us who breaks and enters and teaches them the lessons they so deserve."

"You don't have a case," a shrill, quivering voice piped up.

Harvey glared at the woman in the center of the group, at least a foot shorter than the others and lost from sight until now.

Harvey advanced on her as the others parted to make way for him. He towered over her, darkening her with his shadow. "Excuse me?"

"Someone broke the barrier," she babbled. "A shot broke the

window and hit their car in the street. They're within their rights to come in and—"

A whipping noise sounded around the cave. Harvey's eyes flashed as the back of his hand struck the woman's cheek. She collapsed on the floor, one hand working to stop the fall, the other going to her face.

He stood over her, not an ounce of remorse in his eyes. "Which one of you broke the barrier? What fool was stupid enough to shoot at the window? I hired you to protect the fucking place. We shelter you, and you protect the operation. That's your entire job description."

Another woman spoke up. "It wasn't us, sir."

"Then who was it?" he belted, face flushing red. "Give me a name."

"We don't know," the stubbled man declared. "We only heard the shot. We didn't see anything happen. We were on our way to the entrance as the AJS broke in and came across an intruder. We followed her here, avoiding a showdown with the guys in blue."

Harvey regained his composure, running fingers through his hair. The move pushed an untidy curl back into its pristine formation. "What did she look like, this mysterious red invader?"

The stubbled man swallowed. "It was hard to get a read on her. She was fast."

"You're telling me she broke through the building and sped past all the bodies we have upstairs?" Harvey adjusted his collar, then dug his hands in his pockets.

"She's strong, too," another voice piped up. A man with shorn hair and red cheeks. "Took out a few of the guys on the way here single-handed."

Harvey ran a hand down his face. "She's down here?"

"Yes, sir," the man replied.

"Right this second?" Harvey continued. "As we speak?"

They all nodded. The woman on the ground whimpered.

"Then what the fuck are you standing around for?" Harvey

shouted. "Get your asses in gear and find her before she acquires any evidence." He threw his hands in the air. "Fuck! Do I need to think of everything around here myself?"

He marched toward the car and sat on the hood. He buried his face in his hands as the pack dispersed, lighting their cell phones and torches and heading off into the many entrances leading off from the chamber. Several women peeled off and came to his side, sitting on the hood and flinging their arms around him.

Valentina's eyes went to the bags in the vehicle, but she didn't have a proper chance to look as a handful of people came her way.

She slipped back down the tunnel, careful to lead with her hands. She blindly stumbled on, moving as quickly as she dared to escape the revealing light. She returned to her recess, then pushed farther, following the tunnel blindly as the others stalked behind.

A short distance into the tunnel, Valentina spotted the cross-hairs of light. Ahead, the light grew. Behind her, the light increased. She looked around for a direction where she wouldn't be caught in the middle and discovered an opening above her. It was thin, no more than a small fissure, but it might be enough.

Using the uneven surface of the walls for leverage, she climbed. Her fingers hooked into small pockets within the crevice, and with some effort, she wriggled her way upward. By the time her foot slipped from sight, the light beneath her was revealingly bright.

The groups stopped some distance from each other. They saw no point in crossing over and headed back in the direction they'd come. Before they left, Valentina glanced at the route above her. The light filtered up enough to show that the fissure rose higher and opened into a wider area.

She climbed. The fissure choked and squeezed at a few points, pinching at her clothes and body, but she climbed. Her fingers grabbed the open air, and she pulled herself free, rolling onto her back to stare up at the darkened ceiling.

Or where she assumed the ceiling to be.

She lay there for a short while, simply listening. The cavern amplified the sounds of walking and the occasional mutter of enemies, but she had a distinct sense that she was alone up here, in this strange hollow attic beneath the ground. After a few minutes, she looked around, hunting for the telltale sign of light from the others' torches and devices.

Only darkness met her.

Another few minutes passed before she sat up and found her phone. Her finger hovered over the flashlight icon. The screen cast a dangerous amount of light, but once she was certain that she was free, she pressed it.

The world exploded in light. The cavern appeared around her, melting into sight as if from some artificial reality experience. The cave walls were at least twenty feet high, with passages spreading in either direction, but that wasn't what caught her eye.

Strange sketching and carvings decorated the walls like wrapping paper. They were everywhere, stretching in all directions, filling every square inch of space she could see. She scanned along the length of the walls, as far as the light could reach, mouth agape at what she saw.

"Holy shit," she breathed.

She ran a hand along the surface, feeling the notches and grooves of the carvings. There were unfamiliar symbols woven between crude pictures of men and women. Towers and buildings and animals knitted around each other with seemingly no logic to the structure of the images. There were sigils and bolts of lightning and crests of waves, and amidst it all were orbs of blue, peppering the images and catching the light, the paint glittering in the carvings like sapphires.

"What the hell is this place?" Valentina muttered, searching the wall with the cell phone's flashlight, losing herself for a moment in the stories that the walls told. There were no saber-tooth tigers or mammoths in these images as she had seen in cave paintings before. These were difficult to place in time, almost impossible to describe.

She snapped a picture of a king-like figure sitting on a throne, surrounded by tropical birds. She took another of a crowd of stickmen huddled around the glowing blue orbs. She took a third of what appeared to be a long staircase leading toward a temple, a rising sun behind it, and a thousand-strong army bowing at its feet.

Valentina shook her head. "Bet I could get a pretty mint for leading some eager archaeologist down into this place." She tapped her chin. "Or is it up? How far down am I?"

Footsteps drew her attention as she snapped off her cell phone. She realized a moment later that they weren't coming from her level but from somewhere below. She looked ahead, and several small fissures and gaps crossed the floor, dimly lit by the search parties beneath. Some of the holes were thin cracks, but a few of them she could easily slip down.

A plan formulated in her mind.

She staked out the area and bided her time.

CHAPTER TWENTY-SIX

Harvey Vincent felt the rage boiling inside.

It hurt his stomach, which only added to the pain. Rage was a Mobius strip of self-inflicting wounds, and it took all he had to bring it under control.

His honchos had cleared the dead man from the ground, dragged him away unceremoniously, and tossed him into the abyss—a literal abyss, given that anything hurled down that hole didn't make so much as a peep on the way down. Who knew where the end came in that eternal darkness below.

His rage didn't abate at the women's croonings. Sure, they tried to help, touching all of his sensitive areas as they led him to the back of the Corvette and deposited the bags outside. The pain wouldn't stop, a sharp dagger of hot metal in his stomach that made him grit his teeth and squint.

"Enough," he grumbled at last, throwing his arms out and batting the women away. The sight of the bags, heavy with jewels and diamonds and laid haphazardly on the ground upset him. These were the ones that didn't quite fit in the car. The ones from his collection that he'd have to find a place for in the dozens of vaults he had excavated into the cavern. Built into the walls and stealthily crafted to look as though there was nothing behind the rocky face were hundreds of pockets stashed with jewels. He'd inherited many of them from his mother and father, two wealthy collectors who had used their ill-gotten fortune to stake a claim in Atlantica, while the rest were his acquisitions.

For years Harvey had robbed, killed, and bargained to own the world's largest collection of jewels and precious stones. Now, many years later, and several thousand acquisitions since his original fortune, Harvey realized that to stay at the top, he needed to hide what he had.

His circle was small. Only a couple dozen of his closest allies knew a small portion of the operation. The rest of it was all a front. Harvey would hire goons and bodyguards—mostly innocent Atlanticans in need of a pretty penny—and initiate them into the lower levels. They'd do grunt work, reconnaissance, deliveries, everything that could be achieved by the dispensable.

If they died, so what? There were plenty more hungry Atlanticans with no homes ready to make a quick buck.

None of them knew the extent of what they were all sitting on.

Harvey had grown more paranoid by the day. The cavern beneath his building was a grand discovery and one that he utilized as soon as he could. His team set to work hiding the jewels, the tunnels causing enough disruption to know when an enemy had broken in and potentially causing them to lose themselves in its labyrinth.

Was it a strange operation?

Sure.

Was it necessary? Harvey felt so.

Harvey stood and marched to a tunnel at the back of the chamber. It was the only one the others hadn't gone through, and that was for a good reason. Midway through the tunnel stood a metal door, crudely fitted, with small gaps around the edge. He thumbed a code into the digital lock, and the door swung open.

Only one man followed Harvey, who he now dismissed with a wave of the hand. The door closed.

The small chamber was round. Inside there was a bed, a hot tub, a wardrobe, and several living essentials that could not have looked more out of place in the cavern. Harvey couldn't remember the last time he had gone up to the surface. He hadn't needed to. He was his guard dog for his estate, and his minions performed his deeds for him. There was stale musk in the air around him, and that was how he liked it. "Lived-in." That's what he called it.

He opened a pocket of the wall to reveal a drawer crammed full of topaz jewels. The blue was hypnotic, catching the rays of light cast from torches on the walls and throwing them around the room in geometric rainbows. Another drawer revealed rubies, some as big as his fist. Another showed emeralds, the one after that sapphires and onyx.

He had long lost count of the value of his little stash of jewels. After so many zeroes, they lost their meaning. He was rich. His den of treasures made him possibly one of the richest barons in the whole of Atlantica.

Not that many people would ever know. He didn't carry the wealth in digital bank accounts—too many opportunities to be siphoned out of your digits by fraudsters.

Finally, he wandered over to the far wall where he activated yet another drawer that was invisible against the surface and flush with the stone. The inside of this one was different. There was no mountain of precious gems and rocks and only one color to speak of.

The diamond stood in a cradle that could have been the lower half of a rocket ship. The stand displayed thin metal legs. The jewel balanced like an egg in an egg cup.

Harvey delicately picked up the diamond and brought it to his face. It was larger than any he had ever held before. The weight was substantial, and he feared dropping it and tarnishing its perfect exterior, even though he knew how tough diamonds were.

A hungry look came over him. He licked his lips, then placed the diamond back in its cradle. He gently closed the drawer and inhaled a long breath.

It was still where he left it. That had been confirmed. He prayed that no one would violate his inner sanctum and take what was rightfully his.

He wouldn't take too kindly to that.

No, he wouldn't.

CHAPTER TWENTY-SEVEN

Terra worked with the officers to ensure that they restrained all of the men and women who attacked them.

They had made quick work of them, rifling past them to slap on handcuffs and read them their rights. The attackers became strangely tight-lipped once they were in custody, and two of her colleagues helped them into the backs of the cruisers, ready for the station to send backup and transport them to HQ.

Terra hadn't finished, though.

Something foul was afoot. She could smell it.

She performed a perfunctory examination of the remaining rooms, accompanied by the remaining two officers. They took the building room by room, ensuring that the second and third floors—the places where they'd seen the masses run—were empty.

They were, bar a rather large woman who had been knocked unconscious and lay on the floor of one of the bedrooms.

"This place is weird," Officer Garmin, a man who had been in the force for two years longer than Terra and often made sure she knew that fact was in place. "Never seen anywhere that's so old and modern, so empty, yet lived in."

"You should see my apartment," Officer Gallow replied dryly. She was at least half a head taller than Terra with a cascade of dirty blonde hair. "Amount I work, you'd think it was a show home from the 80s."

"1980s?" Garmin asked.

Gallow shook her head, opening a nearby door with her toe. "1880s, more like." She thrust her pistol ahead of her and scanned the room. A quick examination caused her to declare, "Clear."

"It doesn't make sense," Terra muttered. "There were loads of them. Are they all hiding out on the upper floors?"

Gallows shrugged. "Only one way to find out."

Find out they did. After scaling the several floors of the building and finding their way near the top, they discovered that a window at the farthest reaches of the corridor was ajar. The window was larger than most modern doors, and a wooden board stuck out from it like a monster's tongue. The beam bridged the gap between the nearest building. The remainder of the scum must have escaped into the city.

"Shit!" Terra exclaimed. Anger bubbled inside her. She hated the idea of scum spilling out onto the streets. Her job was to contain the problem, and here they had failed.

Garmin put a hand on her shoulder. "Can't bag them all."

Terra shook his hand away. "We're not done yet." In her mind, she saw the passage where Valentina had darted down. There was still more to discover down there. Valentina hadn't re-emerged. "I'm sure there are still plenty of vermin to flush out. Follow me."

They didn't spot the woman following them down the halls.

A group approached. Valentina couldn't count how many, but she needed to know. That would be key to her strategy.

She saw them coming from their torchlight filtering through the cracks below her. A short distance away in the chamber of cave paintings and carvings, the lights burned brightly. They would dim by one crack, then brighten by another, unwittingly marking their passage.

Valentina crept to the farthest crack and counted them below. She could see two of their heads, but that didn't mean that more couldn't be nearby. She raced to the next chasm and stuck her head lower, able now to count three.

She waited until the trio had passed, then dangled her legs into the fissure. She carefully eased her body down until her legs were free. She hung from her fingertips, then dropped silently behind them.

They were fifteen feet in front of her. She cast a cursory glance over her shoulder to check that no one was behind, then waited.

And waited.

They walked away.

They continued their walk until one of the women raised her nose in the air. She cocked an ear. "Wait. Listen."

The others stopped. Valentina froze.

"What is it?" a gruff voice asked—the man holding the flame.

The woman waited. "I thought I heard something."

"You did," Valentina breathed, soft enough that only they could hear her in the tunnel.

They turned abruptly, alarm written on their faces. Their eyes widened. Before they could say a word, Valentina pushed the button on her phone's screen and activated the devices she'd quietly rolled past them right before they stopped. Smoke exploded behind the three, cloaking them in a thick cloud. The explosion echoed around the chamber. Valentina smirked, pleased with the effect her paraphernalia had that she'd dropped to the ground. Remote control smoke pellets worked like a dream.

She ran into the cloud without hesitation, following her memory of the location of the men and women. They materialized before her, the torch acting as a shining beacon as she worked her magic. The man was down in seconds, a swift blow to the jaw followed by a kick to the gut. The torch dropped but didn't extinguish. Valentina darted at the woman, wrapping an arm around her throat and wrestling her to the ground. She stomped on her stomach, then sent a tough boot into her chin.

The final one of their number tried to run. The smoke chased her. So did Valentina.

She grabbed the woman by the collar and pulled her back. She vanished from sight. Anyone watching would only have heard the sounds of attack and disruption as Valentina beat her into unconsciousness.

The sound of the explosives raised the alarm, and more groups appeared, glancing at the cloud with confusion. Some of them aimed weapons. Others readied their fists. The few that ran into the smoke were quickly taken out and didn't return. The next time their comrades saw them, the smoke had dissipated, and all that remained was a bundle of bodies.

"The hell?" a voice exclaimed.

They advanced slowly, two groups from either side of the chamber. They nudged the others with their toes, their lights highlighting bloodstains and what would soon become dark purple bruises.

"She's here," a man exclaimed.

They hunted all around them, aiming their weapons in all directions. They looked behind, in front of, below, and at the ceiling, but none of them saw Valentina watching from above, the glitter of a single eye as she studied her targets.

She circled them, preparing for Phase Two of her plan. She had drawn them in and thinned a chunk of their number. She knew those below wouldn't be everyone in the cavern, but removing them would at least make her job a little easier.

She held out her palm to reveal a drone, only a few inches in diameter. She placed the drone on the lip of one of the holes, then sat back against the wall, the strange carvings scratching against her back. She unlocked her phone and steered the drone.

Its propellers spun. It gently eased an inch or so off the cold floor. She could see through the camera fixed inside as she guided it into the hole and down to meet the others.

Mixed voices clashed against each other as those below began to panic and scrabble to find an explanation. A couple of snippets of conversation suggested they examine the holes, which was confirmed when the drone appeared between them.

Valentina pictured Deng as she looked through the camera, the mechanism allowing her to swing the lens for a full three-sixty-degree view. They fell quiet for a moment before someone asked what that was. Someone lined up their gun and took a shot.

Valentina jerked the drone up.

The bullet found its target in one of their own.

Shouts erupted once more, and Valentina waited until they started closing in on the drone before she pressed the button on the screen and confirmed her action.

A faint *hissing* sounded from inside the drone as several nozzles appeared in its bodywork. A few yelps of surprise emerged as fingers pointed at the machine. A moment later, sparks erupted as tiny black pellets shot in all directions.

Valentina watched it all from the camera as those closest to the drone went down. It would be only a few seconds before the toxin worked its way into their bloodstreams and forced them into a long slumber. Although the drone could only hold enough ammunition for one expulsion of pellets, it was enough to take a lot of the group out. They slumped and joined their number on the ground.

Only four remained.

Two had guns.

Valentina rose to her feet, keeping her eyes fixed on the phone screen as she steered the drone directly at one of the gun wielders.

The gunman shot at the drone. The bullet missed and ricocheted off the ceiling, finding its bed in one of the fallen on the ground. Valentina took the opportunity to drop through the largest crack in one clean motion, lowering her legs, then catching her fingers on the final outcrop before bending her knees on impact.

A small part of rock caught her side. The graze stung, but a bullet to her head would hurt more.

She turned toward the closest gunman—the one not attacking the drone—and raised her leg high. She kicked him in the chest and sent him back against the wall, where he stopped with a sudden grunt. The gun fell from his grasp. His body jerked. He reached for the gun. Valentina was there to kick it away. It skidded into the darkness, losing itself beyond the reaches of the torchlight. Valentina finished the guy with a swift blow to the temple. The man spat, then fell asleep.

Valentina fixed her attention on the final gunman. The drone had caught him across the eyebrow, and a crimson streak trickled into his eye. He blinked stupidly, trying to focus his aim on Valentina. His finger tensed on the trigger. Valentina stepped off the wall and backflipped away from the bullet's trajectory, swearing she felt it speed beneath her back as it arched.

She landed neatly then zigzagged toward the remaining man. It was an indelicate operation as she used the bodies of the fallen like stepping stones toward her destination. The man's face filled with fear, hands shaking as he aimed another shot.

Valentina drew her pistol so quickly that he didn't have a chance to pull the trigger. The bullet connected with the mouth of the barrel, and the gun spun out of his hand. He drew back as though the action of it had burned him. Then she was in front of him.

She punched his gut, then his shoulder, and his chin. He held up his arms and planted his feet, but the damage was done. She could see it in his eyes. He fought valiantly, throwing a few punches that didn't quite land. Valentina cut across him and blocked them before they could do much damage. Her side burned from the drop into the scene, but she would deal with that later.

The man grunted and wobbled on his feet. Valentina kicked his kneecap. Something crunched. He folded. She slammed her elbow into the top of his head, and he was down.

She stood there, her chest rising and falling as she regained her breath. It wasn't the hardest she'd had to work, but she'd be lying if she said it hadn't taken some effort. The torchlight flickered around her, one of the flames catching the edge of a nearby woman's top. Before the fire spread, Valentina stamped it out. She picked up the torches, then extinguished the flames. Others would come soon. She had made too much commotion. Darkness would have to be her friend.

She noted her position in the tunnel before the last flame died. Somewhere nearby a person groaned. Valentina gave them one final kick to silence them, and darkness consumed her again.

She turned back through the tunnel, away from the places she had been, guiding herself only by the faint light of her phone screen. She wouldn't chance the full flashlight, knowing how bright it was, but at least with the dull light in her hand, she could quickly hide it and slip from view if needed.

She strode ahead, understanding that if a group of the enemies had come this way to look for her, there was undoubtedly a way toward the main hub if she looked carefully enough.

As she took her time in the twisting tunnels beneath the city, her mind drifted back to the art that lay above her. She wondered if those who inhabited these chambers knew they were there and what it all meant.

CHAPTER TWENTY-EIGHT

Archie's eyes stung.

The spread of monitors he'd been staring at for the last few hours was finally getting to him. Each screen blurred with the other, white and blue and black backgrounds, displaying charts and graphs of all types that had long since lost meaning.

The bags beneath his eyes were black. There were red streaks in his scleras. He couldn't count how many times he'd snapped at Friedrich and his team. There was little patience left in his system—if there had been any there to begin with.

Friedrich tapped away on the keyboard, each hammer of his fingers a screeching scratch down a blackboard. Friedrich's eyes darted to the screen and back. Occasionally he adjusted his glasses. He looked as tired as Archie, but he still had the energy to continue.

"Modifying the conduits to the neural pathways..." Friedrich muttered. He had a sickening habit of doing that, talking to himself. It drove Archie crazy. He wanted results, not a goddamn narrative. "Strengthening connections to core nodes within the hypothalamus..."

Archie reached for his mug, ready to taste the sweet savior of caffeine. When he raised it to his lips, he found it empty. "More!" he barked at a timid assistant who had been hunched over Kit's body, double-checking each connection of the multitude of wires that littered his body.

The assistant jumped, then dashed to Archie's side. As he turned to leave, Archie grabbed his wrist. "You know the rules."

"Don't look at anyone. Don't speak to anyone," the assistant replied quickly.

Archie's nostrils flared. There was a strange satisfaction in the power he could lord over these minions, scientists he was paying good dollars for, knowing he could buy their silence and discretion on what was, arguably, one of his toughest assignments to date. "If I find out you have…"

"Understood." The assistant waited until Archie finally released his grip, then scurried away from the medical bubble that Archie had built solely for this purpose.

Friedrich continued muttering.

"How much longer?" Archie asked.

Friedrich adjusted his glasses. His hair fell in threads across his forehead, dark and greasy. "Difficult to say. The last efforts were…"

"I know what happened with the last efforts," Archie snapped. "I was here. You don't need to explain our fucking failures to me."

Friedrich flinched. He screwed his eyes shut. "Yes. Of course. A thousand apologies. It's just that I—" He glanced at Archie as if expecting another lashing. When nothing came, he continued, "I hadn't prepared myself for this operation. I need to understand more data, study the boy, learn more about this code."

Archie rubbed his forehead, then lazily drew his pistol. He held it to his side, out of sight from anyone who might walk in and see them both. Friedrich swallowed.

"You're on my payroll, Friedrich," Archie growled darkly. "Things move fast in Atlantica. I want your expertise on this subject. I'll take your expertise on this subject. You are a man of science, aren't you?"

"No...Well, yes..." Friedrich shook. He removed his glasses and polished the lenses with a cloth, removing the steam that came from his sweating forehead. "I am a learned man in many departments, but medicine and biology isn't my forte. You need physicians, neurosurgeons, people who deal with the everyday..."

Archie gripped his seat until his knuckles turned white. The gun shook in his hand as rage rushed through him. "I don't need doctors. I've tried doctors, and they've gotten me nowhere so far. I need innovation, expertise from outside the lens of conventional science. If this doesn't work, I will look for other sources, but Kirk protests that you're a man of learning and are more than capable of understanding the implantation of systems." He paused, breathing deeply. "You have a sister, no?"

Friedrich's eyes lowered. "I do."

Archie pressed on. "And she..."

"Suffered from RPD." Friedrich's voice was soft, the memory of it all painful.

Archie grinned. "Isn't rapidly progressive dementia a condition that has no cure?"

Friedrich knew where this was going. "The circumstances were different. I..." He sighed. "The circumstances were different."

Archie came closer as the panel to the door buzzed with the assistant's entry code. The door *hissed* as it opened.

"You healed her, didn't you?" Archie's words were mere breaths. "You fixed the impossible."

Friedrich relented, nodding slowly. "I did what I needed to."

"You served in prison," Archie stated.

Friedrich nodded, shame welling in his eyes.

Archie didn't relent. "The medical board revoked your right to practice."

Friedrich put his glasses on and nodded.

The assistant arrived at Archie's side, standing awkwardly, aware that he was interrupting a moment. Archie was certain he could see the gun, but he didn't care. Let the kid appreciate the severity of their situation.

Archie waved the assistant away. He returned to Kit's body, examining the wires for loose connections, trying hard to remain invisible.

Archie continued, "I need this to work. I've done my research. I know your background. You think I brought you to my service to dig with my team and examine the archaeology of Atlantica? You're a Swiss Army knife, Friedrich. Your mind is a toolbox, and it is mine for exploiting. I pay your salary, and I support your pitiful life on this island. You want to see that sister again? You play by my rules, got it?"

Friedrich eyed the gun.

"Got it?" Archie repeated, thumbing off the safety.

Friedrich nodded.

"Good." Archie sat back in his chair and holstered his weapon. "How is Anabelle these days?"

His sudden tone change caught Friedrich off-guard. He fumbled for words, then offered a sincere smile. "She's great. Six years this month since she cleared her original diagnosis."

Archie nodded knowingly. "See? Sometimes you have to think outside the box. Sometimes you have to play in the sandboxes that people don't play in. Every tale can have a silver lining. Help Kit find his, okay?"

It wasn't a question so much as it was a command.

Friedrich glanced over his shoulder, catching the eye of the assistant. He nodded, then returned his attention to the screen, quietly muttering to himself as he tried to solve the unsolvable problem and utilize what could very well be the miracle cure.

From this distance, the city was still.

Wendy Howard didn't often visit the city proper. There was no need to when others catered to her every need. Advantages came to the wealthiest couple on the island of Atlantica. Most of her days were spent with her husband, sitting in the drawing room and playing rounds of chess. They didn't use digital pieces, either. None of the holographic boards so often pictured in the advancing age of digital. No, their pieces were wooden, hand-crafted, and authentic. There was something about the tangible nature of handling the wood that gave Wendy a thrill. It was a powerful sensation to control your pieces and slide them into place, often thinking five or six steps ahead of the competition.

After all, wasn't that what had made her so successful? Hadn't it been her forward-thinking and ability to play the game that had secured her one of the highest seats in the world?

Yet, one main negative came from sitting at the top. There was no real competition.

Stanley tried to offer a challenge, but those days had long passed. His skin was sagging as much as his mind, and the liver spots grew larger on his skin every day. His mind was slower than it once was, and she would often find herself letting him win for the sake of it. He was her love, after all. No sense in letting him know that he was declining faster than a snowman melting down the volcano's side.

The challenge would have to come from elsewhere. Boredom was a dangerous thing to experience so Wendy meddled. Her bi-yearly conclaves were an opportunity to stir the pot and discover what the latest dramas were that were operating in Atlantica. Most of the wealthy kept to themselves or engaged in vicious feuds, but under her roof, twice a year, they called a truce among themselves.

How enlightening a show they had proven to be. Catching snippets of conversation and probing her visitors in the right way allowed her to keep her finger on the pulse of the island. The visitors had no idea that she employed spies among the group to eavesdrop and acquire information. She had bugs placed all around the rooms, and a team spent their time pulling out the key themes and finding tasty morsels from which she could draw inspiration.

Wendy placed Stanley's king in checkmate. The room was gloomy, only a single candle lighting the board and space between them. Outside the door were four of the top security guards in Atlantica, ready to answer at a moment's call. Here she was practically alone. Stanley's head flopped onto his chest, his near-transparent eyelids closed. He snored soundly, a string of drool staining his silk maroon shirt.

Wendy rose and crossed to the balcony. From here, the city twinkled, looking like the looped animation of a city on someone's computer background. A thin veil of fog blurred the lines of the metropolis, but the light shone through. It looked mystical, a realm of wonder and possibility.

And beneath it all...

What *was* beneath it all?

Wendy narrowed her eyes, bracing herself against a sudden blast of chill wind. She drew her robe about her, then heard the chime of a notification.

She twisted her watch to face her. A woman's face appeared in the video on the circular screen. "Sorry to disturb, ma'am, but you have a call."

"Who is it?" Wendy asked.

The face disappeared, replaced by a pale woman with dark hair and harsh features. A green and red icon appeared, requesting Wendy to make a decision. Wendy's lip curled. She thumbed the red button, and Deng Zenim's face faded from view. The guard's face reappeared. "Apologies for the disturbance."

"Screen her calls," Wendy instructed. "Let the children fight it out among themselves."

She strode back inside, the warmth from the large open fireplace instantly heating her bones. She passed her husband, who from this angle could easily have been mistaken for dead had it not been for the gentle purr in the back of his throat. She wondered how long he had left. Over six decades of marriage would end the way that all lives end, with the disparaging grief of one or the other. Likely she would feel the sorrow in time, though she had learned that emotions were hardly advantageous to success.

The guards parted as she exited the room. Two of them peeled off and followed her, ten paces behind, exact and perfect every time, copying her exact footfalls. Left, then right. Left, then right.

She spiraled down the stairs, descending three stories before she directed herself toward a thick oak door. She paused in front of it, and the guards flanked her. Simultaneously they bowed at the two identical control panels and scanned their retinas. They then pressed their thumbs to the panel. After a *beep*, Wendy declared: "Wendy Howard."

"Confirm password," a robotic voice replied.

Wendy recalled the words of John Milton, penned in the hefty tome of *Paradise Lost*, a book that connected so profoundly with her on so many levels. "Better to reign in Hell than to serve in Heaven."

The doors unlocked. Another *beep* sounded. The guards pulled the handles and allowed her entry.

They did not follow her inside. Once the doors *clicked* shut, she entered a chamber of silence and chill. The room was dimly lit, the primary illumination cast by a vast network of screens that formed a sphere around her. It could have been mistaken for a digital astronomy gallery had it not been for the hundreds of viewpoints cast on each screen. From here she could see all the corners of the city: street views, apartments, inside factories, the beaches, the parks—everything.

She eased herself into the deluxe leather throne, her bones

snapping and creaking as she dropped into the seat. On the panel in front of her was a round sphere. She splayed her hand over it to control which screens appeared before her. Her fingers danced, pulling through reels of footage until she found the ones she was after.

Deng Zenim and Archie Fontana stood on the balcony at the conclave, their discussions about the infamous Valentina Winter coming to her in crystal clarity. Another play of the sphere and footage of a woman in red working her way through Tynamo's compound met her eye, a brief exchange with Deng and Valentina through which she couldn't hear the words but could guess the conversation. Another twist of the dials and she played the sequence of Archie's and Valentina's riddles, looking from the viewpoint of the infiltration chest that Deng thought she had so cleverly coded to spy on her enemy.

Now a darkened room, a woman with pale skin harshly lit by her panel of displays. Wendy examined Deng for a long while, trying to get a read on her. She was crafty, intelligent when it came to technology, but Wendy was wiser. Her team was stronger, and her bug in the system was clever enough to exploit the gaps in Zenim's code—of which there were, admittedly, very few—to ride on the back of the rhino and peep into all systems in the city.

It paid to be wealthy. It paid to have contacts.

What was Deng watching on her screen?

She zoomed in as close as she could, then bypassed the feed she was on and hacked into Deng's monitor. Deng was watching some kind of scuffle play out in the city, a group of AJS enforcement officers searching through a private residence.

Why?

For what purpose would that serve Deng?

Deng grimaced. A glass of something clear was beside her, half-drunk, and Wendy guessed it wasn't water.

Another switch of the screen showed Archie Fontana in his

chamber, a duo behind him working feverishly on what Wendy could only describe as a very well-preserved cadaver. They looked exhausted, but there was a smile on Archie's face as the readings on a computer screen showed a sudden uptick in some kind of activity.

Deng banged her fists on the table, her usually passive face creasing into a mask of frustration and annoyance. She kicked her chair back and exited the room.

A grin crept up Wendy's face. That same grin used to paint her expression when she had an ant under the glaring focus of the magnifying glass. The same grin she displayed when she first entered the dating game and learned the power that sex could play over the workings of the male mind. A perfect replica of the smile she sported on her wedding day when they signed the paperwork and Stanley's fortune combined and sealed with hers to secure their place as the wealthiest entity in Atlantica.

The smile of the meddling joker.

Deng watched the monitors with disdain. She was not a loser, had never been one of those. Yet, here she was, falling behind a rival.

Valentina could be her secret to advancing her knowledge of technology, particularly as it pertained to the workings of the human body and the electrical conduits and pathways that composed the human mind. If only she could get her on her side.

Archie had his secrets, but Deng's infiltration had gone as planned. Even with the chest's mobility out of function, she could still spray her code into the networks of Archie's compound. Technology wasn't all wires these days. It was amazing what you could do with the frequencies in the airwaves. Infrared, Blue-tooth, Wi-Fi—they all spoke to each other. You merely had to learn their language.

Now the chest acted as her router, allowing her an increasing amount of access into his machinery and systems. She had only recently gained entry into his private medical sanctum, and the results were illuminating, indeed.

Archie had a test subject. Deng had known this, but she now knew his name, his genetic makeup, and more. The only thing she didn't understand was Archie's connection and dedication to this subject. Nor, frustratingly, had she connected the dots between Kit Carter and Valentina Winters.

There had to be something there.

When a smile appeared on Archie's face, Deng lost the last of her control. He had admitted it on tape although he wasn't yet aware, that he would pull out of their agreement. The technology she had begrudgingly passed to Archie, taking a risk on a fellow billionaire, hadn't paid off. She couldn't say that she was surprised, but she was disappointed. There was a reason she struggled to trust, and men like Archie were part of that equation.

She slammed her fists on the console. She would have to do the one thing that she tried not to do if she could ever help it.

She would have to go in there and take what was hers by force.

No one crossed Deng Zenim.

CHAPTER TWENTY-NINE

Valentina spotted the others a long time before they saw her.

There was a crowd of them near the Corvette, seemingly unbothered by the raucous interruptions from her takedown of the others. Well, the guards were, at least. The women wilted against the wall near a door at the back of the chamber, eyes darting in all directions as they tried to shrink from view.

The remaining obstacles standing in her way were half a dozen men who easily could have been the models for some kind of fitness regime. She had seen these hulking men in gyms, walking around in vests they might as well not have worn, and eyeing their competition.

They looked more intimidating with actual guns in their hands.

Valentina studied them from the darkness, working out the best path forward. She was aware she needed to move faster. She still hadn't seen any sign of Bradley, and that was an issue. All of this commotion and discovery and there was no sign of the man she came to save.

So where the hell was he?

She weighed her options and chose the good old reliable

method. If sneak attacks could only take her so far, then it would be down to confusion and disruption to allow her access.

The metal orb rolled into the center of the room, occasionally jumping as it hit the various bumps and divots on the cave floor. It drew the eye of an eager nearby guard who shot at it, his draw fast, his aim true. The bullet struck the device, which erupted into a large cloud of smoke, and gunfire rained.

Valentina nodded, satisfied. She hadn't expected the burst to happen so suddenly. Ordinarily, the bomb would leak the smoke at an ever-increasing pace, but since they were so eager to attack anything that came their way, she couldn't complain.

She strode ahead, gun prepared. She bent her knees, shrinking away from the bullets that flew. Each gunshot gave a slight clue as to their direction, and when a nearby shot sounded, Valentina didn't hesitate. She swung her arm and fired.

Another gunshot nearby. Pebbles of rock rained down on her. She shot back and missed. Another attempt and the sound of a man falling confirmed the hit.

There were still four more. She wasn't sure that the women weren't a diversion and were actually guards in disguise. You couldn't trust anything in this city.

The world was grey and dense around her. She stopped and focused on her hearing, listening for signs of movement. Somewhere the women whimpered, but the other men had gone deadly silent.

Where are you?

She took another step in the smoke and dimly made out something ahead. The hood of the Corvette appeared like a small rowboat across a lake of fog. She drew closer to the hood, now dented with bullet holes. Jewels had spilled from bullet-torn bags. She crouched low and picked up a handful of them, small rubies and opals and quartz and more.

Something shuffled to her right.

Valentina hurled the handful of jewels into the smoke.

Someone grunted. It was their mistake. The next second she shot, and another went down.

Three to go.

Gunfire rained around her, the others drawn by the report of her pistol. She threw herself to the ground and shuffled beneath the Corvette. She held her breath as bullets *pinged* off the car. Someone shouted, "Not the car, you idiot. Harvey will have your head for this."

Valentina shuffled farther beneath the car as boots appeared through the gloom. She moved until she felt something squishy beside her. She turned her head to find one of the women staring at her with terrified eyes, a single tear rolling down her cheek.

Valentina clapped her hand over the woman's mouth. She held her gaze and placed a finger over her lips. "If you make a single sound, I will kill you," she breathed. "Understand?"

The woman nodded.

Valentina removed her hand.

The boots came closer. Valentina could smell the musk of a man. She delicately eased her hand down her side and found a device that was no bigger than a thumbnail but which would do the job she hoped for.

She just needed him to come closer.

The boots came toward the car. The man inspected the bags, tutting and shaking his head. He was a foot out of reach. Valentina would have to break cover to get him.

Using the woman beside her as leverage to push, she reached out from under the car and slapped the device onto the man's calf. Small prongs emerged that tore through the cotton of his trousers and embedded in his skin. She thumbed a button on the device, and a burst of electricity pulsed through his body.

The man jerked, his words catching in his throat. He fell to the ground with a *thump*, shaking as his head turned and he saw Valentina.

She waved her fingers and mouthed, "Hi."

The woman whimpered.

Valentina glared at her.

Two more.

The smoke thinned. Slowly, more of the chamber revealed itself as the smoke filtered into the other tunnels. When it had subsided, Valentina was surprised to find that the other two guards were gone.

I did count six, right?

She emerged from beneath the Corvette, thankful that the glass was gone before the gunfight occurred. She saw one other woman hugging the wall, face a mask of tears, and shook her head. "Where did your friends go?"

"They ran," she managed between sobs. "They ran. Please don't kill me."

"I'm not going to kill you." Valentina maintained her grip on her gun as she scanned the chamber for signs of the remaining enemies. Her eyebrow raised as she noticed two figures on the floor at the far side of the cave. "What the hell?"

The guards were down. At first, she wondered if some of the stray shots had found their way into the remaining two, but there was no blood on them. There was no visible sign of a bullet wound entry. So what had happened?

Something cracked against Valentina's ankle. It failed to penetrate the leather of her boots, but it still caught her off-guard. She glanced down to find the woman she had hidden with reaching out and attacking her with a shard of onyx.

Before Valentina could react, the woman screamed. She disappeared beneath the car, dragged back and out of sight. Valentina looked through the car and could make out the shape of someone hunched over.

Valentina aimed her gun through the car. "Stop, and put your hands on your head."

"That's my line," came a voice from one of the tunnels.

Valentina's expression fell as Terra appeared from the mingle of shadows and the remnants of smoke.

Terra looked from Valentina to the person on the other side of the vehicle. "She a friend of yours?"

The woman stood straight with a coy grin on her lips. "Hard to say."

Gabby looked unperturbed by the situation as she slid her hands into her pockets. "Hey, Val."

Valentina raised an eyebrow. "What are you doing here?"

"Claiming what was mine," Gabby replied. "Surprised to find you here, though. Well, I was until I saw the trail of destruction you left behind on the way in." She jerked a thumb at the officers and lowered her voice so only Valentina could hear. "Great job using the AJS as a distraction tool. Very smart."

Terra and the officers aimed their guns at the two women. "What exactly is going on down here?" Terra nodded at Gabby. "Where did *you* come from?"

Gabby laughed. "You're not as astute as you believe you are, ma'am. Once someone knows how to employ the shadows to become their friend, it's easy to fade from view. While you were attempting to sneak down that stairwell, I found alternate methods to pass you."

Valentina holstered her gun. "You shouldn't be here, Gabby."

"Neither should you." Gabby's eyes darted toward the mountain of jewels. "Didn't have you down as a jewel trader these days. Thought that diamond gig was a one-off for you."

"It was." Valentina was confused. What was Gabby implying?

Gabby's brow furrowed. "Interesting. Well, if none of you mind, I have places to be."

She managed only a few steps toward the door when Terra raised her voice. "Freeze! This is an AJS scene now."

Valentina cocked her head. "Honey, do you really believe that to be true?"

Terra gave her a threatening look. "You let us pursue this asshole, and we'll pretend that we haven't seen you."

Officer Gallow shifted uncomfortably and stared at the back of Terra's head.

"Deal?" Terra asked.

There was no downside for Valentina. She took a step back and swept an arm toward the door. Gabby, on the other hand, jittered awkwardly. Still, what choice did she have? She was an A-grade mercenary—well, maybe B-grade if Valentina set the standard—but that didn't mean she could easily duck out of a situation that involved three AJS officers and Valentina Winters.

Terra advanced on the door, instructing one officer to keep an eye on Gabby. Gabby held up her hands to placate her, but Valentina knew that meant nothing. They were both Jack-in-the-boxes, able to explode at anything and surprise their victims.

Terra pressed her ear to the door for a few moments, listening for anything happening inside. When she heard nothing, she announced, "Atlantica Justice System. We're coming in. Do not resist."

She nodded at Officer Gallow, who set about working the lock. After a minute of fiddling, the door *clicked* open. Terra narrowed her eyes at Gallow and counted to three. Valentina ducked behind the car, preparing for a sudden onslaught of attack.

Terra booted the door, then ducked out of sight. Gabby joined Valentina at the hood of the car, peeking into the chamber.

Silence bled through the cave as the echo from Terra's kick died. Standing in the center of a room that looked as though he'd lifted it directly from one of the local hotels was Harvey Vincent. His posture was straight, his fingers laced behind his head. There was a strange grin on his face as he stated, "Everyone calm down. I surrender."

Terra glanced at her comrades. She aimed her pistol at Harvey. "Stand right still, scumbag. We have you now."

She circled behind and grabbed his wrist. She wasn't delicate when twisting his arms to place the cuffs on him. "Easy now, easy," he muttered, that same strange smile on his lips.

As Terra worked at restraining the willing Harvey, Valentina and Gabby entered the room. They skirted the walls, examining every nook and cranny. Valentina couldn't understand it. Where the hell was Bradley?

"All set," Terra stated, instructing the other officers to take Harvey by one arm each and guide him from the room. When he was up, she stood before him and stared intensely into his eyes.

Harvey grinned. "You ain't got nothing."

"I have years of DNA evidence linking you to several crimes," Terra replied. "Not only that, but I have you sending your crew out there to shoot at AJS officers with intent to kill."

"I didn't do anything," Harvey replied. "I'm innocent."

Terra's lips thinned. "You have mountains of stolen jewels packed into a vehicle reportedly stolen in 2024 by one of the directors of C-Chain, Inc. Yet another mysterious homicide where your DNA happened to show." Now Terra grinned. "Just because you thought you could hide out forever didn't mean that justice wouldn't be able to drag your ass in when we caught you."

Harvey's grin faltered, but he fought to keep it. "Do your worst. You can't prove shit."

Gabby, who had been running her palm along the rough wall of the room in the cavern, piped up. "You want to say that again?"

She nudged the wall with pressure from the heel of her palm, and a drawer slid open, breaking the perfect illusion of the rock wall. From all angles, they could see the jewels piled inside, arranged and neatly organized by color.

Harvey's grin faded.

"Interesting," Terra crooned. "Looks like we might be able to get you on some evidence after all." She nodded at her colleagues. "Could you take him out of the room so I can talk to these two, please? See what lies you can get pouring out of his mouth."

Harvey growled as they escorted him from the room.

Terra waited until they were clear before she closed the door and trapped Valentina and Gabby in with her. "You going to tell me what the fuck all of this is about?"

Valentina and Gabby exchanged a glance. At the same time, they shook their heads and stated, "No."

Terra pinched her forehead. "Val, you can't put me in a situation like this."

"Like what?" Valentina asked. "I got you entry. I gave you your guy. What's the problem?"

"You shot an AJS cruiser," Terra hissed. "You killed people in this cave. Worse, you stayed around so that I can't deny I've seen you. I have two officers out there who have seen you in the flesh, and you're supposed to be in hiding. We dance around each other. We never take to the floor together."

"How sweet," Gabby offered with a smile.

Valentina rolled her eyes. "They don't know who we are."

"They can guess." Terra folded her arms. "Just because you hide behind the guise of the Red Countess doesn't mean they won't make some kind of connection. Fuck." She ran her hands through her hair.

Valentina chewed her lip. "There are a thousand copycats of me in this city. Pass it off as one of them. Chances are they'll believe it. I've kept my profile low enough over the past few years to fade from the public eye. Make a joke of it. Tell them I'm a kink of Harvey's. Find a way. You're a smart lady. You'll figure it out."

Terra remained unconvinced but decided to let it drop. "What the hell is this place, anyway? Must have had a compelling reason for you to blast your way down here and raid a jewelry den." She ran her fingers through a drawer of jewels.

Gabby fell away from the conversation, busying herself with activating the other compartments, her amazement growing as more and more drawers revealed themselves from the walls.

"They took a friend of mine." Valentina focused on Terra. "I'd heard that he was down here with Harvey." Her jaw clenched as she pictured Bradley under torture. He had to be down here if she didn't want to accept that the blood splattered all over his room was his. "I was mistaken."

Terra drew a few level breaths, weighing a decision in her mind. Gabby continued to explore the drawers.

Terra nodded to the door. "Go. Hunt. Get your ass out of here, now."

Valentina raised her eyebrows. "I don't take kindly to orders."

"I don't take kindly to being ignored," Terra retorted. "You want freedom and space away from my team? Run. Before I change my mind."

Valentina hesitated a moment, her gaze moving to Gabby. Gabby shut the drawer and turned to face them both. "Does that go for me, too?"

Terra nodded. "I don't know who you are, and I don't want to know. It's best if we all forget this ever happened. Go."

Gabby and Valentina affirmed with a nod, then headed for the door. As Valentina opened the chamber, Terra added, "Val. Thanks."

Valentina gave a two-finger salute, then passed Harvey and the AJS officers. They followed her with their gazes as she and Gabby disappeared into the tunnels.

When they were out of hearing range and out of sight, Valentina grabbed Gabby's arm and paused her in her tracks. "We're not done here."

"We?" Gabby asked. "Since when are we now a team?"

Valentina patted Gabby's bag, her hand closing around a large, hard object. "If you don't want me to snatch that diamond from you again, you best help me scan this place. Two mercenaries are better than one."

Gabby frowned. "What have you gotten yourself into, Val?"

"Nothing," Val lied. "Just help me look, okay? Listen for signs of torture. Find any other entrance or chamber where someone could be. I can't leave until I know it's clear."

Gabby told her she'd help. When she turned to move in the opposite direction, Valentina added, "You know that if you try to run away, I'll find you, right?"

Gabby didn't reply, but the message was clear.

They began their search.

CHAPTER THIRTY

"Something's happening." Friedrich stared wide-eyed at the screen, an air of excitement around him. A line that had once been flat with only steady pulsing breaks between had begun to beat a semi-regular rhythm.

Archie stood behind him, casting a shadow over his shoulder. "It's working?"

"Something's working," Friedrich muttered. "See here? That shows electrical activity running between the synapses of the brain. An increase in electrical function could mean—"

"Recovery," Archie breathed. His stomach curdled as he said it, a mix of feelings running through him. On the one hand, he had the power of progress in his hands. If he could truly bring someone back from the brink of years with zero function in their brain, this could be revolutionary. Deng's code and his know-how could combine to make one of the most outstanding break-throughs in medical history in decades.

On the other hand...

He thought of Valentina, one of the most reliable and powerful allies in the city. A mercenary with no limits, with an agreement to execute his every whim. A woman who would do whatever it took to ensure that Kit made a fast and full recovery. What would he do without her? There was no way she'd stick around. If anything, she might exact revenge for some of the uses that he'd gotten out of her in the past. Worse still, what if she united with an enemy? What if she got into Deng's pocket or straddled the lines between Taylor or Vanessa?

Keep your friends close, but your enemies closer.

Was there a greater enemy than Valentina in Atlantica?

The screens flashed as the sounds of beeping increased. Something was happening. The code that Deng had sent Archie had been embedded and was running its sequence. For half an hour there had been a constantly refreshing screen of code as the AI performed its duties, but now that was changing.

Friedrich gave a stunned laugh. "Activity increasing across the parietal lobe, Sylvian fissure, cerebellum, and occipital lobe, with function beginning to engage across the sulcus, gyrus, hypothalamus, and brain stem."

"What does that mean?" Archie was breathless. Nearby the assistant watched over Kit, a tablet in his hand, feverishly tapping away on the screen.

Friedrich shook his head, his mouth hanging open. "I don't know."

Archie grabbed his collar and spun him around. "What do you mean you don't know?"

Friedrich tensed. "I mean it's impossible to know. No one has ever done this before. I'd associate increases in brain function with possible recovery, but your subject has been this way for over half a decade. No one has come back from the brink. It could just be the dust getting shaken from the old structures. The synapses may be working, but who knows what's happened to the nervous system, the digestive system, the adrenal systems? For all we know, we have a Frankenstein monster that acts as an amazing conductor but shows no activity. All we can do is—"

"Wait," the assistant declared. His tablet sat on the desk. He was leaning over Kit, a flashlight passing from eye to eye. "He's responding."

In a flurry of excitement, Friedrich pushed past Archie and stood over Kit. He took the flashlight and passed it back between each eye, pulling the eyelids open as he did so.

Archie, trying to move past the fact that Friedrich had shoved him given the current situation, joined them. "He's awake?"

"No," Friedrich replied. "But his pupils are showing weak signs of dilation."

"What does that mean?" Archie asked.

Friedrich smiled. "It means that he's responding."

Archie examined Kit. The guy barely had an ounce of fat on his atrophied body despite the years of IV drips and sustenance they'd pumped into him. They'd given Kit the utmost care, keeping his body moving and doing all they could to ensure he didn't develop sores and fade further into the abyss. He had dark hairs on his legs. His toenails were a shade of ice blue. There was a scar above his left knee from an accident in childhood, and by his side…

"What was that?" Archie breathed.

Friedrich, who was still examining Kit's eyes, turned to face him. "What?"

"That." Archie pointed at Kit's hand. For years, his hand had lain as limp as a dying flower. Now the finger twitched. Barely there, but something. "That wasn't just me?"

Friedrich and the assistant gazed at each other in wonder before Friedrich moved to where Archie stood and examined his finger. He rested it on his palm and held it steady. "Kit… If you can hear me, tap my palm once. Give us some kind of sign that you're still there."

They waited. Then waited some more. The machines continued to relay the information, declaring Kit's signs of cognitive activity were increasing, but no finger moved.

Friedrich asked him again. Archie repeated the words. After a few minutes, Friedrich sighed and placed his hand down. "Maybe we were imagining."

"No," Archie declared. "I know what I saw—"

An explosion rang from nearby, a booming crash of glass and steel and brick. The room they stood in shook, the metallic grated platforms wobbling precariously as though under the tremor of a low-grade earthquake.

Archie's jaw clenched. His eyes darted toward the only door into the room. The assistant dashed to leave. "No!" Archie cried, drawing his gun and aiming it at the man's back.

The man stopped in his tracks, growing alert under the glaring gaze of Archie and his pistol.

"Don't run *toward* an explosion," Archie growled. He handed the pistol to Friedrich and told him to aim it at the assistant. Friedrich looked uncertain and afraid. "If you so much as point that thing at me, it'll be the last thing you do. I promise you that much."

Archie knew Friedrich wouldn't shoot him. The man was a mouse. An intelligent one, but a mouse nonetheless.

He turned to the computers and sat, quickly drawing up the compound's CCTV system. Many of the camera feeds were out, displaying nothing but static. Of the few that could capture the mess outside, he could make out the shapes of dozens of black-clad figures with assault rifles and pistols in their hands. They'd compromised the glass dome tunnels that led to the chamber he stood in, and figures approached.

Archie pounded a button under the console with the flat of his hand. An alarm initiated, red lights flashing in the room and all around the compound. Within seconds, his men and women were coming to attention, appearing at the far reaches of the hallways and firing their weapons.

The sounds were deafening, even behind the thick walls of the room where they stood. Archie had this room built to specifications, knowing how vital it was to guard his secrets, yet still, the rapid gunshots were loud.

Shouts could be heard and dying gasps. The infiltrating enemy was eager to enter, and it was almost a deadlock as his forces tried to thin their number and stop their approach. Archie grimaced as another camera died and turned to static. His heart raced. Friedrich sweated beside him. The assistant was frozen although his legs shook.

Another handful of his men went down. The shapes drew closer to the door, and in one of their hands, he spotted a package that looked suspiciously like C4. Whoever was running this operation—and he thought he knew—had prepared, and they were there for a single purpose.

A purpose that Archie couldn't let them achieve.

"Hold on tight," Archie cried as his fingers raced on the keyboard and initiated the backup protocol. The red lights turned white. He hit the "Enter" key. The assistant grabbed the nearest handrail and held on for dear life. Friedrich dropped the gun and clutched Kit's bed, his face inches from the lifeless man. The bed was strapped in tight, ready for such eventuality.

It was a good thing, too, as the floor began to rumble. Hydraulic pistons announced movement and the platform lowered, inch by inch at first, then increasing in speed. The floor below them opened like the gaping mouth of a long-lost creature and swallowed them whole.

Wind raced past Archie. The cold depths below the island breathed at them. Lights burst into action to lead their descent, and Friedrich's breath caught with the sudden rush and the wonder of where they were heading.

When the ceiling closed above them, Archie breathed a sigh of relief. It quickly turned to anger as the video feed showed the ongoing fight with his men and the infiltrators. They were putting up a good fight, but the C4 was almost in place around the doors. A few more minutes and the explosion would sound.

The foundations of the compound disappeared as they sank farther into the ground. Eventually, the lights ran out, and all that remained was darkness. Archie and his men were completely blind.

That didn't stop the impression that had been left in Archie's mind right before the last light died. Not one, but two of Kit's fingers wiggling and stretching, attempting to regain their strength once more.

CHAPTER THIRTY-ONE

"Nothing." Valentina grimaced as she punched a fist at the concrete lip of the building. "Absolutely nothing."

Her mind twisted with guilt and rage. Another victim. Another person in her life that she had failed to save.

He's not dead. You don't know that he's dead. It's not even your fault, Val. Bradley got involved with the wrong people.

Yet, somehow deep inside she knew it was because of her. If Isabella hadn't offered Bradley a place to stay, the events might not have unfolded as they had. She raised her head to the murky moon and let the breeze soothe her skin. She tried to absorb it all, to understand what step she had missed, try to fathom where Bradley could have gone.

"He's out there somewhere," Gabby offered beside her. The pair of them sat a short distance apart as they looked down at street level and watched the additional AJS units rounding up Harvey's followers. "You have to keep the faith."

Valentina hadn't told Gabby much, only that she was looking for *someone*. Despite how close they had once been, Valentina couldn't trust—*wouldn't* trust.

She changed the subject, glancing down at Gabby's bulging bag. "Who's the diamond for?"

Gabby scoffed. "You know it's bad practice to discuss personal information about our clients."

"I probably know them," Valentina replied. "I could track it down easily enough. There's a limited pool of people with enough bravado and stupidity to hire goons like us to do their bidding. You could be getting my sloppy seconds."

"More than likely," Gabby replied. She tilted her head, deep in thought for a moment. She scanned Valentina with sparkling brown eyes as if determining the pros and cons of informing her.

There was no loyalty among mercenaries, and as such there was no loyalty among mercenaries and their clients, as much as they stated to the contrary. Mercenaries were in it for themselves. You could buy them for a few hours, but you couldn't hold their silence for life. That was the price of the gamble.

Gabby sighed, head turning to the activity at street level as she spoke. "Vanessa Hatfield."

"The space girl?"

"You've heard of her?"

Valentina leaned back on her palms and crossed her legs. "Real estate phenomenon turned philanthropist, ear to the ground but eyes on Mars. A surprise competitive rival to NASA and SpaceX that seemingly appeared out of nowhere and is racing to place the first Atlanticans on Mars."

Gabby raised a finger. "You mean the first *humans*. Rumor has it she's seeking vulnerable volunteers from third-world countries. Those she deems 'disposable.'"

Valentina shook her head. "No. I meant Atlanticans. You can't call the people who live here 'human.' They don't exist in the same league as the rest of the world. Nothing is the same here."

"Fair point." Gabby drew a long breath.

"Why the diamond?" Valentina asked. "Surely space girl

doesn't need diamonds to man a crew to Mars. What benefit do diamonds have to the mission?"

Gabby shrugged. "Compact carbon? Hardened materials? Resources to sell to fund the campaign? The hell am I supposed to know. She wants, I deliver. Simple as that." Her eyes narrowed. "Aren't you going to stop me taking the diamond to her? You wanted this beauty only a few days ago."

Valentina smiled. "Nope. My job is over. Paid. Signed, sealed, delivered. Do with it what you please." She climbed to her feet. "Now, if you'll excuse me, I have places to go, people to find."

Gabby looked out at the horizon where the faintest notes of pastel were beginning to color the sky. "Very well. I'll still watch my back. Don't take this the wrong way, but I don't trust you."

Valentina smiled. "Then you're learning."

Dawn crowed as Valentina returned to her apartment building. She entered the usual way but didn't linger in her apartment. Sneaking around the side of the building once more, she found herself at Bradley's bedroom window.

The interior was dark. She could make out the police tape at the door marking the crime scene, but no one was in sight.

Strange, she thought. *There should be forensics teams. The whole place should be swarming.*

She eased the window open, the security on the outside of the windows some thirteen stories high not built to protect against invasion. After all, who would climb thirteen stories to enter through the window? She climbed inside and slid the window shut.

There was a smell of metal in the air, but there was no hint of rot or decay. Valentina had been around crime scenes in which bodies were in the early stages of rigor mortis. In those scenarios, she'd had to cover her mouth and nose with a cloth to remain in the room. Here though…here things were different. Things were *wrong*.

Valentina drew her pistol, turning quickly toward the bed. "Make any sudden movements, and I'll add your blood to the crime scene."

She struggled to see her features, but she recognized her shape. When Deng pulled the cord on the lamp, she came into full view, as relaxed as if she was prepping for a night in bed with a pizza, gin, and *Wheel of Fortune* on the TV. "Good to see you again, Val."

"I wish I could say the same," Valentina replied. "Should I be surprised that you're mixed up in all of this?"

Deng shook her head. "You're an intelligent woman. You shouldn't be surprised." She sat forward. "Any luck finding your friend?"

Valentina held the gun steady at her. "Where are the cops?"

"Occupied," Deng replied. "You'd be surprised what cash and leverage can do, even on law enforcement. Bribery is the path to invisibility, didn't you know?"

"I'd heard." Valentina's jaw clenched. "Where is he?"

"You assume that I know?" Deng replied with mock offense. "Valentina, I'm hurt."

Valentina jerked the gun in her direction. "No more bullshitting. Where is he? Why else would you be here if not to toy with me, bitch?"

Deng held up her hands to soothe Valentina, but she didn't look threatened. "Valentina… Calm down, please. We're engaging in a friendly chat."

Valentina held her gaze, adrenaline coursing through her.

Deng's humor dropped. "Fine. You want the truth? Here it is. I have him in my custody."

Valentina almost threw herself at Deng but resisted. Barely. "Why?"

"Leverage, of course," Deng replied. "You think I don't have eyes everywhere in this city? You think you can keep your secrets and never get discovered? You hide your past as though no one will ever find it, but I have ways. I have means. The beady eye of Tynamo is watching you at Archie's. It's watching in your cabs. It watches you enter the building and disappear every single night."

Valentina was shaking with rage. Who was this woman to own the monopoly on security in the city? More than that, what was she going to do with that information? Secrecy was all that shrouded Valentina, and Deng was threatening to steal it from her. "Give me one good reason why I shouldn't put a bullet through your skull."

Deng's face grew serious. She sat straight, looking down for a moment at the stained bedsheets. "Because you need me."

"Bullshit." Valentina couldn't hold back.

"And I need you," Deng stated.

Valentina bit back the retort when, for the first time, she noticed the sincerity in Deng's eyes. "What could I possibly need from you?"

"Everything," Deng replied. "Your friend Archie has drawn back on our deal, hiding away the location of the software I developed to change the world. It did change the world. Archie's theory of neuroprogramming had an effect. Whatever he hoped to achieve, he hit the goal today. Great things will be written about this day."

Valentina's mind spun. Archie was going to use the AI on Kit. Did that mean...

"Still, he stole it," Deng continued. "You were there. You know that he went back on his word."

"Cry me a river," Valentina muttered. "You're all traitorous assholes."

"That's as it may be. I sent my team to extract the software and grab it back by force."

Valentina pictured Deng's forces from her encounter with

them at the Tynamo compound. She wondered how they'd fare in a sudden raid on Archie's facility.

"Archie fought back," Deng continued, gaze fixed on Valentina.

Valentina frowned. "You're telling me your team failed? You were unable to penetrate his place, and now you want me to join your side to help you when Archie's doing all he can to help me?"

Deng's eyes narrowed, a studious look on her face. "No. I'm not telling you that. I'm telling you that Archie is gone."

Valentina's skin prickled. "What do you mean he's gone?"

Have they killed him? What about Kit?

"I mean that he's gone," Deng continued. "Hiding from the world. Lost in whatever cavity of the earth he descended into. All data and information went with him."

Valentina's mouth went dry.

Deng crossed to Valentina. She placed a hand on the gun and lowered it. Valentina didn't resist. "He's gone, Isabella. Archie is gone. So, too, are your chances of ever finding Kit again unless we can work together to find him."

Valentina looked into Deng's cold, dark eyes—eyes that had appeared frequently in her dreams. Eyes that spoke of corruption and betrayal and malice. Her mind raced, filled with thoughts of Kit and rain and swings and parks.

It wasn't until moments later that the knowledge appeared on her face, Valentina registering Deng's use of her alter-ego's name and the connection between her and her brother.

A secret held from the public eye for so long.

Broken.

Three words conjured themselves in Valentina's head, syllables that filled her with chills: *Enter the dragon.*

AUTHOR NOTES MICHAEL ANDERLE
MAY 14, 2021

Thank you for not only reading this story, but these author notes as well.

I'm back in Texas in my old 'stomping' grounds of Trophy Club / Southlake area (between Fort Worth and Dallas.) I'm staring out across the 5th story window at the Harkins Theatres huge movie cineplex that lies dormant.

Empty.

It officially closed on November 1st after issues negotiating it's lease.

For me, it is a reminder that the ongoing residual effects of the Covid pandemic are going to be felt for many years to come. While I'm only here for the weekend (our son graduates from the University of Texas – Arlington) I doubt I'll be back at some point to see which company eventually takes over the lease.

Personally, I'm a big fan of Harkins Theatres and was surprised to find out that this was the only location for the chain in Texas. It was clean, well run and I always liked seeing movies there.

May the company do well in the locations that are still active!

What's Coming in ATLANTICA

LMBPN Publishing has a development project underway to tell a bit of backstory in ATLANTICA's beginning. Back in the 60's to be more accurate.

If you started with the first series JOHN CHAMBERS you met Terra Kris, a member of the Atlantica Justice System. The existing AJS is a result of a handful of individuals willing to bring law and order to a chaotic reality of the early days of this unique island.

When people were willing to push others around and a few stood up and pushed back.

And pushed back hard.

The first book is about half-way through at the moment and I'm pretty excited about how the story is coming along. Hopefully, we will get a pre-order up soon...ish... (we need a cover).

Speaking of covers, we have the third Terra Kris cover completed for her series. Here's a sneak peek at the new series coming at ya.

Have a fantastic day and the future is so bright, we all need to wear shades!

Ad Aeternitatem,

Michael Anderle

www.ingramcontent.com/pod-product-compliance
Lightning Source LLC
Chambersburg PA
CBHW020412110726
47899CB00006B/1948